WIRED

G.P. CHING

Wired, The Grounded Trilogy Book Three

Copyright © G.P. Ching 2015

Published by Carpe Luna, Ltd., PO Box 5932, Bloomington, IL
61704

First Edition: June 2015

ISBN: 978-1-940675-14-5

Cover art by Christ Holland
www.paperandsage.com

v1.5

Books by G.P. Ching

The Soulkeepers Series
The Soulkeepers, Book 1
Weaving Destiny, Book 2
Return to Eden, Book 3
Soul Catcher, Book 4
Lost Eden, Book 5
The Last Soulkeeper, Book 6

The Grounded Trilogy
Grounded, Book 1
Charged, Book 2
Wired, Book 3

Contents

Prologue 1

Chapter 1 *Lydia* 16

Chapter 2 24

Chapter 3 33

Chapter 4 42

Chapter 5 53

Chapter 6 59

Chapter 7 75

Chapter 8 86

Chapter 9 101

Chapter 10 107

Chapter 11 120

Chapter 12 126

Chapter 13 136

Chapter 14 146

Chapter 15 160

Chapter 16 175

Chapter 17 187

Chapter 18 197

Chapter 19 205

Chapter 20 223

Chapter 21 232

Chapter 22 243

Chapter 23 251

Chapter 24 265

Chapter 25 277

Chapter 26 292

Chapter 27 306

Chapter 28 323

Chapter 29 329

Epilogue 337

About the Author 347

Acknowledgements 349

Prologue

Trinity Pierce pushed her breakfast around her plate and smiled sweetly at her father. She hoped the happy act was convincing. It should be; she was an expert. If there was one thing she'd learned from living with the Red Dogs, it was how to fake a smile. Under the persona of Bella, she frequently feigned contentment among the pack, especially when the men in her life acted distressed. And at the moment, her father, Chancellor James Pierce, was clearly distressed. His upper lip curled and his bushy gray eyebrows plunged above his nose as he scrutinized her eating habits. Yep. Distressed. With a side of agitated.

"You've hardly touched your food," he said.

"Just not hungry this morning."

Her father's mouth twisted with disappointment. "You're too thin."

"The people who held me prisoner didn't feed me regularly. I don't think they had a lot of food."

Straight-out lying was also something she learned from the Red Dogs. Actually, she ate well at the Kennel, as did everyone there, fresh food they killed or sometimes grew themselves. Even sewer rat tasted a hell of a lot better than this Crater City slop. She'd stayed thin in the Deadzone due to her workload, not the food.

"Thank goodness we saved you from those monsters. I shiver to think what you've been through these years."

"Thank goodness." She did her best not to sound sarcastic.

"I understand your condition is not your fault, but now that you're home, with a little effort, it should be easy enough to rectify the deficiency." He forked eggs into his clean-shaven maw.

"Deficiency?" Trinity was thin but not so much as to appear ill or weak. Her arms and legs still carried a healthy amount of muscle. The way her father talked it sounded like she was an embarrassment.

"You've been gone for some time. The current fashion is to carry a softer appearance. You don't want to look like a laborer." He chuckled. "The boys at the Ambassador's Club will think I'm abusing you. I'll make sure Cook knows you will require extra meals, and we'll send Esther out to get a padded shaper for under your dresses."

Trinity sighed over her uneaten breakfast. The dresses her father referred to were nothing like the ones she wore in the Deadzone. She didn't mind the extra material, but his choice of style made it clear he still thought she was a little girl. She was nineteen and had lived with the Red Dogs for two years, since the day she'd run away from home following her mother's death.

As rough as things could get with Sting, most of her time was spent doing as she pleased. She valued independence above all else. Now that she was found, or as the media called it—rescued, she had a schedule and social expectations, a chancellor father who was looking forward to introducing her to the Republic elite. Introductions that would occur at the Ambassador's Club, a swanky social destination for government leaders and their families. Just thinking about the sons of dignitaries sizing her up for marriage potential made her claustrophobic.

For the thousandth time, Trinity regretted the night she'd been found. She should have followed Lydia and Ace and taken her chances escaping through the sewer. Being eaten alive by rats would be a better fate than slowly suffocating within her father's tight grip. Not that she missed being owned by Sting. That part had always been an unfortunate side effect of her liberation. But in some ways it was more honest than this. Her relationship with her father was truthfully strained but outwardly affectionate. All about appearances.

"Eat, Trinity," her father said, clearly exasperated with her. The doorbell chimed. Trinity released a held breath as her father's scrutiny ebbed with the distraction of the bell and he turned his face toward the foyer. "Who in the name of the Republic?"

Trinity used the interruption to hide some of the rubbery eggs in her napkin.

"Esther!" her father boomed, calling for the housekeeper.

Esther emerged from one of the bedrooms, dusting cloth in hand. She was undoubtedly cleaning an already clean room. Trinity's father had an unnatural obsession with cleanliness and organization. Everything must be kept in its place. Everything and everyone. He could have answered the door himself or asked Trinity to do it. But he didn't. Instead he used the opportunity to reinforce Esther's lower rank and position. Trinity hated that about him. Undoubtedly, he thought about her in the same way. Daughter or not, she had her place too.

Esther waved her hands in the air. "I will get it, Mr. Pierce." She jogged down the main hall to answer the door.

"Good morning, Dr. Konrad." Esther cleared her throat. "Chancellor Pierce is not currently receiving guests. Can I give the chancellor a message for you? Or perhaps make an appointment for later in the week?"

Trinity wasn't sure whom Dr. Konrad was, but Esther was right to put him off. Her father hated to be disturbed during meals. In fact, he looked quite peeved at the arrival of this visitor as he returned to eating his eggs.

"He must see me," came a gruff voice. The shuffle of feet echoed from the foyer.

"Dr. Konrad, please!" Esther was a ninety-pound Asian woman with a dust rag. Not exactly high security.

The man charged into the room from the foyer, Esther trailing behind as if she could somehow retract him by force of will. So this was Dr. Konrad. He was stern, with a yellowing, sickly complexion. He didn't look like a doctor. He looked like a patient, one with an unsuccessful treatment. The last time Trinity saw someone as thin and yellow, they were smoking Slip, the addictive byproduct of artificial meat production.

She'd met plenty of Deadzoners addicted to smoking the stuff. All of them yellow like Konrad. All of them with one foot in the grave.

"Konrad," Chancellor Pierce said by way of greeting. He dismissed Esther, his thick lips descending into a scowl. The skin around his eyes wrinkled in annoyance. "Is there a reason you are intruding on our family meal?"

"I need a military unit to apprehend the four criminals who terrorized my lab. The commander is telling me I have to get special permission from you."

"He's right. You do."

Konrad's eyes widened incredulously. "They forced me to inhale toxic gas. I only survived because I've worked with the chemical before and built up a tolerance. I'm sure you've been briefed on the attack and escape!"

"Yes. Lydia Lane and Korwin Stuart. I was briefed. Unfortunately, I was not briefed about their original capture. Nor was I informed of the purported torture you inflicted on them and others in that lab of yours."

Trinity's stomach kicked when she heard the name Lydia. It was an unusual name, and her mind went immediately to the Lydia and Ace who'd evaded the Green Republic raid on the Red Dog Kennel.

They'd escaped into the sewer. Of course, none of the Red Dogs used their real names. Still, the coincidence unsettled her. She chewed a bit of toast to disguise her intrigue.

"About that," Konrad said. "I planned to inform you as soon as I dealt with the immediate threat."

"Don't be absurd. According to my sources, we spoke on the phone while Lydia and Korwin were in your detainment. Not only did you conveniently forget to tell me of their presence but you mobilized troops upon their escape without permission or funding."

"It is my right to do so as the director of military science and technology. They are byproducts of the Operation Source Code experiment and are absolutely lethal. They cannot be underestimated."

Pierce bared his teeth. "Yes. We learned that, didn't we, when we had to bury six of the men involved in the skirmish. Talk about a political black eye." He pointed a finger at Konrad's face. "You didn't follow procedure, Emile. Frankly, I'm concerned you are abusing your power and circumventing the system. You don't respect my authority."

"Of course I do, sir," Konrad said in an insincere and condescending tone. "I simply wish to avoid any embarrassment to you. By taking responsibility, I merely sought to insulate you from the brutal and dangerous realities of my position."

"Cut the bullshit, Konrad. I was fighting in the Great Rebellion while you were pushing a writing utensil at that university of yours. I've made my decision; your position has been temporarily revoked, and there will be an inquiry into your office."

"I received no notice of this!" Konrad said through thin, drawn lips. "You can't do this. I know where the fugitives are hiding. Now is the time to strike! You must authorize my use of force to hunt down and apprehend Lydia and Korwin."

Chancellor Pierce held up one finger. "First, I'm notifying you now. It's all the notice you deserve after the stunt you pulled. Second, if you know where the fugitives are, why didn't you mention it before now? It's been weeks since the incident."

"I was recovering," Konrad squeaked. "I wasn't strong enough."

"Well? Now that you are strong enough, where do you believe they are hiding?"

"The Outlands."

Her father scoffed. "We've had people stationed in Willow's Province for months. They would have detected any rebel activity in that sector."

"I didn't say Willow's Province. I said the Outlands."

Pierce chuckled. "If you're right, I hardly see the problem. The radiation levels in the area will kill them off eventually. They might already be dead."

Konrad's eyes shifted from side to side. "I have reason to believe that Korwin's and Lydia's electrokenisis makes them immune to radiation."

"Reasons to believe… What reasons?" Pierce asked skeptically.

Konrad fidgeted and licked his lips. "The girl said as much. I don't think she was lying. Other members of the Liberty Party are helping her. David Snow and Laura Fawn are responsible for their escape. They're still alive, and I believe they've done something to counteract the radiation in the Outlands. They've been hiding there. The Liberty Party was behind the attempt to steal the specimens from Stuart Manor. I'm sure of it."

Pierce shook his head. "You are even sicker than you look. David Snow is dead. We found his remains in the explosion at CGEF. DNA evidence, Konrad. The poison you inhaled is playing tricks with your brain."

Konrad huffed. He held up one hand. "I am fully in control of my faculties. I can prove I'm right.

Give me a small military contingent to investigate the area and I will show you David Snow is still alive."

One of Pierce's meaty fists landed on the table, rattling the dishes. Trinity sat up straighter, her stomach clenching at the violent outburst. "Am I speaking to myself?" Pierce asked. "What evidence do you have that could possibly be strong enough to induce me to put more human lives at risk to search an area where we already have flasher drones safely doing the exact same thing?"

Konrad thrust his hands into the pockets of his lab coat and shook his head. "The flashers are useless. They relay too much information. Every time the wind blows it sets them off. The analysts are weeks behind—"

Face red, Pierce pointed a finger at the doctor. "The evidence, Konrad."

"The girl told me as much when I interrogated her!"

"Did you drug her to tell the truth?"

"The drugs don't work on her composition."

"Obviously a lie then. She chose the one place we can't thoroughly search without injuring our troops. That was her intention. It was a poison pill, Emile. We both know there's nothing alive out there."

Trinity cleared her throat and put on her sweetest, most curious expression. "Excuse me, Daddy, do you have a picture of the girl, Lydia? The name is familiar to me."

Her father did a double take, his face softening. Reaching into his pocket, he retrieved his phone and tapped the screen. Holding it up, he showed her a security photo. "Have you heard of them, sweetheart?"

Trinity stared at the picture. It was Lydia and Ace, real name Korwin. Was it possible they'd escaped to the Outlands? Images of the sketchpad she'd seen Lydia holding in Ace's room came back to her. The drawing depicted strange clothing and surroundings. For a long time she'd suspected the two had known each other before the Kennel. Not to mention, she'd seen both of them exhibit electrokinetic powers, although she'd assumed they were simple scampers. Ace was Korwin. Lydia was Lydia. Her friends were the products of Dr. Konrad's experiment.

"I knew them," Trinity said.

Pierce adjusted himself in his chair. "What's that, honey?"

11

"I knew Korwin and Lydia. They lived in the Deadzone with me. They were Red Dogs. I didn't know their history at the time."

Konrad lurched forward and grabbed her by the shoulders. "How did they get there? Where are they now?"

"Unhand my daughter!" Pierce said, standing.

Konrad lowered his arms but held her within the grasp of his intense stare.

She looked him in the eye and lied like a pro. "Lydia's been a Red Dog forever, since she was a baby. She never lived in the Outlands as far as I know. She left for a while to be part of some political movement and came back with Korwin. They said something about the group they were part of being eliminated. They called the Red Dogs home after that."

Konrad's mouth dropped open. "You must be mistaken. It can't be the same girl. A different Lydia."

"No. That's the one," she said, pointing to the picture. "She could shoot lightning from her hands. Everybody got used to it after a while. She's probably returned there. The Deadzone was home for her."

Pierce grinned. "There you have it, Konrad. We will search the Deadzone."

"With all due respect, Officer Reynolds and his team have scoured the Deadzone for weeks. She's not there." Konrad pressed the tips of his bony fingers together. "My assistant pursued Lydia and Korwin after they escaped my lab. He was found dead just a few miles from the border of the Outlands. He was"—Konrad's eyes shifted to the side—"electrocuted. It had to be them."

"Your assistant?" Pierce raised his eyebrows. "What type of assistant attempts to apprehend dangerous fugitives on his own?"

Konrad took a step back. "One who is familiar with Operation Source Code."

Pierce rubbed the bridge of his nose. "I did not approve a special assistant for that purpose."

"Give me a few men. I'll prove I'm right."

Pierce groaned. "Listen to me carefully. If Lydia was living in the Deadzone until recently as my daughter suggests, that means the Liberty Party is scattered."

"Not necessarily—"

"Shh." Pierce held up one finger. "The Green Republic has never been stronger. Aside from the escape, the Liberty Party hasn't presented an organized attack since the night we assassinated Maxwell. They're weak. Let the girl rot from

13

radiation poisoning in the Outlands or go on with her life in the Deadzone. I don't care. She's nothing to us. The boy is less than nothing."

"She's everything!" Konrad ran his fingers through his hair, leaving it wild and uneven. "It's too dangerous to allow her to live. If the rebellion has hold of her blood, they can reproduce the serum to make more alphas. Or worse, with both her and the boy, they could make an army of gammas."

Trinity laughed. There was nothing funny about Konrad's red face or his temper. The laugh was meant to deceive. If she was right about Lydia, it was imperative that her father believe what she was about to say. "I am positive that Lydia said the rebel group she'd fought with had disbanded. That's why she came back home to the Deadzone." She shrugged. "It's over. We've won. Whatever Lydia and Korwin were doing when you arrested them, I'm sure it was just an effort to survive after their home in the Deadzone was raided. They weren't working for anyone."

"You're a liar," Konrad barked.

Her father's hand slapped Konrad's chest, pushing him toward the door. "You will not talk to my daughter in that tone. Go back to your hole, Konrad. I'll be in touch about the official inquiry into your conduct. Until then, you are suspended on forced medical leave and Operation Source Code is on permanent hiatus."

Esther held the door open and Pierce pushed Konrad through it.

"You're going to regret this, Pierce," Konrad yelled. "If you turn your back on this, they'll do to your daughter what they did to your wife."

Trinity gasped. It was a low blow. Her mother had died of a massive stroke at a Republic dinner. Due to the circumstances, there was speculation she may have been poisoned. She'd been campaigning for peace and a more democratic government, the exact opposite of the Republic's current position with her father at the helm. There was never any proof of assassination. It was gossip. Hurtful gossip after all this time.

There was a pause as if her father was registering what Konrad said. The door slammed. "Esther, do not let that man back into this house." Pierce stormed from the foyer, giving Trinity a small nod before heading for his bedroom.

Trinity smiled, authentically this time. Success. She wasn't sure what Lydia and Korwin were up to, but she hoped they were safe. With any luck, she'd just witnessed the end of Dr. Emile Konrad.

Chapter 1
Lydia

Even though I can tell I am dreaming, it feels real. I explode from the white van and attack Brady. I know it's a dream because in real life I drained him of his electrokinetic energy until he died. It was bloodless and in self-defense. But in my dream, his death repeats in my head, and each time I kill him in a new and more horrific way. A moment ago, I slit his throat. As soon as he dies, I am back in the van, and it starts again.

It feels real. Brady's chin is in my palm and my hand clutches the back of his head. He is on his knees, begging me to spare his life. Korwin is beside me and says, "Don't do it, Lydia!" I twist. Brady's neck snaps. I watch the light ebb from his eyes and I am happy, ecstatic that I've ended the life of a killer. Then the dream changes and I am holding Korwin's head in my hands. And he's dead.

I wake gasping for breath. I'm cold. My nightgown is soaked with sweat and my blankets are on the floor. I'm in my bedroom in the reactor. I sit up, relieved it was a dream but horrified nonetheless. Why would my brain produce thoughts of killing Korwin? I love Korwin and he's proven he loves me. Is it out of guilt? An echo of the pain I experienced in Konrad's lab? Or something else?

A whimper comes from the corner of my room. *She* is there. My wolf. She first appeared to me when I was thrown from David's motorcycle and hit my head against a tree. I saw her again when I almost killed Alpha and once more when I killed Brady. Now she's with me most of the time. I know she's not real. No one else can see her. She's what they call a hallucination—something I don't talk about, not even to Korwin. But she is also my friend. She understands me in a way real people don't. She understands when I have to do things I don't want to do.

"It was just a bad dream," I say to her. Tears well over my lower lids.

She bobs her head and walks to the door, pointing her nose at the Biolock.

With a deep breath, I get out of bed and dress in my training gear, stretchy black pants and a gray T-shirt. "Yes. A workout will help." If I make myself tired enough, I'll sleep without dreaming. I place my palm on the scanner to open the door.

The lights in the corridor are always on. I live in a tower of apartments in a nuclear reactor complex. When I lived in Hemlock Hollow, I would sit in my tree and stare at the reactor with its many concrete buildings and never for a second suppose that anyone lived there. I never even considered it might be inhabitable. But hundreds of people call this home as well as Liberty Party headquarters.

It must be the middle of the night because I don't see another soul as I make my way to the elevator, not even beyond the balcony in the foyer down below. I've rarely seen it this quiet. The wolf growls and walks to the railing. She looks down, across the atrium toward the entrance to the tunnels. That's where we train. It's an underground bunker with a growing arsenal to rival the Republic's.

We take the stairs down to the first floor and jog across the tiled expanse to the circular entrance. A concrete ramp takes me underground. Double doors welcome me into a state-of the-art facility. There's a weight room, cardio machines, padded rings meant for boxing, wrestling, and martial arts practice. I have an itch to spar, but with no one else here, I'll have to settle for a simulation. Luckily, the Liberty Party owns the best simulator ever invented.

I step onto a platform reminiscent of a boxing ring and wait while a ray of blue light scans my body.

"Hello, Lydia," the simulator says in the gentle coo of a forty-year-old mother. We call her Simi. I've often wondered about that voice. Was she a real person? And if so, why did they select her soothing tone to introduce a grueling holographic workout? "What would you like to practice tonight?"

"Simi, random setting, please." I want to be surprised. I want to finish so exhausted I won't dream when I fall asleep.

"Very well. Your last completed level on record is thirteen of twenty. Please indicate level of choice."

"Fourteen, Simi."

"Level fourteen beginning in five, four, three, two…" My wolf jumps into my skin—fur, claws, and teeth blending into my spirit.

The platform around me changes, morphing into the chipped bricks and shattered windows of an alley in what looks like the Deadzone. Four men, at least six feet tall and muscled like rugby players, stand between the street and me. Their chests are numbered, one through four. Behind me is a brick wall. Beside me, a pile of trash.

"Get her," Number One says in a hyper-masculine, computer-generated voice. "She doesn't leave here alive." My favorite music kicks in; a loud blend of synthesizer and electric guitar. One attacks from the front. I jump and kick him in the chin. He's a hologram but what my foot strikes feels solid. Simi has technology to shift molecules for the most realistic experience. She's programed not to kill, but the simulation can hurt.

When I come back down, Four is behind me. He grabs me around the chest in a bear hug over my arms. I drop into a sumo squat, hook my knee behind his thigh, and grabbing his pant leg, flip him off my back. Three's fist flies toward my face. I snatch it out of the air, twist his wrist and slam into the back of his elbow with the heel of my opposite hand. The force comes from my hip and all my weight is behind it.

"Good, Lydia," Simi says. "Shattered elbow in dominant arm. Three is eliminated."

Two kicks me in the gut while I'm focused on One and Four. It hurts and I gasp. Breath knocked out of me, I duck Four's punch and block Two's second kick. I hear One behind me. Faking a front kick, I drop instead into a roll, planting both feet into One's gut before flipping forward into Two and Four. I use the half a second I buy myself to swipe a pipe from the pile of trash. The three men charge me again.

I spark, sending an electric blue charge down the pipe. As Two and Four rush me, I wedge it between them. They fall, trembling to the pavement.

"Two and Four eliminated," Simi says.

One lowers his shoulder and charges me. I rotate the pipe above my head, gripping the end and swinging it like a bat. It connects with his temple. Fake blood sprays the alley.

"One eliminated. Pass to challenge two."

I run from the alley and the scenery shifts. I'm on the grid, balanced on the narrow strip of electromagnetic metal that supports and powers the vehicles in and around Crater City. A truck barrels toward me. I look down. Too high up to jump. I burst into a sprint, pumping my arms and legs like pistons. I can run three times faster than any human, but I can't run faster than a truck on the grid. Before it can barrel into me, I jump straight up. I land on top of the cab.

"Pass to challenge three."

The truck dissolves from underneath me and I fall. I land on a slick of oil. There's a tank rolling toward me, and civilians line both sides of the street. I can't spark without igniting the oil and injuring the civilians. The tank gun points toward me.

"Lydia!" Laura's voice breaks through the simulation, distracting me. The tank fires. Before I can react, fire billows all around me, the platform vibrating to simulate the explosion and my incineration.

"Simulation failed," Simi says. The street scene melts away and I am left standing on the platform, staring over my shoulder at the woman who gave birth to me, then abandoned me eighteen years ago.

"Lydia, what are you doing?" Her voice is heavy with concern. "It's the middle of the night."

I turn to face her, but I can't form words. My wolf is close to the surface. All I can do is growl.

"What's wrong with your eyes?" she asks. She climbs onto the platform and grips my shoulder. "What are you doing up?" she asks more softly.

It's the wolf that answers her. "You're not my mother!" I launch myself at her, hands to her neck and knees plowing into her abdomen. I knock her to the floor, becoming a whirlwind of scratching nails and punching fists. She blocks and deflects me like a pro. Laura is a trained soldier with more than twenty years of experience and a Spark like me. But I have the element of surprise. I connect with her jaw.

"Lydia!" she screams, blocking my next punch.

"Stop!" David yells. I have a second to process his voice and presence, even though I ignore him. "Lydia, stop!" he yells again. A wooden staff whistles through the air and collides with my head. I roll off Laura, my limbs going slack before I pass out.

Chapter 2

Laura and David are hovering over me when I come to. David waves a small medical packet under my nose. I groan and rub the side of my head where he struck me. He casts the medical packet aside.

"What the hell did you think you were doing attacking Laura like that?" David snaps.

What *was* I doing? Why did I attack her? Truth is, I don't know. Confused, I rub my aching forehead and try to sit up. "I don't know," I answer honestly.

"Why were you down here in the middle of the night? The training center is closed. When I heard you in here, I thought we'd had a security breach." Laura places a hand behind my back to steady me.

"I had a bad dream," I say. "I couldn't sleep."

She stares at me, nothing but concern on her face. David's face is another matter entirely. He squints at me, still gripping the staff in one hand.

"I'm going to need more of an explanation than that," he says.

"Do you think you were sleepwalking?" Laura asks.

"Sleep fighting, Laura? Seems a far-fetched explanation." David scowls.

With one arm around my shoulders protectively, she says, "Her eyes were completely dilated. She wasn't herself." She places a hopeful hand on my wrist. I can practically feel her willing a justification out of me. Only, I have none.

I blink at her several times. Maybe I *was* sleepwalking. It's as good an explanation as any I can think of. As I try to recall what happened, it feels distant, like a dream. "Yes. I think I was sleepwalking."

"You're a long way from your room," David says. "Do you remember coming down here?"

"Yeah. I used Simi."

He walks to the console attached to the simulator. "You passed the first quarter of simulation fourteen. Are you saying you did that in your sleep?"

I shrug and shake my head. "I'm not saying anything. I don't know why I did it, David. I have no desire to rip Laura's head off. You know that's not something I'd normally do."

"No, it's not," he concedes. "But this is serious. I've never heard of a person doing something like this in their sleep."

"Maybe you should talk to Charlie about this in the morning," Laura says.

I notice the splotch of red on her jaw where I punched her. I remember doing it, but the memory is foggy, like I didn't experience it personally, just watched it happen in a video clip. "I'm sorry I hurt you, Laura. I didn't mean it."

David softens slightly. Laura is already soft. I get the sense that nothing I could do could make her angry at me. The thought makes my heart ache. Our relationship isn't strong enough for that. She's still barely more than a casual friend to me.

"Come on. I'll walk you back to your room." She holds out her hand and I let her help me up.

"I don't know, Laura. Maybe we should wake Charlie up and have him take a look at her now."

"I promise. I'm better," I say, and I believe it. "I just want to go to bed."

Laura flashes David a pleading glance.

"Fine, but first thing tomorrow morning, promise me you will see Charlie." David points one finger at my face. "I mean it."

I nod. "I promise." Under the weight of his frown, I follow Laura from the training center. She leads me to the elevator and pushes the call button.

"What were you and David doing up in the middle of the night anyway?" I ask, curious about how she found me in the first place.

"Emergency meeting of the council. All of us are concerned. The Greens should have struck by now. It's been over a month since we busted you out of Konrad's lab and he found out where we are hiding."

"Why haven't they attacked?"

"We don't know, but our fear is they are buying time."

"To do what?"

"To leverage the genetic material they stole from the manor."

I step into the elevator, suddenly feeling sore and heavy, like my limbs are encased in concrete blocks. "You mean, to try to make a gamma... a baby. Our baby. Korwin's and mine."

She nods. "We want to stop Konrad before he starts. Get in, destroy what he stole from us, and get out. We're assembling the team."

"How do you know he hasn't already started?"

She looks me in the eyes as the doors open to the second floor. "We don't. Not for sure. However, we have an informant who says Konrad has been on medical leave. It seems the gas I strapped to his face might not have killed him, but it did some serious damage."

"Good. Then there's hope."

"I wish we could be so sure. Medical leave or not, I don't trust Konrad not to tinker with his new toy. Creating a true gamma without a beta mother will be tricky. Between his illness and medical leave, our hope is he's still struggling with the details."

"I'm ready to go." I frown. "I hate the thought of Konrad experimenting on our cells."

"Soon. The council is simply waiting for the right opening to ensure a successful mission." She smiles encouragingly.

Laura walks me to my room, rubbing her palms together.

"Again, I'm so sorry, Laura. I'd never attack you if I was... myself," I say. I still feel awkward in her presence, like she's a ghost. Like her presence isn't truly real. My biological mother. The mother I never knew I had.

"Lydia, these nightmares you're having and the sleepwalking, have they happened before?"

I roll my lips together and cross my arms over my chest. "A few times. Nothing like this."

"When did they start?"

Glancing toward the ceiling, I think back. "After Konrad's lab... and Brady," I answer vaguely. The first time I saw my wolf flits through my brain. I'm too embarrassed to go into all the details. "Maybe it started before, when I left to look for Korwin."

Laura frowns. She follows me into the room but leans against the door, holding it open. "Sometimes when people experience traumatic events, their minds struggle to process what happened. Charlie and I wrestled with seeing life clearly after we escaped CGEF. It would be completely normal for you to experience psychological stress right now. The kind of torture you endured can produce a strong emotional response. Whatever you are feeling is okay. It's normal." Her words are slow and steady.

"I don't know what I'm feeling," I say.

She licks her lips. "I'm concerned these dreams are a symptom. Please, tomorrow, do as David asks and see Charlie. I... *We* need you at your best. The Liberty Party needs you. Tell him everything. Be totally honest. He'll know how to help."

"Okay." I sit on the bed and tuck my feet under the covers, signaling I am too tired to speak. I'm not sleepy, just tired of talking.

"Lydia?"

"Yes?"

"Before you attacked me, you said I wasn't your mother."

"I did?"

She nods, twisting her fingers together. "I just want you to know that I don't expect anything from you. What happened to you was unfair. What happened to both of us was unfair. I carried you for nine months and in ways you couldn't possibly understand, you saved me. It's natural for me to have strong feelings for you. But you grew up with Frank. I don't expect you to reciprocate."

"I don't blame you for leaving me with my father. It kept me safe." I say the words because they are the right words to say, but inside, my chest feels heavy. I don't blame her or wish her harm, but I do feel a sense of loss for my childhood self. She deprived me of a mother, despite her good intentions. It's a difficult pain to bear.

"It did keep you safe. It was necessary. But we can't change the fact that we have no history together. All I ask is that you don't shut me out. I'll take whatever you'll give me. Whatever you want our relationship to be, it can be. I never expected you to consider me your mother."

I sigh. "I hardly remember saying that to you. The whole thing is foggy, like a dream."

"But maybe some part of you feels it."

"Maybe. But if it does, it's not the part of me that's in control. I like you, Laura, and I hope we can be friends." That's all I can promise her, friendship. I am not sure she'll ever feel like family.

"Good enough." She rubs her face where I hit her. "How's your hand feeling? David says I have a hard head, you know."

My hand throbs from punching her. I circle my thumb over my palm. It's the same hand where Dr. Konrad broke my bones. It's completely healed and shouldn't hurt anymore from his torture. The hurt is from the punch. Still, it reminds me of the day I spent strapped to Konrad's steel table. Icy fear comes over me in waves.

"Where did you go just then?"

I blink at her, my mind going as blank as a bare wall. "I don't know what you mean. I'm right here."

She stares at me for a breath or two. "Okay. Charlie, tomorrow, all right?"

I nod.

Backing out of the room, she leaves without another word. The door closes and locks behind her. The lights are off, and without the light from the corridor, I am plunged into darkness. I do not sleep. I stare toward the ceiling not knowing what to do with myself. I try not to think about that day in the lab, but fear grips my throat and flashes come back to me. Korwin's screams. The sound of my bones breaking. The pain of being ripped apart from the inside out. I shiver under the covers, and my eyes swim with tears.

The bed sinks on one side, distracting me. I reach through the darkness, my fingers connecting with the warm, thick coat of my wolf. She's back. She curls into my side, and I stroke her soft fur rhythmically.

I don't need to be afraid. My wolf has sharp teeth and tearing claws. And she's part of me. A part of me I need. A part of me I'm unwilling to let go.

Chapter 3

Charlie shines a small light into one of my eyes and then the other. "Follow my finger." He raises one brown digit above my head, and I follow it with my eyes. "Touch my finger with yours, then tap your nose."

I do as he instructs, even though I feel silly completing the task. Touch, tap. Touch, tap. He has me repeat this exercise in various coordinates around my head and then touch alternating fingers to my thumb in rapid succession. I have no trouble doing as he asks.

"What is the purpose of this exercise?" I ask with a sigh to convey my annoyance.

"I'm testing your neurological function. With everything you've been through, it's possible you have a loose wire or two." He chuckles.

"I fail to see what's funny about this situation."

His lips press together and pull to the side. "Laura says you've been having trouble sleeping."

"Yes. I've been having nightmares." I shift my eyes contritely toward the floor. "Is that all she told you?"

He pulls up a stool in front of me and takes both my hands in his. Charlie has a kind and caring face. A wide scar runs from his hairline to his left eyebrow. I've never asked how he got it, but it isn't the type of thing you get from falling off a bike or even the slash of a knife. It's wider, like the butt of an ax. His eyes, too, hold the darkness of a soldier who's seen the losing end of battle. That's what tugs at my heart. He knows pain and he has secrets, just like me. Yet those same brown eyes are warm with compassion. He hasn't allowed the bad stuff to lock him behind an emotional wall, even though it would probably be tempting for him to do so.

"She also said you weren't feeling like yourself lately. Do you have these nightmares every night?"

I swallow hard. I decide to take Laura's advice and trust him. "For a while now. I usually fall asleep easily, but I have nightmares about Brady or Konrad. When I wake up, *she's* there."

"She?"

"My wolf."

He looks at me, confused. "Your wolf."

"In August, I hit my head. I was thrown from David's motorcycle. Ever since then, sometimes, I see this wolf. I've figured out she's not real. No one else can see her. She's a hallucination. But she seems real. Very real."

He licks his lips and swallows. "This, um, wolf. Does she scare you? Chase you or something?"

I shake my head. "No, nothing like that. She always appears when I'm scared or have to do something horrible like killing Brady. She helps me. She makes me brave. She protects me. Like when I killed Brady, she… encouraged me to do it. It's like…" I place a hand over my heart. "She is a part of me all the time, but when I have to be brave, really brave, I can see her standing next to me or feel her inside of me."

"Was she in Konrad's lab when you were strapped to the table?"

"No."

"But she was there when you killed Brady?"

"Yes. And when I almost killed one of the Red Dog men who attacked me."

"Hmm. And she's been there after your dreams, like last night?" Charlie looks away to scratch some notes on his clipboard.

"Yes," I say softly. "And when I attacked Laura."

His head snaps up to look at me.

"I didn't mean to," I say quickly. "It felt like a dream. It didn't seem like I was in control, more like I was watching myself do it. I looked at Laura and was overcome with this ... rage that she abandoned me. The wolf was in me. I was... seeing the world through her eyes and I attacked."

"Hmm. So the wolf is something you picture inside your mind?"

"Oh no, I can see and touch her. She has soft fur and sharp teeth. I can hear her too. Sometimes she pants at the foot of my bed. But I know she's not real. She vanishes when others are around, or when I feel safe. Like now."

Charlie frowns and squeezes my hand. "What you are describing is a tactile hallucination. They can seem as real as you or me. You said the wolf protects you. I find it interesting that this wolf only appears when you have to hurt someone else to protect yourself. If she protected you from others, she would have appeared when Dr. Konrad was torturing you. Instead, the scenarios you've shared with me were instances when you were the attacker. The wolf may be protecting you mentally—from your own harsh judgment."

I tangle my fingers in my lap. "I was raised to be a pacifist. Acting out violently toward others is difficult for me, even when I have no choice."

"But you did have a choice. When you attacked Laura, you acted on an emotion you would normally suppress."

My face feels hot. "I didn't mean to."

"The wolf makes it easier for you. She's a mental construct your brain has created to do what your conscience doesn't want you to do. Our brains do this for us from time to time. Oftentimes, human beings rationalize their actions or intellectualize them. But seeing the wolf and touching her like you do isn't normal."

I nod. "Is there something wrong with me?"

"Not wrong per se." He sighs. "You've had a traumatic experience, which in and of itself can cause a psychotic break."

"What do you mean by psychotic break?"

He clears his throat. "On top of the trauma of being tortured, you have Nanomem in your system, which was outlawed for the high rate of psychosis it caused. Eighty percent of users have a psychotic break—they reach a point where they can't perceive reality accurately. And just to put a little icing on the cake, you've had a head injury and a possible concussion."

I bite my lip and hug myself. "I am well, Charlie. Korwin healed me. There is nothing broken in me anymore."

"Not your bones, Lydia, your mind. I'm concerned that the hallucinations are a symptom of an altered mental state that could put you at risk for hurting yourself or others. You won't mean to, but if I'm right about your wolf and what she's doing for you, the world may go topsy-turvy. You won't know right from wrong seeing it through her eyes."

A flash of my fist pounding Laura's face comes back to me. I might have hurt someone last night, but it wasn't on purpose. It just happened. "I'm not going to hurt anyone or myself," I say firmly, and I mean it. I'm sure I would have stopped last night, even if David hadn't hit me.

"I know you wouldn't intentionally harm anyone, but I want you to consider that this wolf might be a sign that your mental stability is in question. There are medications that can help. I just need a few days to run some tests to understand what we are dealing with here to know the right course of therapy."

I shrug. "Okay. Do you need to take blood or something?"

He nods. "And until we figure this out, I want you to rest. Try to relax and not worry about anything."

"What would I have to worry about?" I ask with a sarcastic laugh.

"Right. Well." Charlie searches my face for a second. "Does Korwin know?"

"What? That I'm going crazy?"

Charlie tips his head and thins his lips. "I never called you crazy."

"You didn't have to. I got the gist."

"Does he know about the wolf?"

"No. I'll tell him in my own way, what we know for sure, not the speculation that my mind is broken. I'd appreciate it if you kept this private until we know more."

Hands on hips, he shakes his head. "It's better if the council knows, Lydia. You need people around you who can look out for you if this gets out of hand again. And I'm not sure you should participate in this mission."

I snort. "The people around me can look out for me without knowing I'm seeing things. I trusted you with this, Charlie. Having Laura and David think I'm fighting in my sleep is bad enough. It won't do anyone any good to think I'm losing my marbles. They need me on this mission."

He takes a deep breath and blows it out his nose. "I won't break doctor/patient confidentiality, but I don't like this. Depending on what the tests show, your participation in this mission might be a very bad idea. What if the wolf comes back at the wrong time and puts you or the team in jeopardy again?"

"You said yourself this is all speculation. We don't know what's wrong with me yet, do we?" I grit my teeth. "I can control the wolf. Lately, she's appeared at night, after I've had a nightmare. I won't be sleeping on our mission, right?"

"No."

"The wolf protects me. She gives me courage, but I don't *have* to listen to her."

He grabs a basket of supplies off the counter. "Excuse me for pointing out the obvious, but even though you say you don't need her, you sure do seem to like this wolf a lot. If I didn't know better, I might think you'd like to keep her around."

I sigh. "Maybe I do appreciate what she's done for me. I'm not sure I would have had the guts to kill Brady without her. Still, as much as I appreciate her, I don't want a replay of last night."

"Understood. Let me run some tests and see what's going on. I'll need to take some blood, and I want a full body scan."

"So, you'll hold off on making this an issue with the council until we figure out if it's really an issue?"

"You have my word," he says reluctantly. He readies the needle.

I hold out my arm and make a fist, preparing myself for the pinch.

Chapter 4

"You went to see Charlie." Korwin passes his fingers over the bandage secured to the crook of my arm. Charlie isn't the only medical professional working for the Liberty Party, but he's the only one who treats us. As a Spark, our biology is different from everyone else's, and he's the only one who understands it. I won't lie to Korwin, but I won't worry him without good reason either.

"A checkup," I say. "He wanted to do some tests."

"Why?" Korwin leans his face close to mine, running his fingers along the inside of my arm in a way that makes my whole body tingle.

"I've had some trouble sleeping. Charlie wants to be sure there are no long-term effects of what happened with Konrad."

"You mean the gas you inhaled?"

I nod. "And everything else." We're in the cafeteria, having lunch. It's a stew of fresh vegetables and synthetic meat. Not bad, or maybe I'm just getting used to the flavors.

"Is he concerned there might be permanent damage?"

With a half grin, I shrug. "I'm sure there's nothing Charlie can't fix."

Korwin strokes my hair behind my ear. "You seem, I don't know, nervous or something." He looks at our coupled hands. Usually when we touch there's an exchange of energy that feels like the rush of warm water through our skin. Today, it's been reduced to a mild tingle, even though I'm not blocking or holding back at all.

"Maybe I'm just tired from not sleeping well." I scoop stew into my mouth.

He flashes a half smile. "In that case, you should eat the rest of that stew and then you should take a nap in my arms so that I can ensure the quality of your sleep."

I laugh and lean in until my forehead touches his. "Are you trying to get me into bed?"

"Yes," he says unashamedly.

"If I'm in bed with you, the last thing I'll want to do is sleep." I smile wickedly.

His eyes spark and his smile grows wider. The tingle in our coupled hands strengthens and energy pours in and out of our connection.

"There it is," he says, leaning closer. "I wish I had my sketchbook. That's a smile I want to remember." He kisses me on the cheek.

With a shove, David wedges his hands between us and wrenches us apart by the shoulders. "Do you mind? People are eating." He glances down at my Band-Aid and gives me a curt nod of approval. "The council wants to see you two, now." He points toward the level one conference room adjacent to the cafeteria.

"Now?" Korwin asks. "We just started eating."

"Finish up. This is important." He knocks on the table twice and takes off in the direction he indicated.

I shovel in the rest of my stew, barely chewing, and stand to place my bowl in the receptacle near the kitchen.

"Hey, why did David just ogle your bandage like he expected you'd have one?" Korwin's hazel eyes search mine.

I sigh. "I ran into him last night when I couldn't sleep." I hook my pinkie into his and smile. "Stop worrying. I'm fine."

He grabs my face and plants a kiss on my mouth. "Now you're fine." Blue light sparks between our lips and we both laugh.

"You're right. I needed that."

A crumpled napkin hits me in the cheek and I turn to see Caleb, sitting next to Hannah as usual, at a nearby table. "Still eating here," he says, pointing at his food.

A blush warms my cheeks.

"You seemed okay with kissing in public at assembly last week," Korwin says with a half grin.

Caleb glances at Hannah and they both chuckle before resuming their meal.

I take Korwin's hand and lead him through the tables of blue uniforms to the conference room David indicated. We slip inside to find the council already assembled.

"Ah. There you are," Jonas says toward his notes, only his eyes flicking above his bifocals.

We take a seat at the two chairs left empty. The only people at the table who look happy are Warden and Mirabella Grant. Mirabella grins at me over a gigantic onyx ring, her hand supporting her chin as if she is posing for a portrait. David, Charlie, and Laura are shifty-eyed and less enthused.

"There's been an exciting development," Mirabella says. She taps the conference table and a hologram displays at the center. Alexandra Brighten, the news anchor for the Green Republic's official news channel, begins to speak. The sound is muted.

"I can't hear," I say.

Mirabella holds up one bony finger. The scene breaks to a video clip and Mirabella taps a button on the console. The video freezes on a young woman with black bobbed hair.

I gasp. "Bella." I look at Korwin, then at Mirabella.

"Do you recognize her?" Mirabella asks, suddenly transfixed.

"Yes. She was our friend in the Deadzone. We called her Bella."

Mirabella's lips spread to reveal aging yellow teeth. "Interesting. This young lady's true name is not Bella. This is Trinity Pierce, the only daughter of Chancellor Pierce."

"No," Korwin whispers. "She was part of Red Dog leadership. Well established. Been there for years."

"Two years and twelve days. She went missing after her mother's fatal collapse at a Republic function. Before you ask, the mother's death wasn't our doing. We don't know who was behind it, although speculation is that she was murdered. Kate Pierce was a vocal and political force for a more democratic republic."

Korwin shakes his head. "I don't understand. Chancellor Pierce has driven the Green Republic to a military dictatorship. Are you telling me that he used to be in favor of greater democracy?"

"No, I'm telling you his wife was, and then she died. In fairness, James Pierce was clearly more moderate up until the time of his wife's death. Members of the Liberty Party have speculated over the years that someone within Pierce's own party murdered Kate as a way to scare James into his current role. They had to make him feel the country was still at war, or he would have never agreed to a military dictatorship. Unfortunately, it seems our rushed attack on CGEF succeeded in pushing him over the edge and finishing what they started."

I frown at the suggestion that the attack on CGEF brought about the military dictatorship. Her tone is slightly accusatory. Korwin and I were behind that attack. I get the sense that the comment is

47

Mirabella's way of blaming us for the current state of affairs.

"What does this have to do with Bella?" I ask, trying to get the conversation back on track.

"As I was saying, Trinity Pierce went missing the day after her mother's murder. She's back. Tomorrow night, her return is being celebrated not just on a personal level but as a symbol of the effectiveness of the regime that brought about her rescue. Her father is holding a ball in the heart of Crater City at a place called the Ambassador's Club. The leaders of every province, all senators and dignitaries, anyone with any power in the Republic will be in attendance."

Korwin slips his fingers into mine under the table and squeezes. "If you're planning to bomb the place, I have a problem. There will be family members, hundreds of innocent people in attendance."

Jonas holds up his hand and shakes his head. "We are not asking you to bomb the event. The Ambassador's Club is in the Capitol building directly adjacent to CGEF. The location was intentional. The Uppercrust prefer unregulated access to power, and CGEF, as the nation's hub for energy allocation, can provide that power. The two buildings are connected via an underground parking garage. We want both of

48

you, along with Laura and David to pose as a family of dignitaries from Northern Province, a family who is currently our special guest in detention. Once inside, you will infiltrate Dr. Konrad's laboratory at CGEF and find the specimens taken from Maxwell Stuart's home."

"Once we find them, how do we get them out without anyone noticing? Do you have a refrigerated purse or something?" I ask.

Warden taps his fingers together. "We don't want you to take them out. Electrocute the vials. Kill everything inside but leave them exactly where they are. The best outcome of this mission is that the Republic never knows we were there."

"We've worked diligently to convince the Green Republic the rebellion is dead," Mirabella explains. "We want to disable any chance of Konrad using those cells without calling attention to the Liberty Party."

"I don't understand. Isn't your goal to overthrow the Republic? Why not attack now?" I ask.

Mirabella glances at her husband. "Ideally, we'd like to lead a revolution, not a war. If we can convince Pierce that the rebellion is dead, he might revoke martial law and return the country to a more democratic republic. Once that happens, we have people on the inside who will work within the system to enact change. Our supporters grow in number every day. With patience, we might be able to sway the electorate to our ends without shedding a single drop of blood."

I snort.

"You don't believe we can do it?"

"It's hard to believe the leader of the government that sanctioned our torture would ever be willing to give up his power."

She smiles and keys something into the table console. "My second surprise for you."

Alexandra Brighten's face pops up between us again. This time, I can hear her. "*Corruption in the capital. Dr. Emile Konrad, longtime director of military science and technology to Chancellor Pierce, resigned today after an official inquiry resulted in proof of misappropriation of funds. Konrad has been on medical leave for over a month during the course of the investigation. A replacement to his position has not been named.*" Dr. Konrad's scowl flashes across the screen.

"He's been fired," Korwin says.

"Resigned," Jonas clarifies. "Although we expect it was a forced resignation. Seems he didn't follow procedure when he interrogated you two. Good news for us. We believe the only reason the Greens haven't found us here is the doubt raised by his head-butting with Pierce. He's the wild card. He knows we're here but doesn't have the muscle to back it up. We need to ensure his successor doesn't pick up where he left off if we expect Pierce to have a change of heart."

"So, we break in and destroy his research but make it look like nothing is missing," I say.

"Exactly." Jonas closes the folder in front of him. "Of course, this is a delicate operation. They aren't going to allow you to walk through the front door. Discretion is key. You'll need to assume the identities of the Baltik family of Northern Province. David and Laura will facilitate a distraction, a folk dance in Trinity's honor, and you two will do what you do best." His eyes fall on Korwin and me.

Charlie takes a deep breath and gives me a knowing and concerned look. I presume he wants me to tell them about my wolf. I look him squarely in the eye and shake my head. There's no reason to go that far. Sharing will only make them doubt me and could put the mission at risk.

Laura closes the folder in front of her and glances at David. "Are you up for learning a folk dance in twenty-four hours?"

David shrugs and flourishes his arm over his head.

"We'll need disguises. Dress, masks, voice alteration."

"We've got it. The best in the business," Jonas says. His gaze darts between us. "If there are no objections, Operation Trinity will execute tomorrow at 1600 hours."

Chapter 5

"I'm Sal. I'll be helping you with your identity for tomorrow." A short man with small eyes and skin three shades darker than mine leads me into a room filled with clothing and makeup. His voice is all gravel, like he's lived a hard life and earned every one of his gray hairs. "You're an inch taller than the girl you're supposed to be. Any guests who might notice will chalk it up to growth. You're both young."

"Who am I supposed to be?" I ask. Korwin, David, and Laura are with their own stylists, each specializing in recreating a persona in record time.

"Anastasia Baltik." He opens a folder on his dressing table and shows me a picture of a girl who looks nothing like me. Her hair is white as freshly fallen snow, and her eyes are a strange violet color I've never seen on a human being. "We will bleach and cut your hair to look like hers. The eyes, we will have to accomplish with lenses you'll wear over your natural eye."

"Did she have surgery or does she always where the contacts?" I ask, assuming the violet color is artificial.

"Natural. A rare mutation unique to her and her brother. They are technically blue, but her specific genetic makeup gives them that unique violet quality at the right angle. They're going to be a bitch to reproduce, but we've got the best people working on it. They'll be custom made for you with pigment programmed to react to the light the way hers do."

He pulls a dress from the rack. It's sterling gray with a violet sheen when the cloth bends and a high stiff neck that I suspect will reach past my earlobes. Long bell sleeves are cut to hang to the knuckle. The front of the skirt is short but the back extends all the way to the floor. He reaches under the table to produce a pair of silver fur-lined boots with buckles from ankle to knee. "Please tell me you're smaller than a size eight. These are her actual shoes. One of a kind. We'd be hard pressed to reproduce them. Handmade and lined with white tiger that's been illegal for five generations. They do not adjust to the wearer."

I shrug and lift the boots from his grip. Kicking off my shoe, I shove one foot into the unbuckled boot. It's a tight, uncomfortable fit and I can hear Sal inhale as I try my best to force it.

"Oh wait," I say, removing my foot from the boot. I pull off my thick wool sock and stick my bare foot inside. This time, I get it all the way on. I pull the buckles together to demonstrate that it will work. "It's tight, but I'll be able to walk."

He lets out the breath he's holding. "Amen." He pulls the boot off my foot. "Now, with this dress, we will need to pad your figure. You're much thinner and harder than Anastasia. We'll use rubber to add some fat to your cheeks, reshape your nose, and fill out your neck. A thick layer of makeup and you should be a ringer. I can't do anything about the muscles in your arms."

"Good enough to fool those closest to her?"

"As far as we know, there is no one close to her aside from her parents, and they will be played by Laura and David."

"Then why are we worried about accuracy?"

"No one is close to her, but most of the country is familiar with her from the social networks and reality TV. You must learn to imitate her mannerisms and language. Come."

Sal leads me into a room with a large computer monitor and fires it up. A few selections and I'm staring at a video of Anastasia.

"You must not vear dat. You vill embarrass Rayle and I. Vhy must you be zuch a rube?"

"This was taken yesterday, just before we abducted the family. Notice the inflection, and how she selects a fruit from the basket with only her thumb and forefinger. It's fashionable to hold the hands thusly."

He demonstrates, copying the girl on the screen. I try it but don't look nearly as graceful.

"She carries her elbows away from her body," I say, copying what I observe.

"To make herself look bigger." He nods. "In Northern Province, they pronounce their consonants differently, and watch your inflections. Try it."

"You must not vear dat," I imitate. Her accent is almost Pennsylvania German, and I come close.

"Again."

I square my back and select an apple from the bowl with my thumb and forefinger, careful to hold my elbow away from my body. "Vhy must you be zuch a rube?"

"Very good," Sal says.

"My voice is higher than hers. I'm not sure I can match it."

"Don't worry about that. You'll have a voice simulator implanted under your mask."

"She doesn't appear overly friendly."

"She's not. Keep to yourself unless someone approaches you first, and pretend like they have to earn every word from you." He replays the clip. "Watch how she pops one hip out. She's all attitude and entitlement."

I pop my hip out and look him in the eye. "Do not vhine to me about your problems," I say.

"Perfect." Sal smiles. "I almost feel guilty ruining a nice girl like you, even for one mission. Come on. I want to get the bleach on your hair."

I run fingers through my honey-brown layers. "Can't I wear a wig?"

He shakes his head. "Sorry, no. The style is flat and straight to the shoulders, very hard to achieve with artificial hair."

I sit down pensively in the chair he indicates, and he wraps a plastic cape around my shoulders. He dons a pair of gloves and pours a few liquids into a measuring cup. The content is lavender in color and smells toxic. I shift nervously as he pins up sections of my hair.

He meets my eyes in the mirror in front of me. "I'm not a professional stylist. I owned a theater back in the glory days before the Greens put me out of business. Had to learn this for the new role. I don't mind, though. You know why I love working with hair?"

"No. Why?"

He grabs a strand and brushes the purple goo from root to tip. "Because if you hate it, you can always grow it back the way it was."

Chapter 6

At 1600 hours the next day, I join the others in the garage as planned. A sheet of white hair covers one of my eyes and my muscles are sore from practicing, with the discipline of a professional dancer, the way Anastasia moves. For the last twenty-four hours I have lived, breathed and eaten as the child of a dignitary from Northern Province. The skin on my face hurts from having the rubber mask of her facial features fitted and removed and then fitted again. My feet are crammed into a pair of boots a size too small and my eyes burn from the intrusion of the violet-colored contact lenses. But I *am* Anastasia Baltik.

In Anastasia's weighted swagger, I approach three people I've only seen in pictures and video. Korwin's skin is now pasty white, and his normally dark brown hair is platinum blond and slicked over his head.

"Velcome, sister," he says in Rayle Baltik's voice, flashing violet eyes.

"Rayle, Anastasia, ve must be going now," David says, adjusting the rings that adorn his every finger. His impression of Eric Baltik is spot on. Laura curtsies next to him, her blond hair piled in tight curls atop her head. She says nothing, as is the way of Evana Baltik. She cannot be bothered to speak. Instead, she rolls her eyes and climbs into the expensive black vehicle, rearranging the layers of blue and red fabric that make up her skirt.

Once we are all inside and our driver, a disguised Liberty Party soldier named Tom, gets behind the wheel, I depress a piece of rubber near my ear to disable the chip that alters my voice.

"What's the plan?" I ask.

David presses behind his ear, too. "Tom will drop us off at the Ambassador's Club. We all go in together and socialize for a respectable amount of time. Once all of the guests have arrived, Laura and I will demonstrate the dance of the Northern Kingdom."

"Did you learn it?" Korwin asks. "I've heard there are only a handful of people in the world who can still do it."

"Twelve," Laura says, "and the Baltiks are two of them. We are confident we can perform a passable version."

David clears his throat. "Once everyone is distracted with the dancing, you and Korwin will separately and nonchalantly move toward the back of the room. You follow the left wall. Korwin will follow the right. There is a service elevator that leads to the basement. Once there, go right and it will take you to the parking garage. We've arranged for one of our people to pose as a server and cause a distraction, so we expect the hall to be empty. If you run into anyone, stay in character and suggest you need something from your vehicle. If that doesn't work, fry them."

"I'm not killing an innocent kitchen worker," Korwin says.

"I will," I say coldly, without thinking. Korwin gives me a sharp violet stare.

"Good for you, Lydia," David says. "It's about time we all realized this isn't a game."

Korwin makes a rude gesture in David's direction.

"Fine. Don't kill him. Just electrocute him enough for him to question his memories," David says.

Korwin nods.

"Once you are in the parking lot, disable the guard at the door to CGEF and do what you have to do to make it to Konrad's lab. We are expecting there will be a skeleton crew as most of the security will be shifted to the Ambassador's Club to protect the Republic elite. Find the specimens. Fry the vials for a minimum of sixty seconds each, then return the way you came. Understand?"

I snap my fingers. "Couldn't be simpler."

Korwin frowns Rayle's full red lips. "Let's hope. After watching ten hours of Rayle videos, it's clear he enjoys female attention. I'm seriously concerned one of the other dignitaries' daughters is going to punch me in the face."

David smirks. "Look at the bright side, her fist will likely bounce off all the rubber they have packed over your cheeks. Looks like Rayle enjoys his desserts as much as his women."

"There is that," Korwin says, raising an eyebrow.

* * * * *

An hour later we arrive at the Ambassador's Club. I'm restless and fidgety and David whacks me on the knee to focus my attention. He points to the back of his ear and we all depress the trigger to activate our voice enhancers.

"Testing," I say in Anastasia's voice. The others do the same. A man in a green uniform opens my door and helps me from the car. I resist saying thank you. Anastasia would not say thank you.

Silently, we ascend the marble steps toward the entrance to the Ambassador's club.

"Anastasia!" A woman with a microphone waves at me from below. A man behind her focuses his camera. "Give us a pose for Fashion Today."

I pause, one boot on a higher step, and rest my fist on my popped hip. I do not smile. There's a flash and then another. The position affords me a view across the street. A small group of citizens have gathered with picket signs. A skeletal woman with gray hair and dark bags under her eyes holds a sign that reads, *Stop wasting energy.* Next to her, a boy about my age, brown from working in the sun, holds one that says *Equal power for all!* They stare at me as if I've stolen food from their mouths. Eight or nine more are gathered around them. They are silent, aside from their signs, and stay a safe distance from the line of security guards at the bottom of the stairs.

For some reason, I can't tear my eyes away from their tired and wasted faces, and the cameraman seems to notice, focusing on me and then on the protesters.

"Do you need directions?" a harsh male voice chastises me from behind. I turn to see a hefty balding man in formal black attire. He raises one corner of his upper lip, as if he finds me under par. I don't have to fake Anastasia's trademark scowl. With a roll of the eyes befitting her, I continue up the steps, rejoining the others at the entrance while my heckler waddles past me and into the building.

We follow the crowd into a ballroom lit up like a lightbulb. It's unnecessarily bright, obviously a way to flaunt the wealth of the people within. The wastefulness makes my stomach turn. We join a queue of dignitaries waiting to pass through the receiving line. Although we look the part, I fear we've underestimated social protocol. The others are talking and laughing while we wait quietly. I fidget, wondering if I should say something to the man behind me.

"Zmile, Anastasia," David says in Eric Baltik's voice. "Zis vait is to be expected."

It's his way of reminding me that the Baltik family are normally unsociable. I relax and play the part.

When we reach the reception line, it takes all the courage I have in me to shake Chancellor Pierce's hand. Clueless, he pumps my grip once, his eyes glancing over me as if I am of no importance. I move on to shake Trinity's hand, the friend I formerly knew as Bella. I'm not supposed to speak, but it kills me to remain silent. She still has the black bob haircut I remember, but her brown dress is padded to add fifty pounds to her frame and her makeup is a thick mask of pale white with bands of color over eyes and cheeks. I hardly recognize her. I meet her eyes and smile more than I should. I'm about to move on from our handshake when her grip tightens, and she focuses on my bicep.

"Velcome home," I whisper in Anastasia's voice.

Trinity's eyes shift from my muscle to my face. "Thank you." She releases me.

I proceed down the line and a thick stump of a hand pushes into my personal space. I take it and see the long face and portly body of the man from the steps. "Happy to see you've chosen us over your adoring public." His voice is arsenic and his black eyes narrow on the low vee of my dress as if he finds it distasteful.

After two pumps of his hand, I hurry on without engaging him in further discussion.

Once we are all inside the ballroom, I sidle up to David. "Who's the sparkling personality at the end of the line?"

"Vice Chancellor Elias Fitzgerald." David raises an eyebrow. "Best to stay out of his way."

"No kidding."

Korwin whispers in my ear. "Trinity looks so different."

I nod in agreement. Her appearance is contrary to everything I know about her. No wonder she didn't want to be found by the Greens.

A server approaches with tall glasses of sparkling liquid and we each take one. David nudges my elbow. "*Now*, be social," he whispers in Eric's voice, and nods toward a group of young adults gathered in a vestibule to our right. He slips his arm through Laura's and the two promenade toward a group of adults admiring a statue of a twenty-first-century artist.

Korwin glances at me before wandering ahead to join the group. We are supposed to be brother and sister. It won't do for us to huddle together all night. I join the gathering hovering at the edge of the crowd while Korwin edges his way in and takes a seat on a bench.

A dark-haired girl in a poofy red dress is the center of attention. She moves her arms as she speaks, as if acting out every word for her audience.

"It's my body," Red Dress says. "If I want to get retinal implants, I should be able to do so."

"A few of the early adopters have gone blind, Hillary. Aren't you afraid?" a boy to her left asks through a half smirk. He's taunting her. Daring her.

She blinks her eyes slowly. "Of course not. I'd only allow the best doctors to work on me. It's worth the risk."

"Hmm," I say, forgetting myself.

The crowd turns to face me, including Korwin, who looks mortified.

"You don't agree, Anastasia?" the girl snaps. "I've heard retinal implants are quite popular in Northern Province, or are you jealous because they can't perform the procedure on mutant eyes like yours?"

A dozen or more stares drill into me. I press my lips together into a pout. "Ze people ov Northern Province don't need furder enhancing," I say in a perfect Northern accent. "Ve cannot improve upon perfection."

The group bursts into laughter and I take a sip of the drink in my hands. It tastes subtly like champagne but slightly different from the version I had with the Red Dogs.

"It's synthetic. Didn't you wonder why they served it to minors?" A young man about my age smiles at me. He has high cheekbones and a shock of fire engine red hair that makes his blue eyes seem to glow.

I shrug one shoulder, as Anastasia is prone to do.

"It's going to be another long, boring night if that's our only entertainment," Red Hair says.

"Agreed," I say. I turn my attention back on the girl. Her face is still hot with embarrassment over my verbal slap. If she has any friends here, they aren't comforting her.

"Come on." The red-haired boy hooks his arm under my elbow and pulls. He catches me off guard and I almost trip over the high, chunky heels of my boots. I have no choice but to clop after him or fall over.

"Vhat are you doing?" I ask.

"Ana, stop the act." He pushes me behind a potted plant and holds me by the shoulders. "Don't you want to make the most of our time together?" One of his brows raises and his blue eyes twinkle. "I agree with what you said. Northern girls don't need enhancing." His fingertips skim along the inside of my arm and brush the outline of my breast through my dress.

"Don't," I say too loudly and out of character. I compose myself but barely. His hands on me remind me of Alpha's, and I bristle. "Ve do not have privacy."

The boy's jaw tightens. He steps in closer, too close, his hands circling my padded waist. "Since when are you concerned about who is watching?" He pulls me against his chest, my ill-fitting shoes betraying me with tiny balancing steps that tip me into him. His breath falls across my lips. He's going to kiss me, and he's going to expect me to kiss him back. I try to remain calm, but inside, I panic. My wolf appears. I see her approaching over his right shoulder. I know without a doubt if his lips touch mine, I'm going to hurt him. I'm going to like hurting him.

"Anastasia." Rayle's voice snaps like a whip. Korwin has found me. He stands, staring at the redheaded boy in a way an older brother might. "Mother vants to see you."

I succeed in pushing my tormentor away and walk toward Rayle/Korwin, mouthing *thank you*.

"Since when do you care what your mother wants?" Red Hair asks toward my back.

I pop my hip and give him a haughty shrug. My wolf disappears after a last disappointed look.

Filtering back into the crowd, Korwin whispers, "What the hell was that all about?"

"No idea. Not my choosing," I mutter. "They must have a history."

"What are you two whispering about?"

We both raise our heads to see Trinity standing in front of us. Her eyes narrow as she takes us in, one after the other.

I give her a genuine smile before contorting my lips to look like Anastasia's. "Ve vere just commenting on your fortunate return."

"Thank you both for coming," she says, but continues to scrutinize me. "You look different, Anastasia."

"You haven't zeen me in yearz," I say quickly.

Her gaze darts between Korwin and me. "Right. Everyone changes with time. What's important is that we stay true to ourselves." She knows. I'm not sure how, but I can see it in her eyes.

Korwin tries to deflect her inspection. "Lookz like our parentz are honoring your return with a traditional folk dance." Korwin points toward Laura and David at the center of the dance floor.

Trinity glances over her shoulder at the pair. The two stand frozen in place, Laura's toe pointed behind David's right heel, waiting for the music to start.

"How nice of them," she says, narrowing her eyes at Korwin. "That's the first time you've taken an interest in the arts, Rayle. Usually your only interest is trying to stick your tongue down my throat."

We freeze. I beg Trinity with my eyes not to blow our cover.

"Whatever you came to do, now is the time," she says under her breath. She bows slightly and disappears into the crowd. I glance around us, but thankfully no one appears to have been listening. Korwin meets my eyes and raises one of Rayle's eyebrows.

The music starts, a techno-polka I only recognize from the hours of video we watched on the Northern province. David and Laura move, circling the dance floor like a pair of mechanical dolls.

"Excuze me," I say rudely to the couple behind me before walking between them toward the bathrooms on the left side of the room. It's easy enough for me to disappear as the other guests crowd in to see the show. I walk quickly around the periphery, the rows of archways and potted plants that form the corridor providing some cover. When I reach the rear of the grand staircase, I see the elevator David described. I race toward it, only to be stopped short when a hand circles my waist.

"I see how you are. You weren't kidding about wanting privacy."

Red Hair again. Damn. This boy won't take a hint.

"You vill mizz the show," I say, pushing against his chest with both hands. His lips stretch toward me, and I arch my back to keep them from touching my face.

"What is wrong with you?" he asks.

Pop! Korwin's fist connects with his jaw. Red Hair tumbles, taking me with him. Luckily, Korwin is able to catch me and steady me on my feet. Red Hair rolls onto his back, knocked out.

"Thanks," I say.

"No problem. Apparently dignitaries can't take a hint."

"Or a hit," I say. "One punch. Impressive."

He grins under Rayle's round face.

We hurry to the service elevator and press the call button. It has fingerprint recognition, but Korwin uses his spark to confuse the wiring. The door opens almost immediately. We slip inside.

"I thought you were against hurting anyone on this mission," I say when the doors close.

A hint of Korwin's attitude leaks through the Rayle disguise. "He had it coming. Nobody touches what's mine." He steps in closer to me, blue sparks visible on the inside of his bottom lip. His spark is calling to me and my energy responds, pulling me toward him until only a fraction of an inch remains between us.

"Yours now, am I?"

"Absolutely and for always." His lids sink, and he looks at me through his lashes.

I lean forward and our lips touch… just as the doors open.

"Oh!" A slender man in a green server's uniform jumps back as we separate.

"Please excuze us," Korwin says as Rayle. "Ve need something from our vehicle."

"Oh! Of course, Mr. Baltik." The man's face turns a deep, beet red.

"You zaw nothing," Korwin adds.

The man nods and looks toward the ceiling. "Physical displays of affection can be quite common among siblings. I did not mean to interrupt you. I saw nothing." He ducks his head and scurries around us into the elevator.

With one last warning glance toward the server, Korwin takes my hand and leads me from the compartment toward the parking garage. The man disappears behind the closing doors.

I snort. "That might end up posted to the gossip pages," I say.

He shrugs. "Better than making Brighten's most wanted list again."

We rush down the empty hallway, ignoring an explosion of voices and crashing pans from what I assume is the kitchen. "Our distraction," I whisper. "A bit late."

Late or not, Korwin doesn't waste the opportunity. Hand in hand we rush out the door and into the garage attached to CGEF.

Chapter 7

Dr. Konrad brought me this way once, the day he arrested me when I tried to visit my ailing father. The garage brings back horrifying memories of my time at CGEF, and I have to work to force each trembling step. The fear awakens my wolf, and I feel her calming presence at my side. I bite my bottom lip. Whatever happens, I cannot allow her to take control.

"Hold it together. We don't have far to go," Korwin says.

"Who's not holding it together?" I whisper. We may be close, but he's fooling himself if he thinks this will be easy. There are always guards here. The first time I was arrested, I learned that the Crater City Government Energy Facility, CGEF, is the hub for energy allocation and distribution to the provinces, but since then I've learned it's more than that. It is the embodiment of everything the Green Republic stands for and it is never left unguarded. Ever.

"Allow me." Korwin moves toward the door to CGEF and knocks three times.

The door opens to reveal a young man in a green officer's uniform. He straightens his cap and fidgets with the rifle hanging over his shoulder. I can practically see the war within. He knows we shouldn't be here but he also recognizes who we are and is afraid to anger us.

"Ms. Baltik, Mr. Baltik." He bows his head slightly. "Can I help you?"

"Might I uze your facilitiez?" I ask, oozing entitlement.

"Unfortunately, no. No visitors in the building today. I'm sorry. The Ambassador's Club is right next door." He points his rifle in the direction we came. "Everyone is over there. That's where the fun is." He laughs awkwardly. "If you give me a second, I can call for an escort. Technically, you aren't supposed to be down here."

I smile sweetly and beckon him forward. "May I tell you zomething?"

He sighs, blushing slightly. "What?"

I lean in, cupping my hand beside my mouth as if I have a secret, too embarrassing for my brother to hear. As soon as he's within range, I grab his chin and send a zap of electricity straight to his brain. He falls twitching to the floor. I pry his rifle from his hands.

"Nicely done," Korwin says.

"I should have killed him. He'll blab when he wakes up." I slip the rifle strap around my neck.

"With the volts you pumped into his brain? He won't remember. He'll think he passed out."

"You hope."

He frowns and gestures inside. "Come on." He leads me into the building, leaving the body of the officer lying on the floor of the garage. The entrance connects to a stairway at the basement level. Konrad's laboratory is on the third floor.

I break into a jog.

"You know, it used to be *you* who worried about hurting people," Korwin says beside me.

"That was before I decided I'd rather live." My wolf is by my side. I ignore her.

"You don't care about preserving innocent life anymore?"

"Innocent. That's the key word. No one who works for the Greens is innocent, and if I'm going to survive, I can't weigh the goodness of every person who attacks me." A simple stretch of my fingers would invite my wolf inside. I wouldn't be scared anymore, but I also wouldn't be in control. I wrap my arms around my stomach and try to forget she's there.

"Fair enough," Korwin says softly.

"Here it is," I say, reaching the third floor. "Locked. There's a notice." A bright yellow sign says *Keep out. Floor closed until further notice.*

"Probably left over from the investigation." Korwin presses a finger to his lips and pulses the Biolock with his other hand. We enter a long hall, clinical and cold. The floor is white. The walls are white. The ceiling is white. Rows of rectangular lights buzz above of us. One of them flickers near the door where Dr. Konrad once tortured Korwin. I flash on the day I saved his life by carrying his wasted body from that room on my back. The flickering almost unhinges me. For a moment, I smell blood. I sniff again and it's gone. Perhaps it's a memory of the scent of my own blood as I lay dying on Konrad's table.

Korwin nudges my arm and motions for me to follow him to the left, the hall that leads to Dr. Konrad's lab. My legs tremble with every step and the gun I'm holding makes a clicking sound with my shaking. Korwin stops and removes the weapon from my hands, putting the strap around his own neck.

Quickly, he pulls me into a tight embrace, then searches my eyes. He looks so different disguised as Rayle, but the current running between us is unmistakable. "You okay under there?"

I am not okay. I thought I could do this. I thought it would feel good to be here, ruining what Dr. Konrad has built. But instead, my stomach twists, my mouth goes dry, and I can't stop shaking. I'm afraid. I take a deep breath and gesture toward the lab. "Let's get this over with."

Korwin points the gun at the double lab doors. I stand along the wall and use one arm to push the left door open.

He sticks his head in and looks around. "Clear."

We step inside. The place is a mess. Equipment is strewn across the space in no particular order. Medical books are piled on stainless steel tables with dusty and worn covers, antiquated and out of place against the surrounding technology. There are beeping machines, flashing lights, and filthy surgical implements. Nothing makes sense. It's chaos.

"Where should we start?" I ask.

"He'd have to keep it frozen until he was ready to use it." Korwin scans the periphery of the lab. "There." He points at a stainless steel cabinet at the back of the room with a solid green square of light in the lower corner.

We pick our way through the equipment. I step over a tank that reads *Oxygen* and around a tipped basket of plastic-wrapped surgical tools. We reach the cabinet and Korwin pulls the doors open. There's a billow of fog as the cold air hits the warm, and then rows upon rows of vials come into view. Blood and fluids, frozen samples of tissue. Korwin hands me the gun and starts digging through the shelves. He must sense my disgust, my inability to fully process what I'm seeing.

"Found them," he says, removing a tray of metal vials from the back. They are still labeled with his name.

I swallow. There's something off, something wrong with the situation, but my brain isn't working. I'm overwhelmed by the mess, the emotions of being here again, and the sense that we are on borrowed time. "One minute," I remind him. He looks at his wrist out of habit, then laughs. Neither of us have watches. It's not the fashion. "I'll count."

He sparks out and a blue cloud of electricity consumes the rack of metal tubes. "One, two, three..." I count slowly as my eyes trail around the lab. The hours I spent as a prisoner here were the worst of my existence. I want to destroy it. I want to burn the place to the ground, but I have strict orders to leave it as we found it.

"Lydia?" Korwin says.

"What?"

"You stopped counting at forty-eight."

"I'm sorry. I'm distracted. I have a bad feeling."

The vials are still engulfed in Korwin's electric cloud. "I'm pretty sure it's been a minute."

"I can count again."

He shakes his head and extinguishes the flame. "It's done."

"What about the samples he took from me while I was a prisoner here?" I ask.

Korwin digs through the shelves. "L. Lane. It's a good thing Konrad was organized." He flames out and I start to count again.

The wall to the left and behind me keeps catching my eye. It looks like any other wall but I feel a pull from deep within drawing me in that direction. I stare until I see a sliver of green against the floor. What is that?

"…Sixty," I say. Korwin extinguishes the vials and replaces them in the freezer.

"What are you staring at?"

I point to the crack near the floor. "The green looks like the green light on the refrigeration unit."

He squints. "What green?"

"There. Just against the floor."

"All the vials are here, Lydia."

I take a deep breath. "Something's been bothering me since we walked in here. How do we know the vials are... *complete*? He could have removed some and stored it somewhere else. Somewhere more secure."

He closes the doors to the freezer and stares at the unit. "It wasn't even locked."

"Exactly. Konrad is too smart for this. It's like... It's like he left it here as a decoy."

Korwin stiffens under his Rayle disguise. "Let's check it out."

We pick our way across the lab to the wall. I run my hand along it looking for a seam in the area where I can see the hint of light. "It could be a false door, like your father had at the compound."

Without a word, he joins me, stepping over a pile of medical books to run his fingers along the painted surface. "Ah," he says. There's a click and a panel slides back. Behind it is an old-fashioned door with the type of knob and lock that requires a physical key. I've never seen one of these in the

English world, although they are common in Hemlock Hollow.

"Can't just pulse this one," he says.

I touch the knob. A memory comes back to me. "I know how to do this."

"You know how to pick a lock?"

"Yeah. I do." I search the floor and find two surgical implements that are about the right shape and size. I unwrap them and dig them into the keyhole.

"The Nanomem?"

"Not this time. Jeremiah. We once stole candy from the general store."

Korwin chuckles. "You have a dark side."

My hands jostle the tools in the keyhole and the lock gives with a pop. "You have no idea," I murmur, thinking of my wolf. He doesn't hear me or doesn't respond. The hinges squeak softly as the door swings open.

Inside, the overhead lights are off but we can see clearly. The green glow comes from four rows of pods, fourteen in all, made of frosted glass. All but one of the pods are identical, oblong circles with buttons on the side that glow green. In the very back of the room there is a larger pod that takes up most of the row.

The hair on my arms stands on end, and I can't take my next breath. My heart pounds. A prickle forms at the base of my neck. Fear takes over, and *she* is there again. My wolf growls at my side.

"What is this?" Korwin asks, approaching the first pod.

"I don't like it," I say. "We need to get out of here." The wolf urges me to protect myself, to leave whatever this is be.

"What are you talking about? This is some sort of experiment. We need to find out what we're dealing with."

Korwin approaches the first pod and inspects the foggy surface, then runs his fingers down the side. He presses the lighted green button on the end. The frost clears. His body is blocking my view, but his silence and stiff posture let me know I'm not going to like whatever's inside. My wolf creeps with me as I approach. Korwin steps aside.

It does not move or twitch. The thing inside is not alive, but I think it used to be. It has translucent skin and a spine, but everything else about it is wrong. There are no legs. What I think are its organs have grown outside its body and where eyes should be, there are craters in a misshaped skull. A fleshy cord attaches it to a gelatinous red block at the bottom of the canister.

"What is that thing, Korwin?"

He looks at me through Rayle's violet eyes. "These are artificial wombs. I think you were right, Lydia. The vials were a decoy."

Chapter 8

"Dead?" I ask.

"Yes. No heartbeat." He points to a darkened icon of a heart in the back of the canister marked SC-1. "And a living baby would have to be encased in fluid."

The fetus isn't even as long as my pinky finger, and I have a hard time wrapping my mind around the fact that it used to be alive, let alone human.

"Why does it look like that?"

"It's malformed. Konrad experimented and failed."

I wipe a tear from my eye, suddenly weepy. "This is our..." I spread my hands, not knowing what to call the unsuccessful combination of our genetic makeup.

He knows what I mean and nods.

"Why is he keeping it if it's dead?"

Korwin frowns. "I'm not sure, but it can't be good."

I walk to the next canister labeled SC-2 and hit the same button Korwin did. "This one isn't formed at all."

"We should destroy them," Korwin murmurs. "He's using them. Somehow. Probably studying the cells and tissue."

I shrug. "They're already dead," I say sadly.

Korwin's hand flies to his ear. "Mmmhmm. Affirmative. We found them. A few more. Yes. Ten minutes to clean this up. Yes."

"David?"

"They've finished their dance and people are starting to ask questions about us. We'd better hurry. David and Laura have made excuses for our absence but we need to be back in ten."

"Where should we start?"

"You take those." He points to the next row. As I follow his instructions, he rolls up the lid on the first unit and incinerates the tissue in front of him. "Disconnect the power source and fry anything inside."

"Got it." Canister by canister, I reduce the dead to ash and short out the cords that power the canisters. I don't know what purpose the cords serve though, because the lights on the sides stay lit after I disconnect them.

"Looks like there's a battery backup," Korwin says in answer to my unasked question. "Just destroy the tissue. Dead is dead."

I pick my way through the tangled mess of wires between the canisters to the third row while Korwin moves to the fourth. I'm exhausted. My wolf is too close for comfort, but I need her. It's too gruesome a job to do on my own. As it is, even with her help I can hardly muster the will to move to the next canister.

"This one's bigger," Korwin murmurs from the fourth row. "Large as a coffin." He places his hands on the glass.

"Hmm," I say. I'm distracted with the grisly task in front of me. The stink of sizzling flesh fills the air. I make my way up the row, feeling faint. One more to go, and good thing; I could topple over at any moment. Maybe it's the heat. I am stewing beneath the rubber mask and the heavy dress. The air feels thick as I near the last canister in the row, SC-13. Even my wolf dissolves, as if she's too tired to go on. "Let's get this over with, Korwin. I'm not feeling well." I slap the button on the side, and the foggy glass clears.

Blink. Blink. Blink. The heart at the back of the canister beats on and off, on and off. This one is different. A balloon-like membrane of fluid, about the size of a grapefruit, is nestled in the red goo at the bottom of the canister. Abruptly, a ripple courses across the iridescent bubble. A bump presses into the membrane and retracts.

"It's alive," I say. My voice isn't working properly. It cracks and scatters.

"What's that?" Korwin asks.

"It's… it's…" My heart is pounding. What's wrong with me? Why can't I speak? A hum travels from my fingers to my heart and my whole body thrums with connection. The closest thing I have to compare it to is the day I met Korwin. This is our baby. *Ours.* I stare between my hands at the tiny being under the glass and a rush of inexplicable joy fills me. I look up to try to tell Korwin what I'm seeing.

He's oblivious to my reaction as he hunches over the large pod. Absently, he slaps the button on the side of the coffin-sized pod in row four. The foggy glass clears and Korwin jumps. He staggers into the table behind him, knocking over the third row of pods. I catch SC-13 before the cannister can hit the floor. I find my voice. "What's wrong?"

Korwin turns and runs for me, wide eyed. "Go!" He points toward the door, shimmying past me.

I move to follow but SC-13 is still plugged in. I don't know for sure how the pods work. They seem to have a battery backup, but does that power source feed the baby or just the pod itself? If I disconnect it, will the baby inside die?

"Korwin, what do I do?" I yell. He's already at the door.

He shakes his head. "Fry it and let's go. Now! Please!" He doesn't know. He didn't see what I saw.

The glass coffin whirs and clicks, and I turn from Korwin to see what's happening. The lid lifts. Fog rolls over the sides and green light blinks from the depths of the canister.

"Come on!" Korwin yells.

With a twist and a tug, I disconnect the cord attached to SC-13 from the place it's plugged into the floor. There's more clicking from the coffin. I need to hurry. I spark and feed the cord my own power. Done. The tiny heart inside continues to beat as I back away from the coffin.

I almost drop SC-13 when a man's head and shoulders break through the fog. I race toward Korwin, who is screaming and motioning for me to move faster. I look over my shoulder, and the man in the coffin turns his head to face me.

A scream pierces my lips as I recognize Dr. Emile Konrad. His skin is tinged yellow as are the whites of his gray eyes, but his thin, wicked smile and unruly hair are unmistakable.

I trip over a mass of cords in my haste to get away and am surprised when Korwin catches me. He drags me toward the door while I struggle to get my feet under me.

"What have you done?" echoes Dr. Konrad's voice. "Who are you? Who sent you?"

I am suddenly thankful for the costume I'm wearing. Dr. Konrad doesn't know who we are. As Korwin drags me through the door, I can't resist turning back at the sound of slamming metal and shattering glass. Konrad is floating. He's risen up out of the coffin and moves toward us, canisters of burnt remains flying into the walls as he approaches in a rage. His feet never touch the ground. He's hovering. Flying.

I scream.

Korwin yanks me through the door and slams it closed as something shatters on the other side.

"He was floating," I rattle as he pulls me toward the double doors to the lab. "And moving things with his mind!"

"I saw. We have to get out of here." I sprint around the piles of medical equipment, doing my best to keep up with Korwin in my ill-fitting boots.

Konrad pounds against the locked door. *Thump! Crash! Crack!* The wood splinters and flies into the lab. The doctor walks out, his yellow tinge muting as he moves from dark to light. What has he done to himself? I can feel power coming off him like the stench of sulfur. With a simple twitch of his head he parts the medical equipment using nothing but his intention. *What the—?*

We've reached the double doors and I am thrust through into the hall. "Be ready," Korwin says. He has the rifle in his hands and has it pointed at Dr. Konrad's heart.

Dr. Konrad smiles. "Who are you? Party guests come to make out in the scary lab? Wooo. Have I scared you back to mummy and daddy?"

Korwin raises the rifle. "Ztop vhere you are or I'll shoot," he says in Rayle's voice.

"Don't be stupid, boy. Do I look like a bullet can hurt me?" He spreads his hands and rises above the mess, hovering in midair. A metal tray flies across the room and crashes against the wall near Korwin's head. "If you shoot, I'll stop the bullet with my mind. Telekinesis, if you're wondering what it's called."

He floats forward, naked from the waist up, and is halfway to us by the time we back out the door.

"Give me the pod." He holds out one hand. "It's not a toy. You have no idea what you hold in your hands, young lady."

"Vhat is it?" I ask in Anastasia's voice.

"The future," he snaps. "Top secret. I don't want to kill you, but I will be forced to if you do not return to me the Green Republic property you hold in your arms."

I look down at the canister. I've been powering it the entire time and the red heart beats within the foggy glass. On and off. On and off.

Dr. Konrad's eyes narrow on my hands. With horror, I see what he sees. The blue glow. The beating heart.

"The doors," I say to Korwin. As fast as I have ever moved, I slam the steel lab door beside me. Korwin fires the gun as Dr. Konrad speeds toward us, but as promised, he deflects the bullet. Still, it's enough of a distraction that Korwin succeeds in closing and locking the other door. I shift the canister into one arm and snap the other at the elbow. Blue electricity consumes my hand and I throw everything I have into those doors, soldering the steel together.

Dr. Konrad slams into the metal. The melted steel cracks.

"It won't hold!" I say. We run. I trail behind, trying my best to keep up in the dress and boots.

"Why did you bring that?" Korwin asks, staring at the pod.

The banging behind us is a constant reminder that Dr. Konrad hasn't given up, and worse, he knows who I am. He saw my hands glow.

We pulse through the door to the stairwell but stop short of descending, pressing our backs into the wall at the sound of voices from below.

"Did you hear something?" an officer says. "From upstairs?"

"No. No one's up there. It's all locked up while they investigate Dr. Creepy."

"Hey, maybe it's the ghost of one of Dr. Creepy's victims."

"Shut up."

"What do you think happened to Ryan?"

"Who knows? Idiot could hurt himself in a padded room."

I meet Korwin's eyes and hold up two fingers. He nods. I lead the way.

"Excuze me," I say as we approach the men. My heart pounds but I force a smile, smoothing my dress. The two officers are young and inexperienced and I can tell we've taken them by surprise. "Ve are looking for de Ambassador's Club."

"You're in the wrong building. It's next door," the man on the left says. He's pale and narrow shouldered, with a face like a mouse. I wonder how he ended up working in security.

"Our mistake," I say, moving toward the door.

"Wait a minute. What do you have there?" the other man says. He's tall and dark and looks like he was made to be a soldier. He approaches the artificial womb in my arms.

I pop one hip and pucker my lips. "My purze, of courze. It'z de latest ztyle."

He nods slowly but moves between us and the door, placing his hand on his gun. He's not going to let us leave. I lament not using the element of surprise to my advantage.

"How did you get in here?" the mouse says.

"Ryan," Korwin says in Rayle's voice. "My zizter needed to uze zhe powder room and zhe other officer let uz een."

The two men look at each other. I'm close to the big man. One pulse and I can knock him out just like

Ryan. But without my wolf, I hesitate. Anxiety grips me behind my forced smile and latex mask.

I force myself a step closer, but before I can touch either of them, an explosion echoes through the stairwell from above. Korwin's arm sweeps me against the wall as an unhinged door clangs onto the stair landing. Dr. Konrad's disheveled yellow body appears from above. He's covered his naked torso with a lab coat but one sleeve has been torn off and his shoulder is cut.

"Stop them!" Dr. Konrad commands the officers. "They are stealing important research."

The mouse man draws his gun... on the doctor. "Dr. Konrad, we have strict orders that you are not to be in this building and experiments are strictly prohibited. I'm going to have to ask you to leave."

The bigger guard nods and presses his finger to his ear to call for backup. He steps between us and Dr. Konrad, who is seething with rage. Korwin and I back toward the exit.

"Go play somewhere else," Konrad says to the guard. With a flick of his hand the officer's gun flies from his fingers into the wall. "The adults need to have a conversation."

A dark spot appears on the big guard's trousers as Dr. Konrad floats toward us, the tips of his toes barely skimming the edge of each stair. The guard shakes so hard his name tag clicks against the buttons of his green uniform.

The mouse takes a moment to register what's happened and fires. Another wave of Dr. Konrad's hand and the bullet curves and hits the wall. I use the distraction to feel for the door panel and try to pulse it open, but I can't get a solid connection with SC-13's pod in my arms. It doesn't work.

Dr. Konrad raises both hands and twists the air in front of him. The mouse's head whips to the side, neck snapping.

"Your scrambler," Korwin says to the big guard, dropping his accent in the excitement.

Fumbling, the man finds the scrambler on his belt and fires. The probes hit Konrad squarely in the chest. He flinches, descending to his feet on the step and quivering as the volts pass through his body. He does not fall. Does not collapse.

Still it gives Korwin enough time to blow through the lock that wouldn't budge for me. The door opens.

"I will hunt you down!" Dr. Konrad rages, fighting his twitching muscles.

"Code red. Level zero. Code red." The big guard's eyes are the size of saucers. He's turned the device all the way up and holds it away from his body like he doesn't know what to do.

Korwin presses the button behind his ear as we race out the door. "Abort! West corner."

Green uniforms flood the garage behind us.

"Damn. Run!" Korwin yells.

I pump my legs, each step sending excruciating pain through my feet thanks to the ill-fitting boots. The awkward shape of SC-13's pod clutched to my chest slows me down. Korwin breaks out ahead. We circle down the ramp to the west corner to see our driver waiting with the doors open. Korwin doubles back, scoops me around the waist, and hurls me inside. David's hands hook beneath my shoulder blades, and I'm hauled across the seat as Korwin pushes in beside me and slams the door. Tires squeal. Shots echo around us. We flatten to the seat as the driver speeds toward the exit.

"Don't stop," Laura says to the driver from the passenger's seat, then gestures to us to buckle up. I fumble for my seatbelt just as the driver plows through a barricade and I'm sent tumbling into David.

"I'm okay," I say. Before long, things even out and we snap to the grid.

"Are they following us?" Korwin asks.

"Not anymore," Laura says, typing something into the dash. "Our tracking VIN has just been scrambled."

I scoot back into the seat beside Korwin, the pod still gripped tightly against my chest. Slowly, I set it on the seat between us, watching the red light blink behind the foggy glass. I keep the cord gripped in my hand, feeding it power.

"Why did you bring that?" Korwin asks.

"What is that thing, Lydia?" David peers at me through the corner of his eye.

Holding my breath, I tap the button on the side of SC-13 and wait for the foggy glass to clear. The heart light blinks and fades, blinks and fades. The fluid-filled membrane ripples with movement.

Korwin and David lean over the glass and look inside. Korwin shakes his head vigorously and claws at the mask on his face, ripping the latex off as if it's smothering him. He pants and stares, Rayle's image dangling from the side of his jaw. He shakes his head again.

"Lydia, tell me that is not what I think it is," David says.

"I don't know what you think it is, David, but this is the successful product of Konrad's experiments on the genetic material we were sent to destroy. Korwin's and mine. This is our baby."

Chapter 9

Laura pivots in her seat. "Did you just say baby?" Her voice is shrill and doesn't match her appearance, which is still disguised as the sophisticated Evana Baltik.

"He was the only one left alive," I say. "I saw him move, and his heart is beating."

"It," Korwin says. "Its heart is beating. We don't know for sure what that thing is."

"What are you talking about?" I ask, not understanding the tension suddenly palpable between us.

"It might not even be human," Korwin yells, meeting my eyes.

I press my back into the seat, mind reeling. "Human? Of course he's human. He's made from you and me. What else would he be?"

Korwin scowls at me. His expression is tight with fear and anger. "What do you think was going on in that room? That wasn't normal, Lydia!" His mouth opens to say something more but nothing comes out.

David unclips his seatbelt and squats on the floor to get a better look at the pod. "This must be one of those artificial wombs. Whatever he is, his existence is rare and possibly short-lived. From what I've heard, most babies don't last more than three weeks."

"Maybe this isn't what you think. Our intelligence suggested that Konrad was barred from his lab. This fetus could be a product of an experiment that had nothing to do with you two," Laura says. "An experiment from before the theft."

"How many weeks do you think he is?" I ask.

David shakes his head. "I have no idea."

Laura narrows her eyes. "Based on the size of the fluid suspension it's in, I'd guess around eight weeks by human standards."

"That's about when he stole the vials from us."

Laura's face pales and she glances at David.

He frowns and shakes his head. "We'll have to ask Charlie."

"Dr. Konrad was there." Korwin states the fact firmly, as if he still can't believe it and is admitting it as much to himself as to David and Laura.

David fumbles behind him for his seat, shaken. "Talk."

Korwin places his hand on mine supportively before answering. "Konrad was sleeping in a glass pod just like this one but bigger. We woke him up." Korwin shakes his head. "He's... changed. He's altered himself."

"How?" David asks.

"He can move things with his mind," I say. "And he's yellow."

"He looked jaundiced," Korwin says. "But muscled like he was using the Juice."

I remember Bella telling me about the Juice. It's a chemical that makes people strong but at the expense of their health. I chew my lip. "We watched him snap an officer's neck without even touching him."

"He's experimenting on himself," Laura says.

"Based on the reaction of the guards when he came after us, I don't think he was supposed to be in there," Korwin explains.

"Did he suspect it was you?" David asks.

"Not at first. " Korwin rubs his palms on his thighs and looks out the window.

I take a deep breath and admit my mistake. "After I took SC-13, I had to keep the womb working. It was plugged in and I wasn't sure how important that was. So, I powered the pod." I hold up the cord. "I'm still powering the pod."

"Your hand," Laura says.

"He saw," I say. "He knows it was us."

"Damn it, Lydia." David buries his face in his hands and digs his fingers into his hair.

"I couldn't let him die in there!" I yell. "He was the only one with a beating heart. He's a survivor."

"Please. Stop. Just stop." David leans his head back and stares at the ceiling.

No one will look at me. Laura stares straight ahead, out the windshield. Korwin watches traffic go by in streaks of light outside his window. David continues to stare at the ceiling.

"You think I should have left him," I say.

David groans and rolls his eyes. "No, Lydia. We think you should have destroyed *it* and gotten out of there as we planned!"

"But—"

"You can't be so naïve as to think you've saved it? The Liberty Party has enough trouble getting common medical equipment. Do you think for a second that we're equipped to keep an artificial womb operational?"

"But—"

"What you've done, Lydia, is enrage Konrad and put us all at risk, to save a baby that is as good as dead."

"Dr. Konrad is terrifying, but he's not with the Green Republic. You should have seen the way the guards treated him. He wasn't supposed to be there."

Korwin turns to me. I expect him to be supportive; this baby is as much his as mine. But his expression is angry and accusatory. "You think that matters? Dr. Konrad is a dangerous man, as dangerous as any weapon. You know this personally. If my assumptions about what was going on in that room are correct, he will stop at nothing to get that thing back, dead or alive." He points at SC-13.

I shake my head. "You can't think I should have left him there. He's ours!"

"He was wired to them!" Korwin yells. He points a finger at the floor of the car to avoid pointing it at my face. At least he gives me that. "Konrad made himself telekinetic, and I don't think it's a coincidence he was sleeping in that room today with the other experiments. Whatever that thing is, it was helping him *become*."

David straightens. "We should eliminate it. Now." He straightens his arm and his fingers spark with energy.

I don't hesitate. I push the canister behind my back and spark out too, glowing electric blue and crackling next to Korwin.

"You won't touch him," I say to David.

"Lydia," Korwin says.

"No one hurts this baby," I say. "This is our baby. If you want to get to him, you'll have to go through me."

"Be reasonable, Lydia," Korwin says. "It's a monster."

"You're a monster," I snap. "He didn't do anything wrong. He's just a little baby. Our baby."

The heat coming off me is scorching the upholstery. David holds up his hands. "Okay, okay. Calm down."

I pant with the effort of pulling the power back inside. "Back off," I say through my teeth, "and I will."

Chapter 10

As we approach the door to the reactor, the forest explodes with flashes of light. There are flasher drones everywhere. I can see their spider-like bodies carpeting the forest floor and dangling from the trees.

"There's so many. They weren't here when we left," I murmur. Their bodies crunch beneath our tires.

"They've been migrating toward the reactor for days. We've taken precautions," Laura says.

"All the Greens will see is a streak of blurred light. The reflective epoxy on the outside of the vehicle effectively makes us invisible to transmittable imaging," David explains.

"That's comforting," Korwin says sarcastically. The flashing light creates a strobe effect behind his head.

"I'm not comfortable with this many so close to us," Laura says. "I'll talk to Jonas. A concentrated blast of energy might scramble their circuitry."

The garage door opens automatically and descends behind us. The intermittent flashes of the drones are cut off, replaced with the solid overhead light of the garage. Charlie and Jonas are waiting in the bay. They don't look happy. In a heartbeat, they swoop in to open the doors and help us from the vehicle.

"Thank the heavens you are all okay," Jonas says, pulling me into a tight hug. "We saw the broadcast and thought we might not see you again."

"Broadcast? Did they catch us on camera?" Korwin asks. I'm just as confused. I was sure we were fully costumed and well hidden within the grid. Aside from Konrad, the Greens shouldn't have known who we were.

Charlie scans each of us from head to toe, seemingly satisfied with our physical health. "There was an explosion in the parking garage between CGEF and the Ambassador's Club. Two dead. Fifteen hospitalized. Mostly workers and security guards who were in the area."

"Let me guess, the two dead were CGEF security guards," Korwin says, glancing at me.

Charlie raises an eyebrow. "Collateral damage?"

"Not by my hand, but they were dead before the explosion. Dr. Konrad killed them and, I assume, caused the damage to cover up the murders. It was clear he wasn't supposed to be there."

"You ran into Dr. Konrad?" Jonas asks, scowling.

"Ran into him. Almost got killed by him."

"Charlie, we need your help," I say, holding out SC-13.

Charlie looks, then looks again, studying the canister in my arms. "Please tell me this isn't what I think it is," he says.

Why does everyone keep saying that? I lower my eyes to SC-13 and say nothing.

David speaks for me. "It's exactly what you think it is. It is the embodiment of Lydia's lack of good sense."

"Hey!" I yell.

"It looks like an artificial womb," Charlie says.

"From Konrad's laboratory," I confirm.

"Taking this was risky and unintelligent," Charlie says. "We can study it, and I can dissect it after it dies—"

I back away. "You're not going to dissect it. You're going to save *him*." I'm glowing like a star.

The entire garage is awash in blue light. Charlie shields his eyes from my heat.

"Lydia, I don't know anything about supporting an artificial womb. Not to mention, only a few babies have ever made it to term in one of these. Human babies. There is no way to project what a gamma might need."

David jumps on board the *destroy it* campaign. "Listen to Charlie. This isn't your fault, Lydia. You have a huge heart, and I wouldn't expect anything less from you, but you can't save everyone or everything. This baby is doomed. It may even be dangerous."

Tears stream down my cheeks and I hug the pod to my chest. "How could he be dangerous? He hasn't even been born."

"What if he has powers, even in the womb?" Korwin says. "Why was Dr. Konrad sleeping wired to it?"

I weep and burn hotter. "You are not hurting this baby!"

I'm surprised when Laura steps in front of me and speaks. "This *baby* is made from Korwin and Lydia. I seem to remember a time we went to great lengths to protect a baby I was carrying, a baby Dr. Konrad warned us could be born a monster. She turned into the woman standing right here. I don't care if it is in an artificial womb. That's my grandchild in there, and we will protect it at all costs."

I look toward Korwin for support. He mutters, "It won't hurt to try."

Charlie spreads his hands. "I'll do my best."

Slowly, I power down, SC-13 clutched to my chest. I sway on my feet, the room spinning. "I don't feel well," I say.

Arms outstretched, Korwin approaches. "You're sweating and pale."

"Let me take the baby and get started," Charlie says in an even, steady voice. "I think you need to rest."

The next moment, I'm falling and Korwin catches me in his arms. "She needs to get out of this costume," he says. "I'll help her to her room."

Hesitantly, I release SC-13 to Charlie and allow Korwin to carry me to bed.

* * * * *

"I don't know what was wrong with me," I say. Korwin waits for me, lying on my bed. I've showered and changed and don't feel as sick, but I'm definitely not myself.

"You haven't been sleeping well."

"Who told you that?" I ask, my shoulders tensing, thinking Charlie has broken my confidence.

Korwin's brow furrows. "*You* did. At lunch yesterday, remember?"

I hold my head. "Yeah. I guess I did."

"Come here." Korwin pulls back the covers and props his head up in his hand, elbow in the pillow. He pats the space beside him.

"We haven't slept in the same bed since we lived in the Kennel," I say. I crawl into bed next to him and snuggle into the nook between his chest and arm.

"Maybe that's why you haven't been sleeping well."

I close my eyes and inhale the distinctive boy scent of Korwin. He smells of a field after a thunderstorm, rain and ozone and fresh air. "That settles it. You should move in here, for health purposes."

"Good idea. All you have to do is marry me first."

I open my eyes. "Is that a proposal?"

He kisses the top of my head. "You know it is. I'd get you a ring but since Amish don't exchange them and I can't grow a beard, I'm at a loss."

"I'm not Amish anymore."

Korwin presses his lips to the side of my head. "Then maybe I should buy you a ring. We are still engaged, aren't we?"

I pause, thinking back to Hemlock Hollow. Had Korwin been baptized, we'd already be married. So much has changed since then. I've changed.

"Lydia?"

"Y-yes," I say.

"Are you having doubts? Because it's really important that we are honest with each other. I want you to tell me what you're thinking."

"I'm thinking... Now that Hemlock Hollow isn't our home, I don't know what marriage looks like. There's no bread to make or clothes to sew. There's no field to tend. What constitutes a marriage to an Englisher?"

"It's not about what you do for each other but how you feel. If we're married in the English world, we'll be equals. We'll support each other through whatever experiences come our way."

I laugh. "We already do that. Can't we just live together? You could move in tomorrow. No ceremony needed."

Korwin says nothing. Although he doesn't physically move, I feel him retract. Should I say something? The only comfort I can think to give him is to renege and say I'll marry him immediately. I'm tempted, but then I think of what Charlie said, *80% of people injected with Nanomem have a psychotic break*. I'm already hallucinating. It wouldn't be fair to bind him to a crazy person.

"The pastor here says I can be baptized any time I want. I just have to schedule it. The chapel is nondenominational. You can sponsor me." His voice is soft, just above a whisper.

"Are you sure you don't want someone who knows this religion better? I know nothing about practicing nondenominational," I say.

"Nondenominational Christian, Lydia. It's the same Bible, just in English."

"Oh." I consider that for a second. "Yes. I'll sponsor you, but we should do it quickly. This week."

"Not that I don't share your enthusuiasm, but why are you in a rush?"

"You know, in case Dr. Konrad comes for us. Things could change in an instant."

He flattens a palm on my stomach. "Is that what this is all about? You don't want to be married for the same reason you want me to be baptized as soon as possible. You're afraid one of us will die soon?"

"Die or worse," I say.

"What's worse than death?"

I search the lines of his perfect face, the smooth brown skin, the hazel eyes alive with blue sparks because he's near me. "Capture, abduction, impairment. Marriage is permanent. I think before we commit to marriage, things should be more stable. We should have a future."

He licks his bottom lip and glows like a lightbulb as his emotions rise to the surface. As always, I am drawn to him. The stuff I am made of wakes up in his presence and reaches for him. I work hard to hold it at bay. All I can picture is kissing him, touching him.

"We have a future, albeit an uncertain one," he says. "I'd be a loyal husband, Lydia. If anything happened to you, I'd never forsake you. I know marriage is permanent, but I want that with you. Come what may."

"That's what I'm afraid of. I don't want you to sacrifice your future for me. You deserve better. You deserve normal."

"So do you. That's not what God handed us. I feel blessed with what we have. Most people don't find someone to love who loves them back like we do. I could die. On any one of these missions, Konrad or the Greens could kill me. Does it make you love me less?"

115

"No. Never," I say honestly and without thinking.

"And nothing could make me love you less."

"Can I ask you something?"

"Shoot."

"Are you sure you still want to be baptized, after everything that's happened?"

He becomes pensive and strokes my pale hand with his brown one. "Yes. I believe in God and want to take this step. I feel like it's something I should do. Are you still having doubts?"

I pause, thinking. "On Konrad's table, while I was dying, I couldn't feel God's presence. I felt abandoned. And when I think of Hemlock Hollow, I get this weight in the center of my chest. The community I fought to protect, fought to bring you into, rejected both of us. Where was God during all of that, Korwin? You told me once in the Kennel that you didn't know what you believed. I feel the same way. I'm lost and waiting for God to find me again, if he's there at all."

Korwin stretches out next to me and sighs deeply. "I was confused too. I felt just like you when I was living in the Kennel. But the day you revived me in the back of that jeep, I realized that God didn't abandon us. He's been with us all along. He guided you to me. He saved us from Dr. Konrad. He connected us with the Liberty Party. And he helped us escape tonight. I don't think God looks or acts the way the citizens of Hemlock Hollow think he does."

I snort. "What do you mean?"

"I don't think he's only for them, living behind that wall with all the rules and the separation. I think he's for all of us. I think God lives in the people who fight the good fight, who stand up against evil in the real world, even when it means personal sacrifice."

"Hmmm," I say skeptically. "You think God is on the Liberty Party's side?"

He shakes his head. "I think God is on the side of people who do good."

"The people of Hemlock Hollow are innocent. They are completely separate from the evil of this world."

"Not doing wrong because you live in a community that takes away your free will is way different than taking risks for the common good. You put yourself out there, Lydia. Yes, you killed a man, but that man was evil. That man would have hurt the people we love."

"What are you talking about? You blamed me for killing Brady. You went on and on about how I should have let him live."

"I was wrong. After seeing Konrad's lab today, I'm certain allowing Brady to live would have been the worst decision we could have ever made. Bringing him back here would've been too dangerous. You did the right thing. God put you right where you needed to be."

My head spins with fatigue, and I close my eyes. "I can't talk about this anymore."

He strokes my hair and down the side of my face. "Okay. Tomorrow. We can talk again tomorrow." I hear him shift as if he's getting out of bed.

"No. Please. Stay with me," I plead, opening my eyes.

He lies back down, and I snuggle into his side again. "I'll stay with you tonight. Just tell me one thing."

"What?"

"Will you marry me?"

I have reservations. I think Korwin deserves better. But I can't say no. "Of course I will. I love you. And besides, we may have a son or daughter to raise."

Korwin pales. "You mean SC-13. Lydia, the chances…"

"I know." I place my fingers over his lips. "I know. We'll talk more tomorrow."

"Deal."

With a deep, cleansing breath, I lay my head on his chest. The sound of his heartbeat carries me into oblivion.

Chapter 11

The nightmare parts the darkness like a bolt of lightning. I'm in the side room of Dr. Konrad's laboratory, surrounded by the glowing foggy glass of the artificial wombs. There's a rectangular-shaped light above me, flickering. At the head of the room, the glass coffin whirs and clicks. The lid rises and Dr. Konrad's yellow torso emerges from the rolling fog.

Panic floods my veins, burning like acid, and my heart pounds in an attempt to rid it from my body. When I try to run, my feet stick to the floor. The cords from the pods are wrapped around my ankles, tying me in place. I can't move. I can't run.

Dr. Konrad's thin lips form words, although they move independent of the sound, like he's speaking a different language. His eyes are black, soulless pits. "Where are you going, momma bird? You have to stay and take care of our children."

Our children? My stomach recoils.

Around me, the pods open like hatching eggs. The babies inside are full-grown but far from normal. With cats' eyes and snakeskin, they open their mouths and scream like hungry birds. Their voices are a cacophony of animal sounds, tortured wails, and inhuman growls.

Dr. Konrad climbs from his coffin, a plate of raw meat in his hands. He dangles a slice over one of the babies' mouths and drops it. The young swallows it whole. He grins and approaches me, thrusting the plate into my hands. "Your turn."

As I accept it, I notice my fingers are yellow against the white plate. Yellow, like Konrad's. Cords appear around my wrists, pulling and moving my limbs from the ceiling as if I'm a marionette. My head throbs from the cries of the babies around me as the meat drops from my hand.

I wake in a sweat, panting, head throbbing. The room is pitch black and Korwin's rhythmic breathing is soft and regular beside me. Tears pour from my eyes. It's the middle of the night. The hair on the back of my neck stands at attention from the horrifying scene in my head. My heart still pounds.

My wolf is in the room. She whimpers near the door. My head throbs with the need to follow her. If I can just let her run for a while, she'll scare the bad thoughts away. She'll protect me from this feeling of helplessness, of falling, of devolving into a beast like Dr. Konrad.

I creep from the bed. Korwin turns on his side but doesn't wake. Quietly, I unlock the door and tiptoe from the room. I'm barefoot, in my nightgown, but I do not go back for my shoes or robe. We have things to do, my wolf and I. I am trapped inside my skin, and she is assuring me my freedom. Whispers, like promises, seep from her jowls.

"Where did you go today?" I ask her. "You left me when I saw the baby. You didn't help me when Konrad attacked."

She doesn't answer me, just trots faster down the corridor toward the stairwell. I break into a jog, following my wolf down the staircase, through the hallways, and to the garage.

I know what the dream meant. It's my mind's way of showing me my fear of losing myself. Behind the wall, I was innocent, and now I'm a killer. I can make excuses for what I've done. There were reasons. Gray areas of morality. But I'm sliding. More and more I have to do things I once thought I would never do. Was this how it started for a man like Dr. Konrad? Small moral concessions until nothing is absolute, until only his will and desires mattered to him anymore and he became the evil that he is?

I shake my head as I burst from the garage into the night. My wolf will fix this. She'll free me from the guilt that binds me.

It is cold and I am only wearing a thin cotton nightgown. As I slip out the side door, pine needles prick the bottoms of my bare feet. The moon shines weak and useless above me, blotted out by the tangle of branches overhead. Neither the biting chill nor the absolute darkness matter to me. I sprint after my wolf, my white nightgown billowing with my movements, the night air catching around my torso and between my limbs. My unkempt hair floats. The rush of my breath brushes the back of my throat. I am a ghost. I am my wolf. I am the night itself.

Faintly, I am aware that my feet are cut and bleeding, but I do not stop. My head throbs; I do not stop. My fingers are blue with cold. I do not stop. I push myself, faster, harder through the trees. Muscles straining. Breath coming in huffs. I sense something up ahead, something I must do. There. A black silhouette in the distance. Almost invisible to the human eye in the darkness but not to my wolf's eyes. This is my prey. A kill will set it right. A kill will earn my keep. Then I will sleep and heal.

Closer now, it squeaks at my nearing. Run, run, my quarry. Don't you see me coming? Fresh meat. The silhouette welcomes death, opening its arms. I run faster, my wolf blending into me. I collide with the silhouette, and I am ready.

I pounce and bite and scratch and hit. The thing beneath me squeals. A pig. I snap its bones and tear its flesh. It tries to fight back, but I am stronger and faster. Another bone cracks, followed by more screaming and then pleading. The forest flickers like the light in my nightmare and my prey's pain-filled face begs me for mercy. Human squeals, not animal.

Scurrying footsteps come from behind. I see flashes of faces. Light and dark.

"Grab her," David yells. What right does he have to tell me what to do? He's the one who made me sick. I bite and howl and thrash at his efforts to contain me.

"Lydia, stop!" Korwin's hands are on me, pulling me back. I go limp in his arms. There's blood in my mouth. I don't want him to see me like this. I groan and struggle against him. I turn my face away.

"Oh no. Oh no," David says.

"Don't. I can hold her." Korwin tightens his grip.

"Sorry. It's too dangerous. We need help." David's hand grips my head and a sharp prick in the side of my neck is followed by warmth that spreads under the skin. He's injected me. The last words I hear before the medication knocks me out are, "Let's get them inside and wake up Charlie."

Chapter 12

I'm in the infirmary. Was I dreaming? My actions feel far off and hazy. Memories of running through the woods come back to me in blurry flashes. I know it happened though, because I ache everywhere, especially my feet, which are bandaged at the end of the gurney. Bright lights burn above me. A steady throb keeps time behind my right eye. I try to curl on my side but can't. My wrists and ankles are bound.

With one eye closed protectively against the glare of the overhead light, I look around the room. Charlie sits in front of a microscope, examining something with intense concentration. Next to him, the pod with SC-13 inside is plugged in, the red heart light barely visible through the fogged glass.

"You kept him alive," I say.

Charlie starts and turns toward me. "Hi." He rubs the back of his neck. "Yeah, SC-13 is proving stronger than I predicted and, as it turns out, these pods are made to be self-sufficient for the duration of the fetal development period. How are *you* feeling?"

"Sore." I tug against my restraints. "Can you untie me?"

Charlie pulls his tiny flashlight out of his lab coat pocket and approaches the side of my bed. "What's your full name? The one you were given, not your alias."

"Lydia Troyer. Charlie, you know me. Why are you asking me that?"

"Is the wolf you told me about in the room?"

My face twitches. I don't like that he knows about my wolf. Why did I tell him? "No," I say truthfully. "Please untie me. My back hurts and the light is too bright. It reminds me of the lab." I'm parched. I glance toward the sink, longing for water.

He looks me in the eye and then pulls a lever to raise the head of my gurney. Without another word, he moves to the small refrigerator in the corner and retrieves a reusable bottle of water. He holds it to my lips and helps me take a drink. "There's something I have to tell you. If I were smart, I'd keep you tied up while I do. But I've never been accused of being too smart."

"Sounds serious."

He goes to work on my left ankle. "You injured someone last night. You might have killed them if David and Korwin hadn't caught up to you in the woods."

My feet are wrapped in bandages. Flashes of the chase flit through my mind. "I was hunting, I mean, chasing… There was someone in the woods. A spy for the Greens. I set off the flashers. Charlie, I'm so sorry. Ugh!" My head pounds and I squeeze my eyes closed.

"What's happening?" Charlie asks worriedly.

"Headache."

"Do you want pain medication?"

I roll my ankle as he moves to the next restraint. "No. I have a bad reaction to it." A few deep breaths and the pain ebbs.

"I remember. Vomiting and seizures. Only, sometimes the side effects are worth a break in the pain."

"Not this time. You were saying? About the spy I injured."

Charlie shakes his head. "Before we get to that, I finished analyzing the results of the tests we did to try to determine why you've been hallucinating and sleepwalking."

I hold up my wrist and he starts unbuckling the restraint. "Did you find out what's wrong with me?"

"As you know, your cells are different than the rest of ours. Even though David and I have electrokinetic power, our cells aren't stable. We burn energy at the expense of our own bodies. That's why we have to take the serum. We have human cells with electrokinetic DNA. You and Korwin don't. Your cells are different. You don't need serum."

"What does that have to do with my hallucinations?"

"When David gave you the Nanomem, it was the first time that drug was used on a person of your genetic makeup. Nanomem works by copying memory proteins from a donor, in this case David, to a recipient, you. Those proteins take root in the brain. Unlike in human trials, David's proteins weren't a match with your own. Different cells; different proteins. My theory is that your body is viewing David's proteins as foreign substances. For lack of a better way to put it, you're having an allergic reaction to his memories."

I laugh. "I'm not allergic to my own brain. I haven't so much as sneezed."

"Not that kind of reaction. When your brain waves change due to extreme fear or going into deep sleep, the biochemical changes you experience trigger a reaction to the proteins in your brain. That's when the wolf manifests. The wolf is your brain's way of attempting to restore homeostasis. When you are afraid, it urges you to fight. No guilt. No hesitation. When you feel weak or inadequate it tempts you to be strong, to be the predator. Am I right?"

"Yes," I murmur.

"Those new emotions produce chemicals that eventually rebalance your brain chemistry. A nifty self-healing property if you think about it."

"So, the wolf heals me. That's not so bad."

"Unfortunately, there are two problems with this process. First is, while it's happening, you are not in control. The wolf is in control. And the wolf isn't good at discerning right from wrong."

"You mean, she puts me in danger."

"The wolf puts you and everyone around you in danger." Charlie unbuckles my final restraint. "The second problem is, the restoration is far from perfect. The places where these events occur in the brain become like scar tissue. The next time they occur, they don't happen over the same damaged area. The imbalance occurs in a new area of the brain and forms new scar tissue. With less healthy brain to work with, the imbalance is more pervasive. The wolf has to show up more frequently, and she sticks around longer. She makes you do things you would never do if you were mentally healthy."

"Who did I hurt last night, Charlie?"

He ignores my question and taps a monitor on the wall. A body-shaped outline appears on the screen. "This is your body scan. This bright red with a core of yellow-orange is normal for you as is the aqua blue of your skin. These white spots in your brain are the scarring I've been talking about."

The white spots are scattered across my head in the picture. Two are quite large and I can see why Charlie is concerned. "There's more than I expected."

He rubs his chin. "Your body will compensate until it can't. These spots are electrical anomalies. Cool spots. For lack of a better word, you have a short in your electrical system."

I shake my head. I don't understand what he means.

Charlie pulls a watch out of his pocket. "This is the old-fashioned kind with the touch screen, from before they went out of fashion. It runs on a battery."

I take it from his hands. "It isn't working."

"Exactly. This watch has a short. It started with one black square in the corner where the power from the battery couldn't reach the screen anymore. The power that was supposed to go to the screen was bleeding off somewhere inside, going somewhere it wasn't supposed to go. No matter how many times I charged the watch, power could not flow to that square of the screen. The problem wasn't the power; it was the delivery. Over time, the black spot spread until the entire screen went dark. The watch had a short, Lydia. Instead of the power going where it was supposed to go, a part of the current took an unintended path. A path that didn't lead to the functioning of the watch. Now it doesn't work at all."

"The white spots are shorts in my electrical system?" I stare at the pattern of white on my scan.

"The scar tissue doesn't transmit electricity easily. Electricity flows along the path of least resistance. For now, the current is navigating these land mines, but eventually, if the white continues to grow, there will be no place for the red to go. You'll lose your spark."

"I won't be electrokinetic anymore?"

He shakes his head.

"Are you sure about this? I haven't had any problems using my spark."

"No? What about passing out in the garage yesterday? You haven't had any weakness?"

For some reason my mind flashes on a few days ago in the cafeteria, when the current that usually flowed between Korwin and me felt like a trickle.

"Can you stop it?" I ask.

"I don't know." Charlie frowns. "I have a few theories, but you are one of a kind. I need time to consider a viable therapy."

I step gingerly down from the gurney. My feet sting beneath the bandages. "Normally, I would have healed by now."

"Already the flow of energy through your body is compromised."

I take a few experimental steps, wincing from the pain.

"You're a tough cookie. I put over a hundred stitches in those size nines."

I groan. "Stop avoiding, Charlie. I'm falling apart. I get it. Just tell me who I hurt last night. Was it Laura again? One of the Liberty Party soldiers?"

"Come on," he says solemnly. He helps me out the door and down the hall of the medical complex. "I know you, Lydia. This isn't going to be easy on you, but I don't believe for a minute you would have done this if you were healthy. I won't keep it from you though. You need to see what can happen if you don't take your disease seriously."

I cross my arms over my waist and hug myself, dread wrapping like a vine up my body and squeezing. Who did I hurt?

When we reach Room 3, he opens the door for me. I enter a homey medical room with a hospital bed and a bank of bags dripping into a tube attached to a man's arm. The IV is taped to his forearm over coarse blond hair. The rest of the man is more bandage than skin. He has an eyepatch and stitches where his neck meets his shoulder. Most of his face is black and blue. One arm and one leg are casted and there are bandages wrapped around his rib cage.

"What happened?" I ask. "He looks like he's been in a car accident."

"You happened," Charlie murmurs.

I turn toward him but he doesn't look like he's joking. "No. Not just me. I couldn't have done all of that."

"Yes. Those stitches are from your bite. You broke his ribs, his arm, his leg. We have him sedated to jump-start the healing process."

I swallow hard, tears forming in my eyes. "I didn't know. Who is it? One of the patrol?"

Charlie shakes his head. "I wasn't sure who he was at first, but David and Korwin recognized him.

He's from the preservation. Name is Jeremiah
Yoder."

Chapter 13

"No!" I rush to the bed and clutch Jeremiah's hand. The boy I grew up with is pale and his fingers are limp within mine. I rub his arm in one of the only spots that isn't bandaged or injured. "Jeremiah?"

"He won't wake," Charlie says. "It's better to keep him sedated for the first part of the healing process."

"Why was he in the woods? What is he doing here?"

"We don't know. You knocked him out when you attacked him. Frankly, he's lucky to be alive. David said you might have killed him if he and Korwin hadn't intercepted and sedated you."

Tears spill over my bottom lids. "I'm so sorry. How could I?" I sob and can't catch my breath. "How could I do something like this?"

Charlie sighs. "It's like I've been telling you, Lydia, the side effects of the Nanomem are altering your reality. When the wolf takes over, your mind can't process the world as you normally would. It's clear to me that you didn't know you were attacking Jeremiah last night. Not only did you hurt someone you obviously care about, you ripped your feet apart in the process and risked exposing us to the flasher drones. Those aren't things you would do in your right mind."

"No, I wouldn't," I mumble.

"The reason I brought you in here is not to make you feel guilty about what you've done, but to make you see how dangerous your condition can be. To warn you."

"Is he going to be all right?"

"I don't think there's any permanent damage. His bones will need to heal. It will take longer than yours. A week or two on bed rest. Six to eight weeks before we take the casts off and can let him go home."

"What should I do? How do I stop this from happening again?"

"To be blunt, you're a ticking time bomb. It's not only the loss of your power. Your brain's reaction to the Nanomem is getting more frequent and severe as the scar tissue spreads. My feeling is that if it continues unchecked, one day the wolf will take over completely and the person we know as Lydia Troyer will be no more."

"There must be a way to fix me. I'll try anything."

"It might be possible for me to create an injection, similar to the serum I take every day, to turn those white spots red. I'll need time. This is theoretical science."

"What do I do until then?"

"We have to tell the others what's going on. The people around you need to know the risks. Imagine if you would have sparked out last night? Jeremiah might be ash rather than injured. After pulling you off him, David and Korwin suspect the problem is worse than sleepwalking. It's time they knew the truth."

I nod. "Fine. We tell them."

"One more precaution. Until we figure this out, I don't think you should be unattended. We can lock you in your room if you need to be alone. You'll stay safe and so will the others."

Looking at Jeremiah, hardly recognizable under the bandages and swelling, it's hard to argue with his logic. The thought of being locked up like an animal bothers me, but I can't risk doing this to anyone else.

What if I'd attacked Korwin in his sleep? "Okay. Is that it?"

"Rest and relaxation are the name of the game. Do not push yourself. Try not to use your power. No missions. No hard-core training with Simi."

I lean my head back and moan toward the ceiling.

"I mean it, Lydia. You've got to trust me on this one. The scar tissue doesn't just impede the flow of electricity out of your body, it also works the other way. Too much scarring and you won't be able to recharge. When I say you could lose your spark, I mean it. Another incident like last night, and you might do damage no serum can ever fix."

* * * * *

"No stress on Lydia until I can get this under control," Charlie tells the council. "No missions. No hard-core training."

Mirabella Grant scowls. "This couldn't come at a worse time. We need her in the field."

"While I can appreciate your frustration, she'll be no good to you if you burn her out," Charlie says.

139

Ever his wife's perpetual cheerleader, Warden Grant shakes his head and says, "Show them the clip, David."

David types on the console and a news clip displays in a hologram at the center of the table. Alexandra Brighten, dressed all in black, looks into the camera. *"We are grieved to report that the rumors Chancellor Pierce was brutally murdered last night have been confirmed. Pierce, who died of multiple stab wounds to the back, was found alone in his home. No fingerprints or DNA were detectible on the weapons or the body, but it is widely assumed the attack was an act of terrorism. Pierce's daughter, Trinity, is missing and authorities worry that her abduction will result in further threats and coercion from the rebellion."*

"Was it us?" Korwin asks as Brighten continues her babble.

"No," Laura says firmly. "We had nothing to do with this. Our best guess is it was an inside job. Unfortunately, our informants are as clueless as we are."

"Sources at the Capitol say that provincial leaders are convening to elect a new chancellor, a position needed more than ever after this unprecedented terrorist attack by the Liberty Party. In the interim, Vice

Chancellor Elias Fitzgerald has taken the reins to ensure a seamless transition."

"Whoever it was took Trinity," I say worriedly.

"If not us, who could be responsible for the murder and abduction?" Korwin asks.

"Konrad," I say absently, puzzling it out in my head. "Pierce fired him. It could be an act of revenge."

Jonas shakes his head. "Konrad hasn't been allowed near Pierce in weeks. None of our informants have seen him since the explosion. It's a matter of motivation. Konrad wants to keep his nose clean and earn his way back into the fold."

Mirabella clears her throat. "Follow the power, dear girl. Who benefited most from Pierce's death?"

I shrug.

"Elias Fitzgerald," Jonas chimes in. He taps the monitor and a hologram of the torso of the heavyset, balding man I'd shaken hands with at the Ambassador's Club hovers over the table. "Elias isn't simply vice chancellor. He's the chief executive of New Generation Ag and was a contender for Pierce's position when the Republic became a military dictatorship. Rumor has it, he was disappointed when he was passed over and Pierce was selected. The senators feared Elias would be too heavy-handed, but with the violence they've endured, the Greens may elect him out of desperation, and that would have far-reaching consequences."

"Farther reaching than Pierce's election?"

Warden leans back in his chair and presses the tips of his fingers together in front of his light blue sweater. "Elias is an absolutely brutal, soulless man. Pierce was a puppy compared to Elias. Pierce was content to leave well enough alone. All these months, he's never pursued us, not in the way he could have. Now, with the bombing and Pierce's murder, the Liberty Party is being painted as public enemy number one. With Elias in command, the Greens will retaliate. It's just a matter of when."

Laura straightens in her seat. "The Liberty Party has the largest and most organized rebellion in its history but we are drastically outnumbered. A direct attack on our headquarters could be catastrophic."

"Our only hope is that Elias's interim leadership ends quickly and they elect Dorian Brandish instead," Jonas says. The hologram changes and a decrepit man, terribly thin, with knotted hands and a hunched back, hovers over the table. "But at ninety-three, it is unlikely he'd be suggested for anything but replacement."

"We should try to find Trinity," I say. "If she's still alive, she'll know who is behind this. By redirecting the Greens toward the real culprit, we might be able to avoid direct conflict."

"If it was Elias who murdered Pierce, I'm not sure we have a prayer of finding Trinity," David says. "He'll want to frame us for the murder and abduction. His permanent election depends on the Green Republic believing they are under attack by the Liberty Party. She could be anywhere. But you're right about one thing. If we could find her, we could stop Elias from gaining more power."

"So where do we start?" I say.

Charlie slaps the table, surprising a small jump out of me. "Do you remember how this conversation started, Lydia? *You* can't help with this. You need to stay here and rest."

"But—"

Korwin silences me with a knee knock under the table. "She'll stay, and I'll stay here with her."

Jonas groans and grabs his head. "Why don't we all stay here and care for Lydia. We can toast marshmallows and wish on the first star of the evening that this all goes away."

"You need to take this seriously, Jonas." Charlie points at me. "She could lose her power. She could lose her mind."

Korwin shakes his head. "She stays and I stay. What happened last night was a tragedy. Lydia shouldn't be alone. She needs support right now while Charlie works on a stabilizing agent."

"Surely a nurse can spend time with her," Mirabella says. "Charlie will be here caring for his other patients if there's an emergency."

"No. I'm staying with my fiancée. We go together or we don't go at all," Korwin says.

My heart quivers at his words. Is he sacrificing himself for me? Does he want to go on the mission? He knows Trinity and would be an asset to the team. Am I holding him back and possibly costing Trinity her life?

Mirabella and Warden frown at me.

David gives Jonas a dismissive look. "It's probably better we travel light on this one, anyway. Laura and I will investigate the crime scene. I don't believe for a second the Green detectives found no DNA or protein markers. They could be covering for Elias. Laura and I will sneak into the place and collect our own samples. No confrontation."

"You'll have to go quickly. Every minute is opportunity for someone to pollute the crime scene," Jonas says.

"I'm in," Laura says, glancing at me. "With just David and me, we'll be in and out in no time."

Jonas's eyes dart to Mirabella, who arches an approving eyebrow.

"Agreed," Jonas says. He slides a folder across the table to David. "Go. Be careful."

The room clears, and I stand up to follow the others, but Korwin's hand shoots out and grips my wrist. His eyes are dark and his mouth pulls into a straight line. "You've got some explaining to do."

Chapter 14

I should have told Korwin about the Nanomem disease privately. I couldn't. There was no time. Still, finding out this way, after he pulled me off Jeremiah, must seem insulting. Maybe I should have blurted it out as soon as I saw him, but telling someone you love that you are losing your mind is not an easy or quick pain to bear. I dread what he will say about Jeremiah. What must he think of me? Will he still want me, knowing I could lose my spark?

"Why didn't you tell me?" he asks. His voice is soft. I'm surprised he doesn't yell. I deserve for him to yell.

"I just found out myself."

"No. You've known something was wrong. Charlie said this was the second incident."

"I wasn't sure what was happening. I didn't want to worry you."

"It's my prerogative to worry about you, even if we don't know all of the facts."

"That's just it. I don't think you should have to worry about anyone. You deserve better, Korwin. This is what I was talking about when I said there were things worse than death."

He snorts. "This is not worse than death."

"Are you going to stick around while I slowly go crazy? Will you still want me when you're not physically attracted to me?"

His eyebrows dive. "Why would any of this change our attraction to each other?"

"If I lose my spark, we won't have the magnetic draw to each other we do now. The blue light we put off and the zaps and tingling when we touch will be gone. Those things will die with my spark."

He shakes his head. "So what?"

"So what? So, you might not want me anymore."

"Ridiculous."

I shake my head. "You say that, but what if I lose my mind?"

"It's going to be okay," he says. "I'll watch out for you. Charlie will fix this."

"We don't know that Charlie *can* fix this."

"You're right. We don't. But I know I love you. Nothing is going to change that."

I stare at my fingers, gone cold on the table in front of me. "I've lied to you."

"Huh."

"The reason I didn't tell you sooner was not because I didn't want to worry you." I look him in the eye and swallow hard. "And it wasn't because I don't want you to sacrifice yourself for me or to settle for something less than perfect. I withheld the information because I don't want to lose you. I'm selfish and insecure. I can't bear the thought of you leaving me. If you do, I have nothing left."

With his thumb and knuckle, he pinches my chin. "Let's get something straight. The electrical connection between us is not why I want you. And it certainly isn't why I love you. I want you to be healthy, and I want you to feel like yourself, but the love I have for you isn't such a fragile thing to be shattered over the loss of your spark."

"You could be bound to a lunatic," I whimper.

"I told you, I'm not going to leave you. Don't you see? I can't be without you, Lydia. If we've learned anything, it's that we have to stick together." He stands and moves behind me, my skin heating from the electrical charge between us as he leans over my shoulder and wraps his arms around my neck, hugging me. "Don't you want that?"

"I do, but—"

"No buts. I will love you if you lose your mind. I will love you if you lose your power. I'm not going to leave you or forsake you because some asshole pumped you full of chemicals that are destroying your brain. I'm going to take care of you. There's no other option for me." His voice comes warm and breathy in my ear.

I pivot within his arms to face him. "I love you. I love you so much."

His lips press into mine, and the heat of a blush warms my cheeks as my body reacts to the charge coming off him.

"We could lose this," I say into his mouth.

"So let's enjoy it while it lasts."

As Korwin's lips trail to my earlobe, he pushes my newly platinum hair off my shoulder. I tip my head to the side and close my eyes. My mind goes blissfully blank. I am lost in our connection, distracted by the sweet oblivion of our physical touch. My blue glow rivals the conference table console. The heat coming off us causes the glass to discolor.

"Charlie says I'm not supposed to get too worked up," I murmur.

"Somehow I doubt this is what he meant." Korwin rubs my shoulders. "Did it bother you when I called you my fiancée earlier?"

"Of course not." I smile and look away bashfully.

"Close your eyes."

"Why?"

"Trust me."

I do as he asks. There are a few moments of rustling, as if he's digging in his pockets for something, and then a cool weight settles around my neck.

"Okay, open them."

Resting on my chest is a shiny platinum cross. I lift it to admire its simple beauty.

"I can't grow a beard like the married Amish do, and you didn't seem comfortable with a diamond ring, so how about an engagement cross?"

A smile spreads across my face until I feel my ears move to make room for it. "I think it's a fine idea. A brilliant idea." I throw my arms around him. He holds me until I let go first.

Threading my fingers into his, I lead him toward the door.

"Where are we going?" he asks.

"To my room. To my bed. Charlie said I needed my rest, and I rest better with you next to me." I give him a salacious half smile.

He raises an eyebrow. "Good idea. I'm happy to help.

* * * * *

We take our time getting to my room, stopping often to kiss and touch. The magnetic draw that fuels our attraction is a palpable thing. It makes me feel strong. Almost invincible. But all the while we are riding the elevator and chasing each other down the hall, a nagging thought floats wispy and malformed at the back of my brain. Are we on borrowed time? Will we have this connection tomorrow?

"You need rest. Let's get you to bed." Korwin's hands wrap around my waist as he kicks the door closed behind us. His lips connect with mine, and I close my eyes, inhaling deeply through my nose. His fingers work under my shirt. The crackle and zap of skin against skin makes my flesh buzz. My shirt billows and sticks from the building static. I wrap my arms around his neck, digging my fingers into his hair. He's slightly taller than me, but I rest my elbows on his shoulders and pull myself up on my tiptoes.

He backs me against the wall. The glow coming off us lights the dark room like our own personal star. I hitch one leg over his hip and press myself against him. My hands trail down the outside of his arms, around his sides, and up his back. The hard muscles of his shoulders strain against my palms through his shirt.

Deep within, I ache with need for him. All those months in Hemlock Hollow, we held back from each other, hardly touching, barely kissing. I am starved for him. I dig one hand under the tail of his shirt and press my open palm into his lower back. The pressure of his body against mine makes me moan into his lips.

There was a time I would have stopped this, told Korwin it was against God's will for us to be this close outside of marriage. But when I left the world of Hemlock Hollow behind, I abandoned the black and white strictures associated with my faith. I do not feel guilty kissing Korwin. In fact, if anything, I feel silly about waiting so long to do more. In my arms, I hold my soul mate, my other.

There are few guarantees in life. I am not sure how many days I can keep the wolf at bay or trust that we'll both make it to see next week. My relationship with Korwin is solid. It is a truth as real as gravity that we will and should be together.

All this sifts through my mind as formless as sand while Korwin's lips work their way down my neck to my collarbone. His mouth burns.

Click. Scrape. Click. Clank.

Korwin pulls back and glances over my head. "What is that?"

"I don't know." I follow his gaze to the ventilation grate above us in the wall. *Click. Scrape. Click. Click.* A whirring precedes the left corner screw slowly twisting from its place. It drops from the grate onto the floor near my feet.

"What the hell?" Korwin sweeps an arm in front of my chest and ushers me to the other side of the room.

The upper left screw drops, followed by the top and bottom right, and then the entire grate flips from the wall. It clangs to rest where we'd been standing. At first the ventilation shaft looks empty and dark, but then a glint of light catches on a thin metal leg. The glossy black eye of a drone pushes out of the darkness, the whir growing louder as the lens adjusts to the light. Like a shiny metal spider, it grips the edges of the shaft.

Korwin sparks. "I'll take care of it."

"No. Wait," I say as light projects into the room in a beam instead of a flash. It scans down my body, blinding me temporarily as it passes over my eyes. There's a beep and then the light focuses at the center of the room. A hologram forms before us, not unlike the clips we viewed in council chambers. A man's body is built out of blue light from the legs up. My hand goes to my mouth. It's Dr. Konrad.

"If this message is playing, be assured that I am aware my drone has found you, Lydia. Its facial recognition software is remarkably accurate. By this time, your location has already been transmitted back to me." Konrad's thin hologram lips pull into a smile. His image is translucent and flickers. Dust passes through his torso, catching the light. "Don't worry. I won't be coming for you; you'll be coming to me." The hologram expands to show Trinity bound and gagged in a chair. "That is, if you want your friend to live." Trinity's wearing a vest laden with explosives. The room she's in is familiar. Concrete floor. Metal girders. The Red Dog Kennel.

I squeeze Korwin's hand. "Dear Lord, he has Trinity!"

"You took something that belongs to me. Now you must return it. Bring SC-13 to the Deadzone or

Trinity dies. You have one hour. You know where to find me."

Konrad's image flickers twice and disappears, replaced by a clock counting down from sixty minutes. The seconds tick by.

"What do we do?" I press my fingers against my cheeks.

Korwin opens his mouth. With a pop, the drone in the ventilation shaft self-destructs, cutting him off.

"We can't give Konrad what he wants. I'm not handing over SC-13," I say.

"Of course not."

"But we have to save Trinity."

"We need to find David and Laura. They'll know what to do. There has to be a way to get Trinity out. We might be able to catch them, but we'll have to hurry."

We rush from the room and down to the tunnels, to where Sal outfits Liberty Party soldiers for their missions. The squat man looks up from mending a shirt when we barge into the apparel room.

"Where's the fire?" he says in his gravelly voice.

"David and Laura," I blurt.

"We need to find them right away," Korwin fills in.

Sal's eyebrows plunge over his nose. "They just left, maybe ten minutes ago. You might be able to catch them in the garage."

"Thanks, Sal!"

We bolt from the room and race across the building. Several soldiers call to us, "What's the hurry?" and "What's going on?" But there's no time to stop and explain. We almost barrel over a nurse on our way to the garage. She berates us over her clipboard.

"David?" I yell as we burst into the garage. "Laura?" The lights are still on but there's no answer.

"The van is gone," Korwin says. "They must have already left."

He pulls out his phone and taps David's icon. After a few moments, he hangs up and taps Laura's. Cursing, he slides the phone back into his pocket. "They're not answering."

"What? Why?"

"I don't know why. Maybe the call's not going through. The guys in Tech might know."

"We don't have time to ask the guys in Tech. He'll kill her." Panic rises in my throat. "If we leave now we can make it in time to stop him."

He shakes his head. "We can't. Maybe we can find Charlie."

"There's no time, Korwin. He gave us an hour. If we leave right now, we will barely make it in time."

"No. No. Charlie says you can't."

"As of now, I'm fine until I sleep," I say, my voice elevating.

"Or get stressed beyond your breaking point. Charlie said no stress."

"What do you think this is? Waiting for my friend to detonate is not helping my condition. And we can't call Jonas or Charlie. They'll never find someone else to go in time."

"No."

I plead, "If we leave now, we might be able to catch Laura and David."

"It's a long shot. I'm not even sure it's possible. What if we can't?" He rubs the bridge of his nose.

My palms start to sweat. All I can see is Trinity's bound body, the gag pulling at her mouth. "Then we go alone. You and I know the Deadzone. We can steal her out from under Konrad's nose the same way we did SC-13."

"You make it sound easy."

"It could be easy." My voice cracks. The words hold a bravado I don't feel.

"As long as Konrad doesn't kill us all, we don't get caught by the Greens, or run into one of the many Red Dogs with an ax to grind."

"We fry them and ask questions later."

He laughs derisively, but I am deadly serious.

"You're wasting time, Korwin. We can only do this together. As long as we can touch, no one can stop us."

"Charlie isn't going to like this. I don't like this."

"We'll be careful. There's no time, Korwin. I know the risks, but we have no choice. We can't let her die. Not like this."

"You're terribly brave."

"No. Just grown up."

"Jeep," he says, pointing at the refurbished Green military vehicle. "We should stay together. The bikes are too risky."

"Right."

Korwin climbs behind the wheel and keys in the code to unlock the dash. I hoist myself into the passenger's seat above the oversized tires. The dashboard lights up and the engine purrs to life at Korwin's commands. I hastily push the button on the console to raise the door.

Tapping the dash, Korwin silences the engine. "Fuel cells don't have to make noise but all of these vehicles are manufactured with sound. It helps people drive. I think in our case, we'd prefer the silence."

"Agreed." He accelerates into the dark forest. With a tap of the dash, I close the door behind us. We're almost a mile out when I notice something. "What happened to all of the flashers?"

Korwin leans forward in his seat in order to see the tops of the trees better. "They're gone."

"There were thousands of them out here the night we came back from the Ambassador's Club."

"Judging by the message Konrad sent, he's pulling their strings."

"Which means he has eyes everywhere." I stare into the trees, my stomach clenching at the thought. Konrad isn't just pulling the flasher strings; he's pulling ours as well. And I can't help but think, as we speed through the forest, that we're playing the part of his puppets to his satisfaction.

Chapter 15

It's dark in the Deadzone. Our headlights illuminate filthy streets, unkempt sidewalks, and the occasional group of Deadzoners huddled around an urban fire. Vats of Slip boil over the flames. I only know what it is because of Trinity. She taught me about it when we lived together in the Kennel and I was attacked by a man high on it.

New Generation Ag (NGA) supplies all the legally obtainable food to the Green Republic. Farming is illegal, so all meat is made in a lab by coaxing a meat cell to grow and multiply into a full piece of meat. The animal is never alive, just the cells. I don't know exactly how it works, but the byproduct of the process is an acidic substance called Slip. NGA stores Slip in steel vats and dumps them in the Deadzone. Any type of pollution is illegal in the Green Republic, so it's a convenient way for NGA to get rid of a substance they can't eliminate legally. The

Deadzoners boil the Slip into a tar and then smoke it. Trinity told me she suspected it was NGA that figured out Slip could make you high and taught the first Deadzoners how to use it. I'd like to think that no one would be as evil as to purposely addict people, but I have to admit it's awfully convenient for NGA. Their pollution problem literally goes up in smoke.

Slip gives its users almost unlimited energy and a high that lasts for days. Eventually though, it's deadly. People who use it forget to eat and sleep. Longtime users become ill from nutritional deficiencies and have red, swollen eyes.

"Don't stop here," I say, wary of the way the men on the side of the road eye our vehicle. "We'll have to hide the jeep."

"How much time do we have?"

"Twelve minutes," I say. My heart sinks. "We can make it."

"We'll make it," Korwin repeats.

"They're boiling Slip everywhere. I've seen at least three vats in the last mile. Was it always this bad?" A malicious-looking lot watches us pass, sucking on their pipes and darting twitchy glances between each other.

"No. This is definitely worse. I'm not sure I've seen this many Deadzoners in the streets before."

"Yeah."

Korwin quickly finds a backstreet empty of Deadzoners, cuts the lights, and pulls into the first alley. He parks in a three-space parking lot adjacent to an abandoned office building. I jump out and meet him around the back.

"Ten minutes. Which way?" I look up and down the alley, but I don't recognize our location.

He nods and motions with his head. At a jog, I follow him through the office building and out a broken window to another street. I can see the Kennel. The building used to be a prison and is surrounded by a tall, barbed-wire-topped wall. The rows of tiny windows in the cells-turned-apartments are dark.

"It won't do for us to walk in the front door. If we go in the way we broke out, we might have the element of surprise."

When the Greens raided the Kennel, we escaped by blowing a hole in the wall of a private bathroom available only to pack leadership. Dr. Konrad's hologram looked like he was in the Kennel's warehouse-sized main room, where Korwin and other clan members used to prizefight for units. "It's the best chance we've got."

Korwin leads me into the alley where we escaped. A piece of wood has been nailed over the hole, but the job is haphazard. We easily pry the nails out and slip inside, closing the hole behind us.

"No one has been here since we left," I say, running my finger through a thick coat of dust on the lip of the clawfoot tub.

Pausing at the door, Korwin holds out his hand. "Together?"

I nod. He leads the way through the door into the dark hall, the subtle glow from our bodies lighting our way.

Korwin sniffs and scowls. I smell it too. Sulfur. Dr. Konrad is close. Too close.

We approach the end of the hall, and I press my back against the wall. Around the corner is the main floor of the Kennel. Korwin places a finger over his lips and points his thumb over his shoulder. He mouths, *Ready?*

A sinister laugh cuts through the darkness, followed by a woman's sob. "Do you think after all this time I can't sense when you are in the same room?" Dr. Konrad's menacing voice cuts through the empty space like a knife. "Come out, dear betas, and face your maker."

Korwin looks at me and extinguishes his spark. I do the same. Without our glow, we turn the corner shrouded in darkness. I inhale sharply. There is a circle of light in the center of the main floor. Trinity is bound and gagged in a chair under the beam, the heavy black vest of explosives with its looping wires a vivid reminder of the danger we're in.

"I knew you'd come." Dr. Konrad walks into the light and looks directly at us, as if he can see us in the dark. "Your friend Trinity was adamant that you'd been hiding in the Deadzone." He lowers his voice. "She was lying, of course, a liar just like her filthy, politician father. Minds like hers are open books to me now." He tugs Trinity's hair, bending her neck back at a painful angle and flashing us the red rims of her eyes. She moans in pain.

"It worked. We're here. Let her go," Korwin says, taking on a faint blue glow with his anger.

"Where is SC-13?"

"Somewhere safe. We'll hand him over when you release Trinity," Korwin says.

"Tsk. Tsk. Tsk. What did I just say about liars?" Dr. Konrad claws at his unruly hair. "I can tell when you're lying. I hear it. I hear everything. Now, bring me the womb."

"Never," I murmur.

Dr. Konrad narrows his eyes at me. He shouldn't be able to see me in the dark. Or hear what I said. But he did. Without taking his eyes off me, he reaches behind him to a stainless steel rolling table that supports his black bag of horrors. Silver flashes and blood pours from Trinity's cheek. She screams around the gag.

"Stop," I yell. "Please!"

"We had a deal." He presses the scalpel into her jugular. "SC-13 for Trinity's life."

"Take me," Korwin says. "I'll go in Trinity's place. You can do whatever experiments you want on me."

"The knight in shining armor throws himself on his sword. Honestly, do you ever tire of trying to play the hero, Korwin?" Dr. Konrad hunches as if the weight of the world rests on his shoulders. "It bores me. Allow me to put this plainly. I don't want you. Either of you. Although nothing would make me happier than to take you apart cell by cell for my own pleasure. Alas, you are useless to me aside from a petty diversion. What I want is—"

The baby, I think.

"Yes, Lydia, the baby." Dr. Konrad rolls his eyes. "I. Can. Hear. You!"

"He can read minds," Korwin says, incredulously.

"One of my many, new abilities." Dr. Konrad runs his finger through the blood oozing from Trinity's cheek. She whimpers. He rubs the blood between his fingers, then opens his hand to show the gory mess. "Blood is such a precious thing. As it turns out, yours is something of a phenomenon."

"Then why not take us instead?" Korwin asks.

"The gene that makes you what you are is a rare mutation. If I combine the genetic material of two alphas, only one in one million would result in a live birth with your genetic makeup. The fact there are two of you, born at the same time, is nothing short of a statistical miracle." He paces behind Trinity, stepping in her bright red blood and leaving footprints on the concrete.

Trinity weeps. He ignores her.

"The same is true of the gamma generation. The combination of your genetic material took me hundreds of trials to figure out. My creations kept dying. One of the chromosomes bends during gestation and the fetus self-destructs. No one understands. I *had* to have a gamma. I extracted DNA from the dying embryos, accomplished a bit of scientific hocus-pocus, and created a retrovirus that made me what I am."

"You injected the dead gamma cells into yourself?" Korwin asks, as if the mere thought sickens him.

"The gammas were alive when I took the cells," Dr. Konrad says coldly. "I had no choice but to experiment on myself once Daddy Pierce pulled my funding. My new benefactor required complete discretion and quick results. The injection was a raving success. Little buggers gave me a host of new psychic abilities. Unfortunately, the side effects are rather insufferable. I'm as unstable as the Alpha Eight. Radioactive jaundice isn't for cowards. The situation was dire. But then a miracle."

"SC-13," I say.

"Yes. The fetus is the key to my stability. Hair of the dog, you see. I quite literally must have SC-13 back. My life depends on it. Even if you hadn't destroyed all of the remaining genetic material in my lab, producing another living gamma could take years. I need the tiny miracle in your possession. Now."

"No! You can't have him." My voice is strained. I'm on dangerous ground. My wolf appears at my side and my head spins with her need to take control.

"You don't think *you* can keep it, do you? SC-13 needs me as much as I need it. It won't survive another three weeks in that artificial womb without my intervention. You have no idea the delicate balance it took to keep it alive thus far. It is useless to you."

"Shut up!" The tiny baby inside the pod flashes through my mind and I squeeze my eyes shut. The thought of anything happening to SC-13 fills me with fury. I seethe at Dr. Konrad. I will kill him. I will end him before he can lay a finger on my baby. I hold my hand out and the wolf comes to me, melding into my side.

Korwin notices the change, the way I stiffen and become eerily calm. "Stay with me," he whispers.

Dr. Konrad narrows his eyes. "Yes, stay with us, Lydia. Now is not the time to run away. Here's what's going to happen. You are going to bring SC-13 to me."

"No."

"I realize Trinity's life isn't enough motivation for you, but how about Korwin's?"

Korwin's hand is wrenched from mine. I dive for it, but I'm not fast enough. His body launches into the air, arms and legs flailing. He groans as if Konrad's power is crushing him.

Dr. Konrad's lips are still moving. He's spewing threats, but I can't hear them. All I can hear is the rush of breath against the back of my throat and the growl of the wolf in my head. Blue arcs of electricity orbit me.

"Still not enough," I say in a voice three octaves lower than my own. Electricity flies from my hand and plows into Dr. Konrad's chest. His face morphs into a mask of surprise as his body convulses and Korwin drops more than two stories to the concrete. I don't check on him. The wolf doesn't care. I take a step forward, breaking a sweat in my attempt to hold Konrad in my electrokinetic grip.

"Come on, Emile. Why don't you show *me* your new skills?" I ask through my teeth. "You don't want to pick on a girl stronger than you? You worthless waste of a heartbeat."

Konrad writhes, gripped in the throes of blue lightning. I take a step closer. I have him.

Without warning, the blue beam I'm sending into Konrad flickers and fails. I stare down at my traitorous hand. Shaking my arms, I try to call it back, but I can't even manage a glow.

"Be careful what you wish for," Dr. Konrad says, shaking off the effects of my attack. He narrows his eyes on me and my feet leave the floor. I soar through the air, desperately snapping my arm at the elbow, but I can't spark. I slam into the second-floor balcony railing and then drop like a rock. My spark engages enough to protect me from the worst of the impact, and then fizzles, leaving me aching and breathless on the cold concrete.

"You're wasting my time," Konrad bellows. "Trinity won't thank you when her blood and brains are splattered across this building. When I'm done with her?" He steps up to my face so that all I can see are his shoes as I try to catch my breath. There's a rustle of paper. He squats to show me the picture Korwin drew of me in my apron and *kapp*. "Once Trinity is dead, I might find some suitable motivation for you behind the wall of the Amish preservation."

I stop breathing. My vision blurs. Rage coils like a fist in my gut.

"Don't you dare die on me," he says. "I don't give you permission to die."

Oh, but I am not dead. I'm listening to my wolf. With a surge of energy, I drive my fist into his lower leg, all my weight twisting into the punch. The bone cracks and Konrad falls, a howl pouring from his lungs. I tackle him on all fours, kicking, scratching. My nails dig into his face and my thumbs press into his eyes.

With a cross punch to my temple, he sends me rolling off his body. Power grips me like a vise. I struggle to breathe as Konrad's gaze squeezes my torso and lifts me into the air again. He staggers to his feet, limping toward me. My ribs crack.

"Did you forget something, Dr. Konrad?" Korwin says.

My eyes flick to find Korwin holding the explosive vest. Trinity is gone. The chair lies in pieces at his feet. Dr. Konrad doesn't fall for the distraction. His eyes don't move from me. The crushing pressure strengthens.

"If I forgot something, it was to kill you sooner," he says.

My lips curve into a wicked smirk. Korwin knows what to do.

A shot of electricity whips from Korwin's hand and wraps around Dr. Konrad's ankle. The doctor topples, knocking over the cart and his bag of terrors. Metal implements rattle and clang across the floor. I'm released from Konrad's hold and fall. This time, my spark doesn't protect me. I land on my back, scalpels and pliers stabbing into my flesh.

The doctor seizes as Korwin hits him with another blast.

As I struggle to pull myself up, extracting a scalpel from my shoulder in the process, I see a plastic detonator among the tools scattered across the floor. I dive for it, blood dripping down my arm.

I hold up the detonator. "Throw the vest, Korwin," I yell.

He looks at me in confusion. "No. No, Lydia." He shakes his head and doubles his efforts to fry Dr. Konrad.

In a wide arc, I round Dr. Konrad's seizing body to Korwin's side. "He won't stop. He won't ever stop," I say. "He knows about the preservation. I have to end this." It comes out as low as a growl. I am not afraid. My wolf has made me carelessly brave.

"Put it d-down, girl. D-Don't be stupid. You'll t-take down the entire b-building. Without your spark, you'll be crushed," Dr. Konrad warns in the throws of electrocution. He peels his lips back from his teeth.

My finger hovers over the button. He's right. Without my power to protect me, I'll die. My heart races. Sweat drips from my hairline. I have no spark left, but my wolf doesn't care. She chants, *push, push, push,* in my head.

"Please, Lydia, no," Korwin says. His eyes dart toward me, even while he concentrates on holding

Konrad within the lightning that flows from his hand.

The wolf howls within my skull. She wants Dr. Konrad dead. So do I. The hand holding the detonator trembles as I try to hold her back.

"You d-don't have the guts," Konrad says through clenched teeth. "You won't hurt your beloved boyfriend."

"Ten, nine, eight, seven," I say loudly. I grab Korwin's forearm. He groans as hot energy flows up my arm and into me. My spark flames to life. It takes all my effort, but drawing on Korwin, I'm able to produce a shield.

Korwin's head shakes. The beam between him and Konrad weakens. "Lydia," he pleads.

"Four, three, two..." My hand steadies over the detonator and I grin at Konrad. Any doubts I may have had about pushing the trigger melt away with the wolf's howl in my brain and the revolving blue atoms that tell me my shield is in place. I am going to end this, once and for all.

Korwin throws the vest and covers his head with his free arm.

Abruptly, Dr. Konrad's persona shifts from confidence to fear. He turns on his heel and tries for the exit. But my wolf wants blood.

I push the button.

Chapter 16

Everything hurts. I lie under a heap of rubble and blink my eyes in the darkness. The spark usually protects Korwin and me. It forms an electromagnetic bubble to keep us safe. But unlike before, it didn't fully deflect the explosion, and Korwin's hand is no longer in my grip. We've been blown apart. I'm thankful to be alive. The Nanomem disease has made me weak, and clearly, it could have been worse. I'm not burned or crushed even though the remains of the Kennel are strewn around me.

Flickers of light reach me through gaps in the concrete above. Is it Korwin? I can't move, so I yell, "Over here!"

"Lydia? Lydia?" Trinity's voice. The flash of light comes again above me.

"Yes. I'm here. I'm okay. Where's Korwin?"

"I'm here." His voice, weak and raspy, comes from my left, from under the rubble.

"Help him first," I insist.

Trinity's fingers wrap around a section of concrete above my head, and she grunts with the effort of rolling it off me. "You're closer to the surface. I'm going to need your help getting him out." She reaches into the hole she's created and grabs my hand. By strategically shifting and shoving aside the rubble, I am able to slither my way to the surface with her help.

"I thought you said you weren't hurt," she says as I gain my footing atop the debris. I follow her stare and see a bloody gash on the side of my leg.

"Your back is bleeding too."

"Nothing to worry about. Where's Korwin?"

"Over here."

By Trinity's light, I find a piece of pipe and use it as a lever to roll the chunks of concrete away. "Where'd you get the flashlight anyway?"

"The kitchen on my way out. I remembered the Red Dogs kept one in there."

"That was stupid. You were seconds away from being on the other side of this wreckage."

She frowns. "Thanks for saving me. That psycho was going to eat my skin for dinner."

"Speaking of the psycho, did you find Dr. Konrad's body?"

She snorts. "No, but hell if I'm looking for him. He's got to be dead. The whole place came down on you three."

"Am I dead?"

"Uh… Is this a trick question?"

"Never assume Dr. Emile Konrad is dead, under any circumstances." My eyes dart over what used to be the Kennel, fearing Dr. Konrad might appear at any moment.

A moan comes from the rubble near my feet. Korwin. He's stuck under a slab of metal that used to be a heavy steel door. I toss the pipe aside and grab the metal with both hands. Even before I became a Spark, I was strong. When I lived in Hemlock Hollow, I could run faster and carry more weight than any boy. I brace my foot for leverage and throw my bodyweight into it. It doesn't budge. Trinity puts her flashlight between her teeth and clamps her hands on the side.

"On the count of three. One… Two… Three."

Together we slide the massive door two feet. Good enough. I can see Korwin's bloody shoulder through the gap.

Trinity cups her hands over her mouth at the sight of the blood and broken bones. Korwin is in bad shape. Worse than me.

"Is he dying?" she asks.

"Probably. But as long as he's still breathing, I can help him." I lie across the concrete and reach my arm into the hole to grip cool flesh, sticky with blood. I can't see well, but I feel my way from his shoulder until I'm cupping the back of his neck. I start the engine that is us and light up like a star.

"Holy heavens. What the hell are you?" Trinity asks.

"I'm a Spark," I say, the flow of energy through me making my voice tinny. "Korwin and I are the products of an experiment Dr. Konrad did twenty years ago. Now he wants our child."

"He's completely lost his mind," she says. The light from her flashlight bobs. She's shaking. Probably going into shock.

"I know it's hard. You've been through so much," I say. "But hold it together, Trinity. I'm going to need your help to get out of here. Walk. Walk it off."

She doesn't say a word but the flashlight steadies and travels with her pacing.

Korwin's body glows, shooting beams of light through the spaces in the rubble. I use my newfound strength to push aside a large chunk of concrete.

Thankfully, Korwin's head is undamaged, but his legs are crushed.

"Korwin? Korwin?" I look at Trinity. "He's passed out. I think he's lost too much blood. I thought if I could reach him, I could make him strong again, but I can't. And I'm not healing properly either." It's my turn to shake. "You'll have to get the jeep. We can use it to free him."

"Just tell me what to do," she says.

I give her the location and the key code for the dash.

She nods. "Got it." She repeats the number to herself and takes off into the night. She takes the flashlight with her. I don't need it, not with the glow coming off us.

"Korwin, come on, baby," I say. I've never called him baby before—it's an Englisher term of endearment—but somehow, it seems appropriate with his life cradled in my hands. He's not healing, and I fear I know why. I should have listened to Charlie. My wolf, in her quest for revenge, drained him to protect herself. I left him vulnerable.

"Well, isn't this an unlikely reunion?"

I'd recognize Sting's voice anywhere, and I turn my head to see his silhouette standing on the edge of the ruins. He steps into the light of our glow. For a moment, I'm taken aback by his appearance. He's lost a good fifty pounds and has the red eyes and broken skin of a long-term Slip addict.

"Sting," I say, because I can't think of what else to say. He's not a friend, but I entertain a flicker of hope that he'll help me dig Korwin out. "I'm glad you weren't inside the Kennel when it blew."

"Ain't no one been inside the Kennel since just after the raid. When Alpha died, the pack disbanded. I'm living with Knight clan now."

"Alpha died?" The revelation is a twisting vise. When I left him, his heart was still beating.

"Shot himself rather than be processed by the Greens."

I squirm with relief on the sharp wreckage. I didn't kill him. Considering the circumstances, I'm not sure why it matters. But it does.

"All of us still above ground are registered now. Official Green citizens, whatever that means." He picks at his thumbnail. His eyes shift as if my glow has exposed him, and he backs into the shadows.

"Congratulations," I say.

He clears his throat in a way that sounds like a laugh. "Why you gone all lighthouse? What you doin' up there?"

"Scamping," I say.

"Thought so."

I consider asking him for help, although my gut tells me it would be a bad idea. He looks strung out, erratic. Thankfully, Trinity arrives with the jeep, tires squealing. I should have asked if she knew how to drive. Just as well. She figured it out. She rolls down her window. "What now?" she asks.

"Bring the chains from the back. We'll use the jeep to pull this off him," I say.

Trinity jumps out and slams her door.

"Bella?" Sting's tone is somewhere between a question and a hiss.

Trinity is startled by his presence. He breaks from the shadows to approach her. She takes a moment to process his appearance before saying, "Stay away from me."

Turning her back on him, she drags the heavy chain across the wreckage. Trinity works to loop it around the heavy slab of metal we couldn't move. Breaking my connection with Korwin could be deadly. I can't take my hands off him, but I help her as best I can with my free hand and kick the chain into position with my boot.

Behind Trinity, Sting spreads his hands and tucks in his chin as if he's been sorely offended.

"That's all the hello I get? After all the years we spent together?"

Trinity bounds back down the rubble to secure the chain to the hitch but pauses before climbing behind the wheel again. "You mean after the years you kept me prisoner?" She curses and makes a gesture with her hand that is clearly meant to be offensive.

"Come on, Bella. You know it wasn't all like that. We had something, you and me."

"We had an abusive relationship that I couldn't leave for fear of my life," she says through her teeth. "Now get the hell out of here before I run you over." The jeep lurches forward and Sting dives out of the way, but rebounds and reaches through the window to grab Trinity by the throat.

I raise my hand, but I'm weak. My power fizzles before it reaches my fingertips, despite my contact with Korwin. The attempt leaves me exhausted, and I lay my head on the rubble.

I needn't have worried. Trinity pulls her arm back and clocks Sting in the jaw. It's not enough to knock him out, but it is enough to knock him back. She uses the space to roll up the window. He barely gets his fingers out in time.

"It's bulletproof glass, Sting," I say. "If I were you, I'd run for home, while you still can run." Trinity revs the engine.

Sting points a threatening finger at Trinity. She accelerates forward, barely missing Sting as he jogs into the shadows again. His curses fade with distance. As she keeps going, she drags the door off Korwin. With everything I have left in me, I get my arms under him and lift him from the hole.

"Something's wrong. He's not waking up," I say. The problem isn't just with Korwin. I stagger toward the jeep, head spinning. Trinity meets me and helps us into the back.

"You need medical treatment," Trinity says, her expression distraught. "But I can't go back to Crater City."

I swallow. "Neither can we." I pant, curling my head between my knees. I can't take my hand off Korwin, but I want to. I am not well.

"You're sweating and pale," Trinity says.

"I need help. Get behind the wheel. I'll give you the coordinates. Not in Crater City."

Trinity slams the gate and does as I ask.

I'm exhausted, but I force myself to hold my position. I can't fall asleep. My wolf sits beside me, waiting, watching my drooping eyelids with cruel intentions. She wants me to give up on Korwin. She thinks we'd do better on our own. If we'd run away and hide, life would be easier. My wolf would put him out of his misery.

I relay the coordinates of the reactor to Trinity, and the jeep lurches into motion.

"You're an Uppercrust." I'm too weak and tired to elaborate, but this is the first time I've spoken to her since I found out she is Pierce's daughter. I'm hoping the conversation will keep me awake.

"And you're a product of Konrad's experiments, wanted by the Greens. Seems like we both kept our share of secrets when we were living with the Red Dogs."

"Fair enough." I lean against the wall of the jeep, my head knocking into the metal with every bump.

"Tell me something, was that you two posing as Anastasia and Rayle Baltik at the Ambassador's Club the night of my party?"

"How did you know?"

"For one, your hair is still white. Also, Rayle didn't hit on me once during the entire party. That's never happened before. You were way too nice to be Anastasia. I knew there was something off the moment you looked me in the eye and shook my hand."

"Hmm. I thought I was convincing."

"You were to the others. Most of the Uppercrust are too busy looking in the mirror to notice the person standing next to them."

My head lists on my shoulders. I have to stay awake. I squeeze Korwin's hand. "Why did you run away before?"

"You mean when my mother died?"

"Yeah."

"I suspected my father did it. It was an inside job. Everybody knew it was, but no one was investigating." She snorts. "Dr. Konrad killed my father in front of me. He used his telekinesis to stab him in the back. No fingerprints. And when he brought me here? He told me I reminded him of my mother. He admitted he was the one who poisoned her. My father didn't do it. All those years hating him and he was innocent."

"I'm sorry," I rasp.

Her voice cracks as she answers. "Thank you."

"Konrad said he had a benefactor. Do you know who it is?"

"No." She shrugs. "It could be anyone. Half the Republic wanted my father dead."

My eyelids droop and the wolf presses in. "Stay away from me."

"What?" Trinity asks.

"Drive faster," I say louder.

I don't like my wolf anymore. She's overstayed her welcome. With my free hand, I grab the cross around my neck that Korwin gave me and I pray. The cross jewelry may not be Amish, but my prayer is, and I say it in the language of my youth, Pennsylvania German. I pray with the cross poking into my palm and both eyes on Korwin.

And I try my best to ignore the wolf who pants and growls in my peripheral vision.

Chapter 17

"Are you certain about this?" Trinity asks as we cross the border into the Outlands.

"Yes." I slur the word. I can hardly hold my head up. "The radiation is a lie. It doesn't exist."

She sighs. "Okay. I'm not sure why I should trust you, but I do. I'm betting my life on it."

I blink my eyes and when I open them again, we are near the reactor. I must have blacked out. There are miles and miles of winding terrain between the border and Liberty Party headquarters. The wolf hovers over me and my hands have moved to Korwin's neck.

"Stay away from him!" I yell at the wolf. She retreats a single step but lies in wait.

"Are you okay?" Trinity darts a glance over her shoulder at me. "No one is touching him, Lydia. No one but you."

With a shaky breath, I ensure Korwin is still breathing and force my eyes open wider. "I'm not okay," I sob. "I'm not okay." I'm so tired. I can't stay awake anymore, but I can't allow the wolf to take control.

"Almost there," Trinity says. "I see a garage door. It's opening on its own."

Through the window, the forest gives way to white walls and fluorescent lighting, rows of vehicles, and metal shelving. Six officers with weapons are our welcoming committee. Trinity holds her hands up. "I have Lydia and Korwin in the back. They're hurt." She yells the words without rolling down the window.

There's the clamor of voices and then the jeep gate opens. Charlie curses. My mind can't make out the words. I'm on my side next to Korwin. I try to raise my head and my cheek sticks to the upholstery. Blood. We are lying in a pool of our blood.

"Keep them together," Charlie orders. I'm hoisted onto a gurney, Korwin tucked in next to me.

I reach out and fist the tail of Charlie's lab coat. "Don't let me sleep. She's here. She's dangerous."

His eyes widen with understanding, but he shakes his head. We are rolled into the surgical suite.

Charlie leaves my side and returns to press a mask over my nose and mouth.

"I'm sorry, Lydia, I have no choice."

* * * * *

I am only aware that days have passed through flashes of consciousness. A nurse changes a bag of fluid attached to my arm. I throw up on her shoes and fall asleep again. I open my eyes to the steady beep of a machine I can't see. It's dark. I try to sit up but I pass out again. David's and Laura's voices wake me. They bend over me and rub my arms and shoulders. I cannot process what they're saying. I close my eyes again. Charlie is in the room. He injects me with blue fluid. It burns, but I'm too weak to cry out. I sleep.

When I finally wake fully, I have no idea what day it is. A wave of nausea comes over me. I grab a basin from the nightstand and heave into it. Nothing comes out but a rush of air. There is nothing left in my stomach. The IV in my arm keeps catching on the edge of the basin. Charlie rushes into the room and presses a cold cloth to my head. "Easy, Lydia. It's going to be all right."

"Where's Korwin?" I rasp. My throat is bone dry.

"He's right next to you." Charlie points to the other side of the room.

I twist to look over my shoulder. Korwin is in a second hospital bed in the same white room. He's sleeping with the head of the bed up and the blanket pulled to the chest of his hospital tunic.

"Is he going to be okay?"

Charlie's face falls. He scratches his jaw and lowers himself to the edge of my bed.

"What happened, Lydia?"

"A building fell on us."

"Right. Trinity told me. Dr. Konrad again." Charlie's face reddens. "It was very, very stupid of you to go after Trinity alone. I'd ask what you were thinking but it is all too clear to me that you simply weren't."

"We had no choice. He was going to kill her."

"Why didn't you tell anyone where you were going? Ask for help? I was here. You could have come to me."

"There was no time." My mouth opens but the sharp look Charlie gives me halts the rest of the excuse in my throat. "I'm sorry," I say instead.

He puts one fist on his hip and looks at his toes. "Korwin's spine was severed. That's why you couldn't heal him. The electrical impulses you were sending weren't making it to his lower body."

"What does that mean?"

"It means, if he were biologically average, he would never walk again."

My stomach clenches, and I grab the bin and heave again. I shake my head. "No. There has to be a way."

"I said he'd never walk again if he was biologically average. He's not. I was able to apply electrical stimulation directly to his spine. It healed, but it's still weak. He's not out of the woods yet."

"Is he able to walk?"

"He's slept most of the last six days, but yesterday he wiggled his toes. It is a long way from being able to walk, or run, or fight," Charlie says. "We'll start physical therapy tomorrow."

"Why are we separate? Why didn't you put us together to heal?"

Charlie frowns. "You had multiple wounds in your legs and back. You must have a guardian angel, Lydia, because if the debris had hit an artery, I don't believe you would have survived. As it is, it's a wonder you didn't bleed to death."

191

I place the back of my hand against my lips and swallow repeatedly to keep from vomiting again. "But why didn't you keep us together?" I press. "I don't understand. Why didn't *I* heal when we touched before?"

"It's what I warned you about. The Nanomem proteins have spread. Your cells have become unstable. You're not as strong as you used to be. Your cells are replicating to be more like David's, more human. You may have passed the point of no return."

"I have a short in my circuitry," I say absently.

"Yes. Exactly. As I showed you with the watch, you can give your power to Korwin, but it can't come back to you—not in the way it once could. It's like drinking through a narrow straw; only a small part of you can use his energy now. You drained your battery trying to heal him. You probably kept him alive, but you almost died in the process."

I picture the watch with the black face he showed me. I believed I understood at the time, but I didn't. "I thought this was just about me, but what you are saying is that Korwin might have died because I can't heal him the way I once could."

"You can't even heal yourself."

My eyes burn with impending tears. "I'm sorry. I shouldn't have put him at risk."

192

Charlie groans. "You shouldn't have put yourself at risk!" When I start to weep, he puts one arm around my shoulders. "Lydia, I know you two, all right? You didn't twist Korwin's arm. He knew the risks and that you were sick. You guys went to get Trinity. You thought it would be easy. You thought wrong." Charlie's talk is meant to be comforting, but instead my heart sinks with guilt at our stupidity.

"Where is Trinity?"

Charlie smiles. "Working."

"Working?"

"After a day or two of interrogation, it was clear she was on our side. She was sworn in and chose to train as a nurse. She's been helping me in the ward."

"She's a good person. She can be trusted," I say.

"The council thinks so." Charlie walks to the wall and turns down the lights in the artificial window on the wall. "Now, I want you to get some rest. Try not to worry about anything. Just heal."

He exits the room, and the lock engages with a metal-on-metal grind. Turning on my side, I face Korwin, watching his chest rise and fall with each breath. I flash back to my hands around his neck. What if I fall asleep and my wolf tries to strangle him again?

Korwin's eyes open, their hazel color making my breath catch. "Hi," he whispers.

"Hi. Charlie was here. I can call him back in if you want me to."

"No."

"He's locked us in. He's afraid my wolf will come back and I'll kill someone," I say honestly, although Charlie didn't admit it in so many words.

"Apparently, he's not worried about you killing me."

"He should be. You tried to warn me against pressing the detonator. I couldn't stop."

"We were weak. I wasn't sure we'd survive."

"I wasn't sure we'd survive either, but my wolf didn't care. I'm losing my mind."

"We did survive. You were right to take out Konrad. Even if we'd died, it would have been worth it."

"No. It was crazy. I tried to strangle you in my sleep on our way home. I'm sick, Korwin. You shouldn't trust me. I could hurt you." My voice is heavy with guilt.

He turns his head on his pillow to face the ceiling and the corner of his mouth tugs up toward his ear. "Love hurts. Haven't you heard?" He chuckles and turns back to face me.

"This isn't a joke. We should call Charlie back and have you moved to a different room."

His smile melts away. "How are you feeling? Still nauseous?"

"No. It's passed. How did you know I was nauseous?"

"Heard you. A few times." With one hand, he pulls the blanket aside and pats the mattress next to him. "Come here. Lay with me. You won't hurt me."

I widen my eyes at him. "You don't know that."

"I know." He pats the bed. "Please. I literally can't come to you. As of today, I can barely wiggle my toes."

"I shouldn't."

Korwin's expression turns serious. "You owe me." He pats the bed again.

Carefully, I sit up and use my IV pole as a crutch to stand. My back throbs. There is a scratching noise as my bandages brush against my hospital tunic. It takes me more steps than normal to get from one bed to the other, despite the short distance. In tiny, measured movements, I lower myself to Korwin's mattress. His side is warm and welcoming. I tuck my head into the nook of his arm, my face resting on his chest. Our skin touches, but only the faintest glow blushes my skin.

"You shouldn't trust me," I say again.

"But I do." He kisses my forehead. "Judging by your journey across the great four-foot cavern between our beds, I don't believe you will be capable of injuring me. Sleep."

He has a point. I can barely lift my arms. With a deep sigh, I close my eyes. As I drift into repose, my right hand wanders to my neck and finds my cross. I'm happy that Charlie either didn't remove it or returned it to my neck after surgery. With it gripped tightly in my fist, the only prayer that comes to me is: *Thank you, thank you, God, for giving us another day.*

Chapter 18

Hot breath on my face wakes me. She's back. The wolf is lying between Korwin and me, staring at him with her lips drawn from her teeth in a silent growl. Korwin's chest rises and falls rhythmically, indifferent to her latent threat.

"What do you want?" I say to her.

Her yellow eyes shift menacingly toward Korwin's throat.

"No," I whisper. To prove I won't bend to her ways, I wiggle off the bed and land ungracefully on my toes. Everything hurts. The skin of my back tugs beneath the bandages, like it might split open at any moment. I clench my jaw to stop from crying out.

The wolf moves to the door, whimpering, demanding to be fed. If she can't have Korwin, she needs a substitution. I can't deny her. I want to, but I can't. As I move to unlock the door for her, the wheels of my IV pole catch on the legs of the bed. Digging my fingers beneath the tape and translucent bandage on my arm, I pry the catheter of the IV from my flesh. Blood bubbles to the surface of the resulting wound. I ignore it. The wad of tape and plastic drops from my fingers. Fluid from the bag drips out the catheter and pools on the floor. I make no attempt to stop the flow or clean it up. My wolf is waiting.

With blood trickling down my forearm, I trigger the Biolock. It's harder than usual in my condition, but I manage. I leave a bloody handprint on the scanner. Our hospital room is connected to Charlie's laboratory and office. He's not there. The lights are off, but a soft glow comes from the corner near the door. The large button on the side of SC-13's artificial womb lights my way. I almost forgot about him. The reason for Dr. Konrad's ire. The gamma experiment. My baby.

My wolf growls at the frosted pod. Usually, she makes me brave, but there is nothing to be brave about here. SC-13 isn't a threat. Instead, my wolf seems to fear the womb. She backs away, separating herself from me.

Step by step I proceed to the glass case, swallowing hard. "Nothing to be afraid of," I tell her. "Since when are you afraid of anything, anyway?"

The wolf pulls her lips off her teeth.

I tap the button on the side of the pod and the frosted glass clears. The tiny red heart still beats, but slower than before, sluggish. He looks like he's barely grown at all. "Dr. Konrad wasn't lying. You're not going to make it in this thing, are you?"

I press my hands onto the glass, enthralled by the blinking light, the tiny ripple of movement inside the sac of fluid. The womb vibrates under my palms. I am transfixed by how the pinkish light permeates my skin, revealing the veins and bones of my hands. I can palpate his heart beating beneath the glass, a small rush of vibration that tickles my skin. *Wub-woosh, wub-woosh.*

Amazed, I glance over my shoulder, smiling. There is no one in the room with me. Even my wolf is gone. I look back at the peanut-sized human. "I think you scared my wolf away."

Wub-woosh, wub-woosh.

"You don't even know how special you are," I say. "You're a miracle. A blessing. I won't let that monster have you."

"What monster are we talking about?" Charlie stands in the doorway, a concerned look on his face.

"Dr. Konrad," I explain. "He told me that he used gamma embryos to create the virus that gave him his power. He's unstable, just like you and the rest of the Alpha Eight, and he needs SC-13 to keep his cells from breaking down."

"Trinity said the building fell on him. She thinks he's dead."

"I'll believe it when I see his rotting body," I say. "And then, maybe only if I kick it a few times."

"Can you frost the glass? I want to turn on the light. It's not good for him."

Reluctantly, I peel my hands from the glass and push the button again. I've left a bloody handprint. My arm still bleeds where I removed my IV.

"Lydia, damn, did you yank the catheter out yourself?" Charlie rushes to my side, grabs a square of gauze from a jar on the counter and presses it against the trickle of blood.

"It was my wolf," I say.

He pulls back slightly. "Is she still here?"

"No. SC-13 made her uncomfortable."

Charlie's mouth twitches like he's trying not to laugh. "An artificial womb made your hallucination uncomfortable?"

"She backed away as soon as we saw the womb, and the closer I got to him, the less I could feel her."

Charlie raises an eyebrow. "Hmm." He pulls me over to the sink and washes the blood from my arm while maintaining pressure on the gauze pad. As he's toweling my forearm dry, his face is tense with thought. His eyes drift to SC-13. He rips a piece of medical tape from a roll he keeps in his pocket, replaces the bloody gauze with a fresh piece, and tapes it to my arm with enough pressure to make me believe he's angry at my wound.

"What's wrong?" I ask.

Charlie frowns slightly and pauses to choose his words carefully. "SC-13 isn't growing."

"Dr. Konrad told me SC-13 couldn't survive much longer without his intervention. Unfortunately, he didn't say what that intervention was."

Charlie scowls. "In this case, the mad doctor might have been telling the truth. The womb is self-contained. SC-13 has enough fluid and nutrients to develop to term, but something is missing. He's not thriving." Charlie turns off the overhead light and hits the button again to clear the foggy glass. "I'm not entirely sure what's normal for a gamma in an artificial womb. His physical development puts him at about eight to ten weeks gestation in human terms. When we brought him in, the amniotic sac was six inches in diameter. It is still six inches. His heartbeat was 169 beats per minute. It should have increased to

175, but instead it slowed. It's now 135. And he rarely moves."

"I noticed. He's dying, isn't he?"

"I think so. Konrad told you that SC-13's biochemistry had a stabilizing effect on his own, right?"

"Yes."

He takes a deep breath. "I have a theory that it might work the same for you. If I learn more about SC-13, I should be able to replicate whatever stabilizing agent Konrad was using. I'll have to extract a bit of his blood and tissue for the analysis. And I need to do it before he dies."

"Will it hurt him to extract the blood?"

"I don't think so. I'll use a tiny needle. I only need a few cells. Complications are rare." Charlie's eyes shift away from me.

"How could you possibly know that?" I gesture toward the artificial womb and the miracle inside. "SC-13 is one of a kind. How will you get in there without opening it?"

"In a normal woman, I'd go through the skin."

"There's no skin, Charlie. You can't open that thing. We have no idea what will happen."

Charlie sighs. "You're right, I don't know for sure, but it's a relatively simple procedure in a pregnant woman, and you said Dr. Konrad had extracted cells to make his own retrovirus, so it must be possible."

"He used gamma cells from gamma embryos. I never said he used SC-13's. There were twelve other bodies in that lab. Dead bodies." My voice cracks and I try my best not to cry. "He was creating them to destroy them. He was creating them to *use* them."

"I know this is hard for you to accept, but he's going to die anyway." Hanging his head, Charlie looks at me through his lashes, the scar cutting through his left eyebrow more pronounced than usual. "If SC-13's cells have stabilizing qualities, it could help with your condition. Analyzing his cells might give me much-needed information in my quest for a serum for you. It could save you from losing your spark."

"If I were going to die, would you hook me up to a drainer? Use the last bit of power left in my failing body?"

"Of course not."

"Then don't you dare do anything to hurt SC-13. He lives until he dies." I take a deep breath. I'm tired. This is the most I've been up in days. "What if I slept in here? Next to him? He scared away the wolf before, maybe he can do it again, no tests involved." I grab a towel from the counter and wipe my bloody handprint from the lid of the artificial womb. "If he is dying, maybe my presence will give him some comfort."

Charlie nods slowly. "Harmless enough to try. But Lydia, we have to do something about your condition. You can't go on like this."

"I know."

"Come on. Back to bed. I'll wheel him in there."

I give him a slight smile. "Thank you, Charlie."

I return to the room where Korwin is still sleeping and lie down in my own bed. Charlie wheels in the cart, parks it next to me, and plugs in the womb. I wait until he leaves before sliding SC-13's pod onto the mattress and curling around it.

I don't fully understand my bond with SC-13. Can any mother explain the bond she has with her baby? Love doesn't have to have a reason. I love SC-13 unconditionally and will protect him, even at my own expense. Our bond just *is*.

"I won't let anyone hurt you," I whisper to the tiny being beside me. "I'll love you for as long as you live, however long that is."

My words are answered only by the steady blink of SC-13's heart.

Chapter 19

For the first time in weeks, I wake up having slept a full eight hours. The artificial window on the wall depicts sunny skies, and the clock in the lower corner of the glass reads 9:00 a.m. Late morning. Unheard of for me. Korwin sleeps soundly in the bed next to mine.

I am still wrapped around SC-13.

I tap the button on the side of the artificial womb to clear the foggy glass. SC-13's heart blinks at me. Is it faster than last night? It seems so. I glance at the clock and start counting beats. After a minute, a wave of joy rushes from my toes to the crown of my head. One hundred seventy-five beats per minute. Normal, according to Charlie. As if to prove he's better, SC-13 tumbles within his iridescent sac of fluid.

What does it mean? Perhaps my presence and love have leant more than emotional support. After all, if I'd been pregnant the natural way, he'd be close to me all the time. I have to show Charlie.

Stiff from lying in the same position all night, I push the womb back onto the cart and sit up to stretch. I feel good. With curiosity, I note that my back doesn't hurt anymore. I climb from the bed and take a few experimental steps toward the bathroom.

The journey is surprisingly painless. A distance that was agonizing yesterday is an easy walk for me. There's a full-length mirror on the bathroom door and I twist so that I can see my back. Once I've wriggled my hospital tunic off, I work my fingers under the bandage on my shoulder and manage to bend the tape and white gauze away. My wound is completely healed. There's a dark pink scar where I was injured, but no blood, no scab. Frantically, I tear the rest of the bandages off, my back, my leg, even the piece of gauze on my arm. Everything is healed. Completely healed.

I snap my elbow and my hand tingles blue with electrical charge. I can feel the energy run in a ribbon from the tickle at the back of my brain to my fingertips and I stretch and massage the power like blue taffy between my fingers. How is this possible?

One look in the mirror and I know. SC-13 has stabilized my cells. My wolf was afraid of him because

SC-13 has the power to send her away for good. He's allowed me to heal myself. Charlie and I were wrong about Konrad. He wasn't using blood or tissue as the stabilizing agent. It was proximity. Simply being near SC-13 is stabilizing. I don't understand the science of it, but it's real.

I have to tell Charlie. I don my tunic again and rush from the bathroom. I'm about to leave the room when Korwin says, "Where are you going?" His voice holds an edge of desperation. He can't move from the waist down. It must be agonizing.

"I was going to find Charlie, but it can wait."

I approach his bed and climb in next to him. My fingers stroke through the hair over his ear. His eyes flutter and then lock onto me, pupils constricting in the light.

"You look… amazing. Healthy. You're feeling better?" he asks softly. His cheek twitches. He removes my fingers from his hair and places them on his chest.

I smile and cuddle in closer. "Yes. Much better. In fact, there's something I want to try."

He winces. "Do you mind hitting the call button first? I need Charlie," he says.

"Why? What's going on?"

"It hurts. My legs burn." There's a note of panic in his voice and an ache of embarrassment.

"Maybe I can help."

"I hate you seeing me like this," he says.

Frowning, I say, "It doesn't bother me. I want to care for you."

"Shouldn't you take care of yourself?" He snorts. "You could barely walk last night."

"Something wonderful has happened, Korwin."

He lifts his eyes to meet my gaze. I work my hand under his shirt and place my palm just above his belly button. With a deep breath, I allow the ribbon at the back of my brain to unravel and flow into him. His lips part and his abdominal muscles tense beneath my touch. Blue tendrils dance across his skin, glowing through his hospital tunic.

He hooks his fingers behind my neck and pulls me closer, his lips finding mine. The full weight of my body shifts against his. I slide my palm over his bottom rib and up his back, shifting our tunics to allow the skin of our bellies to touch. I hitch one knee over his hips, the way I did the day we escaped Konrad's lab.

Our kiss is hot, liquid butterscotch. It is the sizzle of a drop of water on a hot griddle, the smolder of August sun on packed earth. Unlike the night we escaped Konrad, a longing awakens in me. This is not just about survival or healing. I ache to be closer to Korwin. My heart and soul pour into him and I burn. My eyes are closed during our kiss, but the blue glow brightens the inside of my eyelids.

Korwin smiles against my mouth. The bed moves as he bends one knee and then the other. His fingers dig into the sides of my hair, and he nudges me back. His eyes, usually hazel, are lit from behind, making them appear as green as mine. I feel slightly weaker, like our energy exchange wasn't exactly equal. It doesn't matter. His legs are moving; that's the important thing. He bends and straightens his right and his left.

"You fixed me," he says. "It worked. The pain is gone."

"We've got to tell Charlie." I shift toward the edge of the bed.

"Wait." He grabs the sides of my face. "I love you, Lydia. I've loved you since the first time I met you." A tear runs from the corner of his eye. I wipe it away.

"I love you too," I say.

"This thing with Dr. Konrad, it's made me understand how short life is. Fleeting. Unpredictable."

I nod. "I was scared too. I wasn't sure we'd make it."

"I'm done waiting. I want you to be mine, permanently. I don't want to lose another day to tomorrow or what-ifs. We are adults now and free. Marry me. Marry me while it's still our choice to make."

I place my hands on either side of his face, my heart pounding with the force of our connection. A barrage of memories comes back to me. The day I lifted him from the healing machine at Stuart Manor. Our first kiss. His hand on the small of my back, turning me away from Alpha in the Kennel. The hope in his eyes as we lie dying in Konrad's lab. I have lived a feline existence with Korwin, nine lives, each one more intense than the last. Our existence is intertwined, destined, and symbiotic. I cannot know myself anymore without knowing Korwin.

"Yes," I say. My voice is breathy but certain. "Let's do it today."

As if he'd never been injured, he sits up and wraps me in his arms. We're still embracing when the door opens.

"Whoa," Charlie says, shielding his eyes with his hand.

I scramble off Korwin. "It's okay, Charlie," I say, laughing. "We're fully dressed."

"I saw nothing." He lowers his hand, and his eyes widen with surprise. "Korwin, your legs!"

Korwin climbs out of bed and stretches his arms above his head. "Good as new, doc."

"How? How did this happen?"

Korwin opens his mouth to answer and then balks and looks at me. He doesn't know. I never told him.

"SC-13, Charlie. I slept next to him last night. I woke up healed. My back is better. I'm better."

As if he doesn't believe me, he approaches and turns me around. Discreetly, he checks beneath my tunic. After peeking through the neck, he lifts the back and runs his fingers over my healed skin while I hold the front of the tunic in place. "You're completely healed, Lydia. This is incredible."

"It's a miracle," Korwin says.

"It's the baby," I say. I straighten my top and circumvent Korwin's bed to reach SC-13. "It helped him too. Look, Charlie. He's stronger. Whatever he's made of needs me, and I need him. Konrad wasn't using his cells. He was using his proximity."

Charlie approaches the womb and examines SC-13, noting his heart rate and movements. He shakes his head in amazement. "I want to do another scan, Lydia. And take some blood."

"Okay."

"Meet me in Room 4 in ten minutes?"

I nod. Distracted, Charlie leaves without another word.

"I think Charlie's overwhelmed," I say.

Korwin approaches and wraps his arms around me from behind. "You're overwhelming." He kisses me on the cheek. "While you're being poked and prodded and having your organs looked at, I will make preparations. Our wedding isn't going to plan itself."

I turn to wrap him in a full embrace. "Today, Korwin. I want to marry you today. It's all we have, and even this isn't guaranteed. I won't wait another minute."

* * * * *

Korwin and I kiss goodbye in the hall as if he's going to war rather than to the chapel. We're both still in our hospital tunics but he doesn't want to wait to talk to the pastor. I have never met the pastor, and I wonder what the ceremony will be like. Then again, I'm beyond caring.

WIRED

When I first left Hemlock Hollow, it was as a tourist. Jeremiah and I expected to see the world and then return to our roots behind the wall. The second time I left was a rescue mission. I intended to dive into the outside world, slip my arms around Korwin, and tow him back to the place we both belonged, behind the wall. I've left again, but this time it feels permanent. The day I fought my way back from death, I realized what the *Ordnung* did to Korwin and me was wrong. Bishop Yoder and Deacon Lapp betrayed us. They refused to accept Korwin because he was different and refused to accept me because I dared to love him. During the months I've been away, I've made a life for myself. I've learned God is there for me, with or without the *Ordnung*. It is time for me to move on, to start new traditions and a new life.

I practically skip toward Room 4, anxious to get the tests over with and to help Korwin with preparations. But to get there, I have to pass Jeremiah's room. The sight of him through the window in the door is a two-ton weight on my chest. He's awake!

Have they told him I was the one who attacked him? I have to talk to him, to know he's all right. Fingers trembling, I push the door open.

"Jeremiah," I say breathlessly. I rush to his side, straight into his one-armed hug. I'm crying, trembling with guilt over what I've done to him.

"You're a sight for sore eyes, Lydia Troyer." His cornflower blues search my face and he squeezes my hand. "Shh. None of that. Don't cry for me. I'm okay." He wipes under my eyes.

I kiss his cheek with lips wet with tears. "I came before but you were unconscious. I'm so happy you're awake."

He tugs at my hospital tunic with his one good arm. "Looks like I'm not the only one needing medical attention. What happened to you?"

"I'm fine. A little banged up from my last mission for the Liberty Party. Hardly worth mentioning." I wipe the tears from my face with both hands.

He doesn't believe me, but he doesn't press the topic. "How long have I been here? The doctor won't tell me, and I don't remember anything."

"A week."

"A week! My mother must be beside herself. She'll think I defected… or died."

I squeeze his hand. One of the nurses must have cleaned him up because his hair's been washed and all the blood is gone. The eyepatch has been removed. "Do you need some water?"

"No. I have some. The nurse was just here." He gestures his chin toward a cup on the tray next to his bed.

"Jeremiah, I am blessed to see you again, but this place isn't… safe. Why did you come? Why now?" I put off telling him the truth about how he was injured, and the omission eats at my insides.

The corner of his mouth twitches. "Always straight to the point with you."

I sniff. "It must've been important for you to come all this way."

He nods and licks his lips. "The week before I left Hemlock Hollow, my grandfather passed away of natural causes."

"I'm so sorry."

"Me too. It was a sad day for my family. But I came to tell you—we had to elect a new bishop." His eyes search mine. "It's your father."

"Father is the bishop?" I can't believe it. "But he already has so much responsibility with the farm and me gone. How will he ever do this too?"

"He's marrying Katie Kauffman. They've been courting since just after you left."

"No. Truly?" The thought of my father with Katie warms my heart. It's a good match. I wonder briefly if it's a match based on love or simply shared responsibilities, and then think how little it matters in the *Ordnung*. If it's what my father wants, it's for the best. He would not commit to marriage without prayerful consideration.

"That's wonderful news. I can't wait to congratulate him," I say.

"You know what this means? You can come home."

I search his face. My mind tries to grasp this revelation but can't make sense of it at first.

"Everyone misses you. Well, maybe not Ruthie Mae or Deacon Lapp, but the rest of us." One corner of his mouth lifts.

As the news settles in, my heart sinks. I should be excited about it. With my father as bishop, Korwin could be baptized, and we could be married this November. But my stomach twists at the thought. The life I thought I wanted before could be mine again. A safe, peaceful life without trouble or war.

"It's exciting news," I say.

"What's wrong?" he asks.

"Nothing, I just… I've made a life here."

"You do want to come home, don't you? Are you afraid Korwin won't?"

I shake my head and force a smile. "It's not Korwin. I've changed. There's something you need to know." I can't put it off any longer. To do so would be deceitful.

"Uh-oh. Sounds serious."

"It is."

He flashes his eyes at me, willing me to continue.

"Did anyone tell you what attacked you?" I know the answer, but it seems as good a place to start as any.

With a sigh, he shakes his head. "No one will talk about it."

I retract my hand from his and tangle my fingers in my lap. I could lie. If he doesn't remember, he doesn't have to know the truth. But lying isn't who I am. "It was me," I say mournfully. "I attacked you. I didn't know who you were."

The smile drains from his face. "You didn't recognize me? Not even when you were tearing my arm from its socket?" There's an edge to his tone.

"No. It was dark." I shake my head. "Pitch black. You were the last person I expected to come across. You didn't see me clearly either." Ashamed, I hold back the part about losing my mind and following my wolf.

"I don't remember the attack." He narrows his eyes at me. "Was it just you? The doctor told me my attacker broke my bones in multiple places."

"Just me."

"You've gotten stronger."

"Yes." In truth, I was always strong, but training with the Liberty Party has made me superhuman. I'm faster and tougher. My presence has changed too. I no longer hide my strength under mounds of fabric. Anyone can see my muscles, my speed.

"Well…" Jeremiah stares at my bicep, bulging under the exposed skin of my upper arm. "Make a note to not approach Lydia Troyer in a dark barn."

"And I'm marrying Korwin… tonight," I blurt.

His lips pull into a smile and he laughs through his nose. "Not anymore though. You'll want to come home to be married the Amish way."

I shake my head. "No. No more waiting. No more hoops to jump through or people to appease. It's tonight."

"But… but… what about your father? Surely you'll want him to attend."

It pains me to think he'll miss it, but I know in my heart I'm doing the right thing. "I won't wait another day. All we have is today. Korwin and I are ready for this. I can't wait for the *Ordnung* to be ready too."

He scowls.

"You don't approve." I look down at my hands.

"I'd like to tell you you're wrong, but even with your father as bishop, it would take time," he says. "Who am I to say what you should do? I'm not your husband." His lips curl slightly, just north of neutral.

"Then you understand."

He slaps my shoulder with his good hand. "Understanding a woman is far beyond my intellectual abilities."

"Jeremiah…"

He shrugs. "I can't say it's what I'd choose for myself, but I can see why you might consider it. Promise me you'll think on it, Lydia."

"I will. And I'll help you get back to Hemlock Hollow, as soon as you are strong enough."

We both look up as the door opens and Trinity enters the room, a covered tray cradled in her arms. "Lydia, you're awake!" She rushes to place the tray down on Jeremiah's bedside table and gathers me into a tight hug. "I'm so glad you're okay."

I return her embrace. "I'm so glad they didn't throw you into a prison cell," I say. "I heard the council questioned you."

"With the amount of insider information I gave them on the Green Republic, I think I made it very clear whose side I am on."

"I want to hear all about it," I say.

"It will have to wait until I'm done with my shift. They've made me a nurse's assistant. I'm here to feed the patient." She looks at Jeremiah and grins.

"This is your nurse?" I ask Jeremiah.

His cheeks warm to a slight red. "Yes. I see you two know each other."

"Old pals."

He waves his good hand lightheartedly. "I can feed myself. Go visit."

Trinity laughs. "Jeremiah isn't good at accepting help with things."

"You don't say?"

She lifts an eyebrow in his direction. "I doubt very much you could hobble down to the kitchen to get your own tray, and I'm not cleaning you up after you try to feed yourself with your left hand."

Jeremiah scratches his temple. "You have a point. You win. You can feed me."

220

Trinity moves to the side of the bed and helps to put the head up, tucking the bangs of her long black bob behind her ear. She wheels the tray over and removes the cover. Chicken soup. The Englisher version is nothing like what we eat at home and smells as bad as it tastes.

"Looks delicious," Jeremiah says.

She digs a spoon into the dish and brings it to his mouth. Smugly, I wait for him to make a face. He doesn't. He locks eyes with her, chews and swallows. He can't possibly like it, but he whispers, "Thank you."

Suddenly, I feel like a voyeur, as if I'm interrupting something intimate. I sense a connection between them that charges the air in the room. I shouldn't be here. I'm intruding.

"Excuse me. I need to find Charlie," I say.

Both of them turn toward me at the same time, as if they've forgotten I was in the room. "I think he's finishing up in Room 4," Trinity says.

"Thanks." I move for the door. "I hope to see you both at the wedding."

"Wedding?" she asks. "What?"

"Jeremiah can fill you in." I give a slight wave.

I'm not even out the door before her attention is back on Jeremiah. He's not complaining. For the first time in my memory, he doesn't even notice me leave, let alone say goodbye. His cornflower blue eyes lock onto Trinity. I could be mistaken, but it looks to me like his old sunshine is finally back.

Chapter 20

"The white zones in your nervous system are significantly smaller than in your previous scans." Charlie points to the monitor and the side-by-side images of my brain. As before, most of me appears red with a few cool white spots that are smaller in the after picture. "Spending time with SC-13 definitely ameliorated your condition."

"And I helped him, right?"

"As far as I can tell. His heart rate is up and he's moving. I'd say the outlook is positive." He says *positive* but his tone is pessimistic.

"You don't sound overly thrilled."

"The spots are smaller, but they're still there. You're not cured. There's no guarantee SC-13 will survive to term. Still, what I'm seeing is hopeful."

"What are you seeing?"

"Every person puts off an electromagnetic field, or EMF. Yours, being what you are, is stronger than

223

mine and exponentially stronger than the average human being's. SC-13 also gives off an EMF, but his is complementary to yours. I can't prove it without testing him, but I think…"

"What?" I press Charlie to continue by placing my hand on his forearm and shaking it gently.

"I think this is your baby, and I think nature designed the gamma generation to have a symbiotic relationship to its parents. His EMF is healing to you because in a natural pregnancy, keeping you healthy would keep him healthy. We see this in nature. A virus or a parasite won't kill you quickly. Keeping you alive to spread the organism to others is a part of its survival."

"Are you calling my baby a parasite?"

"I'm just saying that nature may have wired his nervous system to stabilize yours. We'd asked the question how SC-13 had kept Dr. Konrad alive without him extracting blood or fluids. He'd done that to the previous twelve, and each had died. As you now know, he didn't extract anything from SC-13. It was SC-13's proximity, not his chemistry that kept Konrad stable. Which means, the pod you saw Dr. Konrad sleeping in was most likely designed to magnify SC-13's EMF."

My lips part as realization dawns. "And Konrad didn't inject SC-13 with anything to keep him alive. Konrad's EMF enabled his growth."

"Not as well as yours would, but yes. In theory, any of us could provide what SC-13 needs."

"And Dr. Konrad would have kept him forever. He would have been poked and studied until he had nothing left to give. Dr. Konrad told me my existence is due to a rare mutation. He didn't think he could make another gamma, even if Korwin and I hadn't destroyed the rest of our genetic material." The thought alone makes me hate Dr. Konrad all the more. I hope he is dead, flattened at the bottom of that collapsed building. I wish I had dug for his bones. I wish I'd seen his bloody and broken body.

"He'd likely try to clone him eventually. Why settle for one gamma when you can have an army of them?"

In Hemlock Hollow we used to talk about the Devil, the incarnation of evil. When I picture the Devil now, I don't see red pointed tails or pitchforks. I see Dr. Konrad. "He killed Pierce. Said he had a benefactor on the inside."

"I don't suppose he mentioned who it was?"

I shrug. "No. Trinity thought it could be anyone."

"Pierce had few friends in the capital."

I turn my attention back to the scan of my brain. "Should I be with SC-13 now? Do you think this healing happens all the time, or just when we're sleeping?"

"There's only one way to find out. Stay away this afternoon and let me monitor his vitals. I'll call you if things turn for the worse. Once I know how long the effect of your presence lasts, we'll know how long you two can be apart. Then we'll test the effects of keeping you together."

"Wouldn't it be safer if I stayed with him?" I look down at my stomach, guilty that I can't provide the safe home for him that nature intended.

"I can't implant him into you, if that's what you're wondering. The artificial placenta won't adhere to your womb. The Greens have tried it before. While your biology is different, I don't think you'd have a better outcome. Even with the most cutting-edge technology, which I don't have, it's never been done successfully. If SC-13 is going to live, he's going to develop to term inside that artificial womb. We need to figure out your limitations."

"I just... I'm his mother. I should take care of him. I should be with him."

Charlie shakes his head. "You can't, Lydia. Not all the time. It's not practical," he says in a low and apologetic voice. "Especially not now. War is coming. The Liberty Party needs you more than ever."

"War? What are you talking about?"

"The council delayed meeting with you and Korwin because of your physical infirmity, but now that you're better, they'll add you to the team. No doubt about it."

"What team?"

"After talking to Trinity, the Liberty Party was able to connect a series of intercepted messages from Green Party headquarters. As we've feared, they've named Elias Fitzgerald as chancellor in place of Pierce. There's already chatter about retaliating against us for the murder of the chancellor."

"But now that we know Dr. Konrad killed Pierce, can't we tell someone it wasn't us?"

"There's no proof. Konrad was too careful. The Greens would never believe it wasn't us."

"You believe they'll attack us here."

"They know we're in the Outlands. The flashers don't just up and leave in a swarm like that. Our intelligence is firm. They're readying an attack. Probably spreading the drones out to survey the border and record our coming and going."

"Dr. Konrad was controlling the drones. That's how we found out about Trinity. A drone came to my room."

"What?"

"It came through the ventilation shaft and played Konrad's message to us."

Charlie rubs his forehead as if his head hurts. "Is it still there?"

"I haven't been back, but we didn't move it."

"Konrad *must* have a benefactor on the inside. There's no way he got access to drone technology on his own."

"Any estimate of how long we have until they attack?"

"Best we can tell, they don't know exactly where we are or how we've survived. Trinity has shared that the size of our rebellion is hotly debated among the leadership, and our intelligence backs that up. The Outlands are vast and uncharted for the most part. They still believe the radiation is real. But fear of the unknown won't hold them back forever. We're just waiting for them to make the first move. We have a better chance of winning the war on our turf than on theirs."

Tension starts under my ears and works its way down my back. "I'm the reason the drones found us at all," I confess. "Konrad programmed the drone to track me specifically. I think they flashed on me when I attacked Jeremiah and Konrad used that, along with the data he had on me, to find me. I led him here." I hold the sides of my head and squeeze my eyes shut.

Charlie places his hands over mine. "It was only a matter of time until they found us. Don't beat yourself up. Crying over the past won't prepare us for the future."

"So, the Greens will attack. And then what? Can we possibly win this thing?" I shake my head. I don't mean to be defeatist, but it seems like a lost cause.

Charlie leans forward and grips my shoulders. "Yes, we can. The Greens have spread themselves too thin over the last month trying to control the ever-widening gap between the Uppercrust and everyone else. They've completely militarized the Deadzone and have troops permanently stationed in all provinces. Their military is vastly underfunded. They won't pull everyone in to attack. They can't. At every angle, they are threatened with mutiny."

I remember the picket lines I saw outside the ball at the Ambassador's Club. People aren't happy. It isn't just the Liberty Party on the verge of revolution. The Green Republic is coming apart from the inside out.

"Will you excuse me?" I say. "I need to find Korwin."

"Of course. He needs to be briefed on what I told you. The council will want to talk to each of you. We need to bring you two up to speed as soon as possible and resume your training. A week in bed and a broken spine have taken their toll, but we'll have you ready to fight in no time."

"We're getting married today," I say softly.

Charlie's eyebrows lift. "Married?"

"Today. Hopefully, today, if the pastor will do it."

"Have you told anyone about this yet?"

I shake my head. "No. Why?"

The corner of his mouth twitches. I can't tell if he's forcing himself to smile or forcing back a smile. "You're so young."

"Most people are married by my age in Hemlock Hollow."

He shakes his head. "It seems like bad timing. Maybe you two should wait until things are more settled."

"There's never a good time. We can only guarantee today."

"With more time, I could explore the implications." His eyes flit to the desk where he takes interest in some paperwork that is upside down.

"I'm through waiting. His father, my *Ordnung*, everyone in our lives has tried to protect us from each other. But they don't get it. All we really have is each other. We are two manufactured creatures. You know, I spent my entire childhood worried about my soul and never questioning what was under my skin. A madman wired Korwin and me. We are human and machine. We belong together in every way. If you're worried about sex, don't be. Korwin and I have more control over what we are than anyone has ever given us credit for."

Charlie lowers his eyes and stares at his hands. "There's so much we don't understand."

"Hasn't anyone ever told you, Charlie? That's why we have faith."

Chapter 21

By the time I make it to my room, Charlie has called in a team to examine the remains of the drone that carried Dr. Konrad's message. Blue uniforms swarm my personal space with beeping gadgets and ticking machines. Jonas meets me at the door. I frown. It must be serious if he's come in person.

"The team will need a few more minutes," he says, placing a hand on my shoulder.

"I would have told someone sooner if I'd been conscious," I say. "I'm sorry if I put anyone at risk."

Jonas shakes his head. "Both the drones self-destructed. Thank God they weren't programmed to be weapons."

"Drones? We only saw one."

"There was a second, deeper in the ventilation shaft. A spare in case anything happened to the first. We're still not sure how or where it got in from the outside. No place a human could reach." He points at the burnt bodies of the drones lying on a small table at the center of the room. "The alloy is engineered to be flexible and can compress to less than an inch in diameter. Adhesive tiles coat the legs, engineered with a reusable polymer. Adaptable suckers. These drones could climb a vertical sheet of glass. They can effectively go anywhere."

The back of my neck prickles. I pray Konrad is dead. With access to this kind of technology, he'd be more dangerous than ever. "Are you sure these are the only two?"

"As sure as we can be. We have our own technology searching the shafts and the immediate area surrounding the reactor."

"What will you do with them now?" I ask. A woman in a blue uniform climbs a ladder to screw the ventilation grate back onto the wall.

"I'll show you." Jonas dons a pair of white gloves and uses a metal tool to spread sections of one of the drone's apart. Inside is a small blue disc.

"What is that?"

"This is a mistake. There is no doubt in my mind that this chip should have been destroyed when the drone detonated. Its counterpart *was* successfully destroyed in the first drone, but this one was in an elongated position at the time of self-destruction. We think that anomaly preserved this chip. This, Lydia, is the drone's brain. Our technology analysts will be able to use this and track the IP address of the party sending and receiving information."

I'm confused. "But we know. It was Dr. Konrad. He admitted it."

"Dr. Konrad was in the Deadzone when this machine was doing its dirty work. He may have been behind the message, but he was not pulling the strings. And these are some technologically advanced strings."

"How so?"

"When the drones were swarming, Laura got nervous. Tech came up with a method to block all radio and wireless communication from the reactor and surrounding area. Without a key that changes every thirty seconds, communications can't get in or out."

"Wait, was that why Korwin couldn't call Laura and David on his cell phone the day we went after Konrad?"

Jonas nods. "Had you spoken with anyone in Tech, they would have given you the key code." He scowls accusingly.

I glance down at my hands.

"Oh, well, never mind. What's done is done. The fact remains that this chip tells us that Konrad had help. He couldn't have controlled this drone from the Deadzone. Even if he designed the drone, there's not enough power there to run the systems necessary to get this here or for him to receive any transmitted data. But, with this chip, our analyst will find out what system this drone was communicating with and where the signal originated."

Jonas carefully slips the disc into a paper pouch and hands it to a man wearing the same white gloves. With a nod, he disappears out the door with it.

I stare, transfixed, as the team packs up, carefully wrapping the drones in cloth before packing them in boxes and leaving with them. Jonas gives my shoulder a squeeze before following them out.

Konrad wasn't lying. He had a benefactor. Someone wealthy and well connected, to pull this off. I've been praying that Konrad is dead, that SC-13 is safe from his reach. Only, now I have to wonder, is there another out there with the same evil intentions?

* * * * *

In Hemlock Hollow, little girls grow up dreaming about getting married. Weddings are never rushed affairs but long, planned courtships that end in permanent relationships. The ceremony itself isn't grand. The focus is on the long term, the marriage, not the wedding day.

Although the consensus in the reactor is that our wedding is rushed, I feel like I've been waiting forever for this day. Korwin and I courted for almost a year in Hemlock Hollow, lived together for weeks in the Deadzone, almost died together more than once, and have loved each other for what seems like forever. My marriage to Korwin will be the prize at the end of a long and hard-won battle. My mind is set on the future. It doesn't matter to me that I only have my uniform to wear, or that there will be no flowers, or that my new community is on the brink of war. What matters to me is that we begin forever today. We join before God and man, committed for always.

I've just finished showering when there's a knock at my door. Laura.

"I heard about the wedding from Charlie. Actually, Charlie and Korwin. He's very excited. Telling everyone."

I smile and blush.

"I thought you might like to borrow this." She holds up a pale blue dress. "I think it's about your size. I thought about having Sal embellish it, but you seem to prefer your clothing plain."

"I do. Thank you," I say, taking the dress from her. "You don't mind?"

"I'd mind if you didn't use it. It doesn't fit me anymore." She stands in the doorway, the awkward silence wedging between us.

"I should get dressed," I say, holding up the dress.

"May I come in? Just for a moment?"

"Yes, of course."

As the door closes behind her, I brace myself for the inevitable continuation of Charlie's warnings. We're too young. It's too dangerous. It's too soon. But she doesn't say any of that. For a long time, she doesn't say anything.

"When your father and I escaped CGEF you were ten days old. Ten days. That's how long I got to hold you, to feed you, to watch you sleep. We loved you a lifetime in those ten days. When Michael convinced me that our best chance of survival was splitting up and hiding you with a citizen, I fought it at first. Charlie had to tear me away from you. And I never saw Michael again."

"Why didn't you come for me, after you discovered I was living in Hemlock Hollow with my father?" I've asked her this before. I know the answer, but I need to hear it again.

"You had a life of safety and security. You were happy. It felt wrong to ruin that. I only broke my silence when you made the choice to leave. Otherwise, I would have spared you this, if I could have."

I give a tight, closed-mouth smile. "Well, if I'd never left, I would never have met Korwin, so I guess everything works out for the best."

"I think so," Laura says. She wipes a tear from her cheek. "I'm happy for you, Lydia. I wish you a love as strong as the one I had with your father. I know he'd have given you his blessing, just as I am giving you mine." Her voice cracks and she covers her face with her hands.

I do not know the woman in front of me. Not really. Although she is my biological mother, I've had little time to bond with her beyond our work together. Still, in that work she's proved herself my ally. She may have abandoned me as an infant, but I believe she loved me.

"Laura, I've heard that it is customary here for the father to walk the bride down the aisle. Since neither my adoptive father nor Michael could be here today, would you do it? Give me away?"

Laura clasps her hands in front of her chest and smiles. "Yes. Of course. Thank you. Thank you, Lydia." Crying, she backs toward the door as if she's afraid I'll change my mind. "Thank you. I'll let you get ready."

As she exits the room, another hand grips the door and holds it open for her. David. He narrows his eyes on the tears streaming down Laura's face. He frowns and invites himself in.

I hold the dress in front of my towel-wrapped body. "I'm getting dressed. This isn't a good time," I say.

He closes the door. "This will only take a minute."

"What do you want?"

"I heard from Charlie that there is hope that SC-13 can counteract the negative effects of the Nanomem."

"Yes, David. The baby you wanted to kill may be the only hope for combatting the effects of the poison you pumped into my system." I turn away from him and lay the dress out on my bed.

"Poison that saved your life on multiple occasions," he snaps, stepping closer to me.

"Poison that could make me lose my mind and eventually my spark." I'm hot with anger. "This mess is your fault, David. Maxwell would still be alive if not for you, and I would have never needed the Nanomem."

He pulls back and runs his fingers through his hair. He's wearing it longer these days, too long for his age. And he's colored sections of it red and black. It's vain. It makes it hard to tell his true age.

"I. Am. Sorry," he says, spreading his hands. "I had reasons for doing what I did. My wife, Natasha, for one."

"And look where she ended up."

He goes ghostly pale. I almost apologize, but then stop myself. David needs to feel guilty. Next time, maybe he'll think twice about messing with people's lives.

"I didn't come here to fight," he says through his teeth.

"Why did you come?"

"I came to apologize for what I did to you and to congratulate you on your coming nuptials. I hope that you and Korwin will have a long and happy life together. I've also talked to Jeremiah and heard the news about your father. I can't take away the past, but if you need my help returning to Hemlock Hollow, I'll do it. War or no war."

"You mean leaving the Liberty Party when they need me most?"

David hangs his head, his hands propped on his hips. He groans toward the floor.

"I'm not like you. I keep my commitments."

He inhales sharply. "Fine. Good luck today." David turns on his heel as if to leave but stops at the door. Squeezing his eyes closed, he says, "I'm not sure why Laura was crying just now, but there's something you should know."

"And that would be?"

"You have never carried SC-13 in your body, but it's obvious you love him. I'd bet you would do almost anything to keep him safe, even give him up, though it would break your heart to do so. You were Laura's SC-13. You are the baby she saved... all of us saved. Dr. Konrad wanted to kill you. He thought you'd be a monster. She kept you alive. Maybe you should respect that her life hasn't been easy." He turns to look me in the eye. "Plus, if you make her cry again, I'll punch you in the throat."

He slips out the door without looking back. My chest constricts. I didn't make Laura cry, not for the reason he thinks. Still, his words cut me to the quick. I was SC-13. I was the monster child, the loose cannon, the baby the Alpha Eight risked everything

241

to keep safe. My heart sinks. I have never truly appreciated their sacrifice, not on a personal level. Worse, the seed of thought sprouts in my brain that perhaps David has made sacrifices too. He's made choices that have only shown themselves as good or evil in hindsight. I cast the thought aside, not ready to forgive him or understand why he did what he did. Instead, I turn my thoughts to Korwin and continue getting ready.

Chapter 22

"Do you reject Satan?"

"I do."

"And all his empty promises?"

"I do."

"And all his works?" Pastor Blake continues, but my mind is on Korwin. The pastor arranged for Korwin's baptism to occur just before our wedding. I am told that it isn't customary for the groom to see the bride before the ceremony, but just like every other custom, we break it. I stand by his side, acting as his sponsor, while Pastor Blake pours water over his head and then makes the sign of the cross in oil between his eyes and on his wrists.

"You are sealed with the Holy Spirit."

Korwin blinks at me and smiles. He takes my hand as the pastor announces there will be a short break before the wedding ceremony begins.

My mother appears by my side and gestures toward the door. "Come on. You'll want to walk down the aisle properly." My fingers slip from Korwin's and I follow Laura out on the heels of our well-wishers. Hannah and Caleb have attended together and give me the thumbs up as I pass by their row.

I'm barely through the door when Trinity grabs my wrist. "Jeremiah wants to talk to you," she whispers in my ear. "I'm sorry. I don't know why, but he's so upset." She points to the common area, where I see my childhood friend sitting in a wheelchair next to a bench.

I squeeze her hand. "It's okay. I'll talk to him." Excusing myself from Laura's company, I cross to his side. His face is flushed with emotion. I expect him to tell me he's in pain or frustrated that he can't do more for himself. But his anger is directed at me.

"Can't you see this is wrong?" he says.

"I thought you said you understood?"

"I thought I did, but…" His eyes trail to a spot on the floor. "I want you to be happy, but what about home? What about your father and the *Ordnung*? I'm going to have to tell them you did this. It will break their hearts."

I sit down next to him on the bench and smooth the material of my dress over my knees. "I'm sorry I put you in an awkward position, but the *Ordnung* rejected me—"

"I told you. Things have changed. They'd take you back."

I place a hand on his. "Maybe. And after a period of reconciliation and Korwin's baptism, and another year of proving ourselves to the community, we could be married."

Jeremiah nods. "Yes. Exactly. You don't have to do this."

I shake my head. "I can't wait another year. I won't."

"Your father, Lydia! Your own father isn't going to see you marry."

"He gave me his permission a long time ago. He loves Korwin. My father was the one who urged me to leave Hemlock Hollow to find Korwin in the first place. He'd be happy for me. He wouldn't want me to waste another day."

Jeremiah shifts in his chair, and his face betrays his pain. He winces and stiffens.

"You're hurting. You need pain medication."

"No. It will make it harder to go home. I've asked David to take me back tomorrow."

I tilt my head to the side. "You can't. It's too soon. You're not strong enough."

"Excuse me? For someone who clearly cannot be told what to do, you seem awfully good at handing out orders." He widens his eyes at me.

My jaw tightens. "I just mean, what's the rush?"

Jeremiah glances back at Trinity, who is waiting outside the chapel. She's turned to the side, talking to David as if trying to disguise the fact that her eyes dart to Jeremiah every ten seconds.

"That's what this is about. You're taken with Trinity," I say. "You are afraid of your feelings for her."

He glances down into his lap. "She's a lovely young woman."

"That's why you can't wait to get out of here. Not because you hate it, but because you *like* it."

Jeremiah's blue eyes lock onto mine. "I don't *want* what happened to you to happen to me. I don't want to lose my faith in order to gain worldly companionship."

My mouth drops open and I stand from the bench, placing my fists on my hips. "Jeremiah Yoder, I did not lose my faith. I may have left the *Ordnung*, but I did not turn from God. You can believe if you want to that following their rules keeps you safe.

You'll do what they tell you to do and never think for yourself what's right or what's wrong. And when you die you will trumpet into heaven riding a horse built of preaching and promises. I don't have that luxury. My life, the life God gave me, cannot be lived without breaking the rules. When I stand before my Lord and Maker, I will tell him one true and honest thing. I did not live my life in fear, hiding behind a concrete wall. I used the brain in my head, the brain He gave me to trumpet into this world and do the good I was put here to do, the best I could do it."

"You can do good without betraying who you are," he snaps.

I step forward and lean over him so that our faces are almost touching. "I am not the one betraying who I am or what I believe. I'm getting exactly what I want. I'm marrying Korwin. I know who I am, and I know what I believe. I don't need anyone's permission. Not even yours."

Jeremiah rubs his forehead. His gaze shifts toward his feet. There's a long awkward pause. Neither of us move or make a sound, although it's clear people are staring outside the door of the chapel.

"I'm sorry," Jeremiah finally says. The apology is soft but sincere.

"You should be."

"I don't mean to be self-righteous. You have to understand, I always pictured our families growing up together, our kids playing together the way we did."

I squat in front of his wheelchair and gather his hand in mine. "I imagined that too. It could still happen. We don't know what the future will bring."

He lifts one side of his mouth in a tired grin and meets my eyes. "I guess we'll just have to have faith that the crooked path leads to where we want to go."

I nod.

Laura approaches, clearing her throat. "It's time."

"Okay." I stand and turn back toward Jeremiah. "Are you coming? Or is it against your religious convictions to watch me get hitched in an Englisher church?"

A burst of laughter escapes his lips. "Don't make me laugh. It hurts too much," he says. "Nah. I wouldn't miss it."

I walk around his chair and start rolling him toward the chapel, but Trinity intercepts me. "He's in good hands," she says.

As I relinquish my control on Jeremiah's wheelchair, he catches me by the side of my dress. "You look beautiful. Korwin's a lucky man."

"I'd say we're both lucky."

He nods his approval.

A few moments later, with everyone back in their seats, a man in a Liberty Party uniform pulls a guitar into his lap and strums a song I'm not familiar with. My mother, dressed in a simple linen dress, thrusts a bouquet of fake flowers into my hands and hooks her elbow into mine. We proceed slowly down the aisle, Korwin waiting at the front for me next to the pastor. It is a short walk. A simple stroll between rows of folding chairs filled with friends, old and new.

As much as I'd believed every word I'd said to Jeremiah, I am relieved that my childhood friend is there at the back of the church. It is comforting that he, along with Caleb and Hannah, representatives from my past, help to usher me into the future. Even David sits near the back next to Charlie and Jonas. When I look his way, he doesn't make eye contact. He focuses on Laura. He seems happy to find her on my arm.

My mother kisses my cheek, and I join Korwin at the altar. The pastor begins with a prayer and then there is more singing. I hardly notice. I can't take my eyes off Korwin in his dress tunic with braided sash. Finally, he is mine, and I am his.

"And now, the exchange of vows. Who has the rings?" Pastor Blake accepts two rings from Korwin's pocket. They're silver and I have no idea where he's obtained them. He repeats after the pastor and slides the smaller onto my finger, and I follow, sliding the larger onto his.

"I now pronounce you man and wife. You may kiss the bride."

Korwin leans toward me, his eyes twinkling with anticipation. Our lips touch. A shower of sparks causes the pastor to take a step back and the crowd of onlookers to gasp collectively. My heart races. The kiss is short and chaste and makes us glow like a lightbulb. When I pull away, our guests erupt in applause.

The man with the guitar begins to play again, and Korwin takes my hand to lead me from the chapel. David, Charlie, and Jonas, along with my mother, who has joined them, stand and cheer as we make our exit. My eyes fall on Trinity. She's clapping and smiling next to Jeremiah.

I'm still looking at her when a soul-shattering explosion sprays concrete toward her head.

Chapter 23

I f I hadn't been holding Korwin's hand, we could not have saved our friends in time. Our protective shield snaps into place instinctively, but it is by force of will that we push it out, a glowing blue circle that keeps the worst of the explosion from shredding our wedding guests. We are too late to spare Trinity a nasty gash on the head. It bleeds, but she manages to grab Jeremiah's wheelchair, shove through the crowd, and roll him from the room without looking back. Trinity is a survivor. I have no doubt she'll keep Jeremiah safe and get out alive.

"We're under attack!" Jonas pulls out his phone and starts jabbing the screen at the back of the crowd. "The force field is jamming the transmission." He bolts out of our protective sphere as another bomb detonates across the building. He dodges a chunk of ceiling and races for the tunnels.

The emergency siren wails and the lights flash on and off above us. "Everyone to your stations," David yells. "This is not a drill." He shakes me by the shoulders, his face awash in blue from the power coming off us. "They're going to need us on the front line."

Laura grabs David's elbow. "We need our dose of serum or we'll be useless!"

Gesturing toward the hall, Charlie scowls at the buckling floor and crumbling walls. "We have to get the stores of serum from my office."

"That's the direction of the blasts," David yells. "Without the serum we'll be weak, but we won't be dead."

"We have to try. If the serum vials aren't damaged, we may have enough to survive a few weeks out there. I won't be able to replicate it right away, David. This *is* life or death!"

I turn to Korwin in horror. "SC-13!"

"He'll be okay, Lydia. The material that pod is made of is strong as hell," Korwin says.

"Charlie, where is SC-13 now?" I yell.

"Still in my office." He shields his eyes to look at me, his forehead wrinkled with a question unasked.

"We go together," I yell. "Stay close. Korwin and I can protect you."

"You don't know how long your remission will last."

"Stop thinking so hard, Charlie." David pushes the doctor into the hall with both hands, and we run for it. We are the only ones running in this direction for good reason. The walls buckle and groan. No one in their right mind would risk the reactor coming down on their heads. All of the others have escaped through the underground tunnels to the armory and are probably suiting up for war at this very moment.

The door to Charlie's office has lost power and the Biolock won't work. I push him out of the way and pulse it open. Inside is chaos. One wall has fallen in. Wires and steel girders are exposed and poke dangerously into the room. The gurney has toppled and is covered in bandages, needles, and instruments thrown from medical supply cabinets.

David and Laura rush past me to the cabinets along the opposite wall. The entire section of drawers is warped and blue drips from the corner of one. Charlie finds a strip of metal that's broken loose from the gurney and wedges it into a crack in the skewed cabinet. He pries the drawer while David and Laura pull against the bent metal.

Korwin and I surround them in our force field, repelling chunks of concrete that fall from above.

"Where's SC-13?" I say, but only Korwin hears me over the clatter. With our hands coupled, I help him right a fallen rolling cabinet and search beneath it.

David plants one foot on the counter and pulls the drawer they've been working on. "I've got it," he says. The screech of metal on metal fills the room as the drawer gives way. Charlie forms a makeshift bag out of his lab coat and the three start loading vials into it.

"Where's the baby?" I yell again.

Charlie blinks at me as if he's just figuring out what I'm asking. His eyes dart around the room. "He was here. He was right here."

My heart races. Panic grips me by the throat. What if the Republic took him? I turn, the room blurring. I can't breathe.

Korwin shakes me by the shoulder. "There." He points behind the fallen gurney and yanks me over to it. Together, we toss the rolling bed aside. Under it is SC-13's toppled cart. I dig through the splayed clutter, and kick aside the fallen mattress. The artificial womb has skidded from the cart and is hidden under it. I lift SC-13 from the rubble and breathe a sigh of relief that his heart is still beating.

Korwin hooks his hand through my arm and pulls me toward the door. The walls groan ominously. "We have to go. The building's not stable."

I see Laura pull the serum gun from her thigh. "I'm ready."

Carrying SC-13 slows me down. "Let me," Korwin insists. I shake my head. He's mine. My responsibility. We race for the atrium and the tunnels, but we are too late. The hallway collapses, blocking our path.

"Out the garage," David yells. We follow him through a storage area, down a hallway, and out into the garage at the front of the reactor. Before I know what's happening, Charlie yanks SC-13 from me.

"What are you doing?" I lurch at him.

He ducks my swipe. "If you insist on carrying him, you need a better way. We can't fight like this." He slides the pod into a leather satchel. I slip the entire thing on my back while he moves the vials wrapped in his coat to another knapsack.

"Guns from the trucks!" David slams a loaded pistol into my hand. Korwin releases my elbow to arm himself. He hangs a rifle around his neck, grabs a pistol in one hand and tucks another into the back of his waistband.

The *rat-tat-tat* of bullets rings outside the doors. They pierce the windows, shattering the glass. I duck behind the jeep and cover my head. When the bullets stop, there's a rattling thunk outside the far wall.

"Move!" Laura yells.

At superhuman speed, we race out the front door. Korwin and I have to separate to make it. We take shelter behind the largest trees we can reach. An explosion rips through the garage, igniting the automobiles within. I huddle behind the thick trunk of a sycamore as fire scorches my shoulders and the sides of my face. Burning branches rain down around me.

A flaming limb hits the backpack, and I beat out the fire. This isn't safe. SC-13 can't stay with me if I need to fight. It's too dangerous.

The rustle of marching footsteps comes from a distance. I expect to see Green soldiers, but instead I see walking dead. Dark circles under red eyes, meatless limbs, hollow stomachs, open sores. Our attackers are Slip junkies from the Deadzone. I recognize some of the faces but can't recall a single name.

The Deadzoners may not be in uniform but it's clear who they work for. Each holds a weapon bearing the seal of the Green Republic. So much for not having the numbers to attack us.

Korwin meets my gaze and widens his eyes. The footsteps close in.

David breaks from his tree and comes out shooting with both hands. He won't waste his electrokinesis unless it's his last option. Deadzoners drop like flies. Every one of David's bullets is true, hitting the head and neck. Our attackers try to shoot back, but they are clumsy with their weapons, bodies weak and slow from their addiction.

A woman dressed in rags with cornrow hair dodges behind a tree and throws a grenade.

"David! Run!" I yell. He does, but his feet still leave the ground when it detonates.

Enraged, I become foolishly brave. I chase the woman, gun drawn. She bolts into the woods and I follow. My mind is clear. My feet are fast. And I know these woods. I chase her deeper into the forest. When I catch her, she reaches for her belt, but she's out of grenades. Instead, she grabs a knife, her dead eyes latching onto mine. She bares her teeth.

I shoot her in the head. Her body hits the forest floor and wriggles in the pine needles. My aim was true. The hole from my bullet entered her temple and blew out the back of her head. But she's still moving. Breath rushing in my ears, I approach her. Her limbs twitch as if her body is still trying to work without her brain.

"Lydia." The whisper comes to me from a group of trees to my left. I leave the dead woman and jog toward the voice to find Trinity and Jeremiah hiding, the wheels of his chair caked in pine needles.

Trinity grabs my wrist. "They're Deadzoners," she says. "New Generation has spent decades making them addicts. Fitzgerald must be using their addiction to bribe them into service for the Greens."

"Elias Fitzgerald is the new chancellor," I recall. "The Greens needed a bigger army, and he knew just where to get one. But this is more than addiction. That woman's body wouldn't stop moving. Whatever chemicals they've given them are pulling their strings."

Trinity pales. "Is that even possible?"

"How else do you explain this? When we were in the Deadzone, Sting told me they'd all been registered with the government. I think they've been planning this for some time."

"But they're Slip junkies. Eventually, they'll physically crash so hard the Green Republic will need a spatula to pry them off the ground."

"How long does a Slip rush last?"

Trinity frowns. "If they loaded them up before sending them out here... I've heard of people lasting three days."

I shake my head. "It's too long. The Liberty Party militia won't last."

"What are you going to do?" Jeremiah asks.

I take the singed leather backpack from my shoulders and rest it in Jeremiah's lap.

"What's this?" Trinity looks at the pack, then looks at me.

"Something very important. Guard it with your life." I meet Jeremiah's eyes. "Don't open it. Hide it where I keep my secrets. I'm counting on you."

He nods. "I promise."

Trinity's eyes dart between us. "Where should I take him?"

"Jeremiah will show you the way. He'll take you someplace safe. Home, to Hemlock Hollow."

Trinity's forehead wrinkles. "Where is that?"

"The preservation. Behind the wall."

"No way. It actually exists?" Trinity's eyes widen with terror and excitement. No doubt she's heard there's only dead or wild men behind the wall.

I don't have time to ease her fears. "It's several miles and it won't be easy pushing him in this, but you must do it, Trinity." She nods. "I'll hold off the Deadzoners here. They won't get past me."

Jeremiah grabs my arm. "Be careful. Stay safe."

I kiss his cheek.

Trinity pulls me into a quick hug and doesn't waste a second more. Pushing Jeremiah back on the path, she sets off jogging behind him.

A bullet whizzes past my shoulder, barely missing Trinity's head. I toss up my shield to protect myself and bolt for my attacker.

Dead eyes lock onto me. He aims and pulls the trigger. I spark. The bullet melts in the shield I throw off. He tries to adjust, to shoot again. I drop my shield and snap the electric ribbon from my head to my hand. Lightning coasts from my fingers. His gun drops and he falls, twitching.

I walk over to him, raising my gun and pointing it at his head. The man shows no fear or remorse. His fingers work through the pine needles, reaching for his gun.

I put a bullet in his brain. His red-rimmed eyes stare blankly into the gray sky above, fingers still twitching.

The pistol in my hand has a magazine that regularly holds ten bullets. But I have no idea how many are left in it. Charlie handed it to me from one of the vehicles in the garage. It might have been used before. I press the panel on the side and it lights up. Five left. I have to conserve ammunition, but I'm also weary of overusing my spark. The snap of twigs to my left brings me around. Another Deadzoner, and another. I'll have to do the best I can with what I've got.

I engage. Running straight for the first, I avoid his bullets, weaving between the trees. He's a poor shot. I reach him in no time and snap his neck. I'm on the second before he has time to react. He turns the gun around and tries to hit me in the jaw with the butt of his rifle. I duck and slam my elbow into his knee. When he falls, I shoot him with his own gun.

I have blood on my hands. I don't think about it. My wolf is silent. She isn't here to protect me, but I know to my core this is necessary. This is war. It is kill or be killed. No. If it were just that, I would sacrifice myself for peace. This is kill or watch others die. Trinity, Jeremiah, SC-13. I owe it to them to be brave and strong. And Korwin, I picture him on Konrad's table, tortured within an inch of his life. I'm doing this for him too.

Another set of footsteps shuffle in the pine needles behind me and I run full force in the direction of the sound. I raise the rifle I've taken from the Deadzoner, only to lower it again when Korwin emerges from the trees. A second later, Jonas follows in his footsteps. They rush to my side, positioning themselves so we are back to back. It's the first time I've ever seen Jonas hold a gun.

"Thank God I found you," Jonas says, glancing at us over his shoulder while keeping one eye on the woods. "I need your help."

"To do what?" I ask.

"The analysts traced the chip from the drone in your room, Lydia. It had NGA's digital signature and was controlled by the communications hub at CGEF. Konrad was working for Elias Fitzgerald."

I can hear gunfire and explosions in the distance. "So what? We suspected it was Elias or another dignitary. How does that change anything?"

"We think the Greens put a mind control substance in the Slip," Jonas says. "The ones we've killed aren't thinking for themselves. They're like zombies. The communications hub is sending out a signal, similar to the type they used with the drones. It's working with the drug to control them neurologically. The Liberty Party can hold the Deadzoners back, but there are too many. If we're going to win this war, we need to take out the hub and stop the signal. You two are our best hope of breaking into CGEF and destroying the hub."

"What?" I shake my head. "But the war is here! You need us on the front lines."

"Laura and David are already there. You two are faster and stronger. Plus, you have access without going through the battle to get to the grid." Jonas turns to Korwin. "Take the tunnel under 54 Lakehurst in Willow's Province, the one your father used for scamping electricity. It leads to Stuart Manor."

I'd forgotten about the tunnel. It's how Maxwell's people abducted Jeremiah. "Fifty-four Lakehurst has been heavily guarded since the Greens arrested me," I say.

"Eliminate any officers that are still watching the place, take the tunnel, and then gain access to the capital from there. With any luck, Maxwell's cars are still in the garage."

"Stuart Manor will be guarded, too."

"We fry first and ask questions later," Korwin says. They're the words I used to convince him to rescue Trinity. His eyes flick to mine. "Jonas is right. We are the best chance of success."

"Then you'll do it?" Jonas asks.

"I'm in," I say.

Korwin nods. "You can count on us."

"Godspeed," Jonas says, giving us a nod. He takes off running toward the front line, leaving us alone at the edge of the wood.

Korwin's hand touches my back. "Where's SC-13?"

"I sent him to my father's with Trinity and Jeremiah."

"Good. We'll have to travel light."

"Not exactly the honeymoon I expected," I say.

He meets my eyes and pecks me firmly on the lips. "We'll have it, Lydia, someday. The whole thing. A home, our own family, each other. Do you believe me?" His hazel eyes flash and sparkle.

"I do."

"Close your eyes." He wraps his arms around me from behind. "Picture it. Picture our life together."

I'm almost afraid to let my imagination go there. If I picture it too clearly, I have more to lose. But I do picture it. A farmhouse, children, good friends, and hot meals. I open my eyes.

"We will find a way."

"I know."

"Then let's go. The sooner we win this war, the sooner it can be real." He tugs my hand and we take off at a jog in the direction of Willow's Province.

Chapter 24

Sparks move fast, faster than any human can move. Korwin and I aren't just Sparks, we are soldiers, spies, and trained fighters. The things we've endured have left us calloused and resilient. They've left us desperate to succeed. Compared to the day I left Hemlock Hollow, I am solid muscle, exponentially stronger and faster. That's the good news.

The bad news is I'm hungry and my nerves are shot. I'm running on adrenaline in a blue dress that is tearing apart with every step, and I'm not sure how long my remission from the Nanomem disease will last. Still, as I approach 54 Lakehurst Drive, the place where my metamorphosis began, I feel free. I feel like God has a purpose for me, and I am living it. It's not a quiet and gentle purpose like I thought it would be when I lived in Hemlock Hollow. It is a mighty purpose. I am an archangel, fierce and terrible, sent to bring justice.

A squad car with the Green emblem painted on the side is parked in the driveway. The Greens have had one here since the day they found me. Aside from the vehicle though, the place has the overgrown appearance of abandonment. The front line of the war rages in the distance, but no one watches from the windows and all the lights are off.

Korwin takes the porch steps in one leap and approaches the door.

"Be careful," I say.

"I don't think there's anyone here." He peeks in the side window. Backing up, he kicks the door and it breaks away from the old-fashioned lock. No protest meets us at the threshold. We enter glowing blue and prepared for anything.

Inside, the family room is just as we left it, only stuffy and dust covered. I stop short.

"What's wrong?" Korwin asks.

"The lamp. This is where it all started. The first time Caleb turned on the light, I was electrocuted and became a Spark."

"I thank God every day that you did. You saved me, Lydia, in more ways than one."

I stare at the blue porcelain base and ivory shade for a second more. "I feel the same way."

"Come on." I follow him to Caleb's old room, to the closet where Englisher clothes still hang. Korwin peels back the carpet and knocks on the floorboards. When he finds one that sounds hollow, he digs his fingers into a knothole in the wood and yanks out the board. The tunnel beneath is dark and dank. We'll have to drop into a space barely large enough to accommodate Korwin's body.

"I can't do this in a dress," I say. My mother's blue dress is torn and tattered. It keeps catching on my legs. I rummage through Caleb's old clothes, then remember I have another option. "Hold on."

Sprinting to Hannah's room, I find her closet filled. I strip out of the dress and pull on a pair of jeans, a T-shirt, and climate-controlled hoodie. Better. I ball up the dress and throw it in the trash.

When I return to Caleb's room, I find Korwin has changed as well. "Do you think we should destroy the clothes?" he asks.

"Why bother? There's no disguising what we did to the front door."

He agrees. "You go first. I'll lower the board over us after we're both below."

I approach the dark hole in the floor with trepidation. Korwin snaps his elbow and lights his hand. There's a ladder.

Reluctantly, I climb down into a concrete corridor. It's better than the sewer, but only marginally. The air is thick, and there is no natural light. A smell, similar to wet dog, permeates the cold and dark. I would not want to be here alone.

As Korwin's foot hits the top rung, a low growl comes from the shadows.

"Who's there?" I ask, igniting my own hand to see. In a flash, a narrow snout and sharp teeth lunge at my face. More than one hundred pounds of matted fur and slashing claws barrels into me. I howl as the skin of my cheek is torn open. I topple to my back on the concrete, a raging beast's neck between my hands. Saliva drips through its teeth onto my face.

"Lydia, spark!" Korwin yells.

I shake off my initial astonishment and free the electric ribbon at the back of my brain. The smell of burning hair meets my nostrils. The beast's eyes bulge and its tongue protrudes. I squeeze harder. It succumbs and goes limp. I roll it off me and find out it wasn't alone. Korwin has fried another two animals and eliminates a third before I can get my bearings.

"Sewer rats," he says. "He got you."

After checking for the rat's brothers and sisters, I place a hand over my torn cheek.

"Here. Let me." He cups the wound. The corner of my vision lights blue from his touch. The pain stops but he doesn't pull his hand away.

"All those times we traveled through the sewer we never saw one sewer rat, and this is where we run into them?"

"The good news is, we didn't run into the really big ones."

"The rats we killed were as large as full-grown pigs!"

"Just joking. They were enormous, especially the one you killed."

Slowly, he pulls his hand away but his attention doesn't leave my face. "That's concerning."

"What?"

"The wound stopped bleeding but it hasn't completely healed."

"It's the Nanomem. Charlie said SC-13 didn't cure me, he just helped stabilize my cells. The more energy I use, the less I can take in. I'll eventually burn myself out."

He frowns. "You should hide here and recover. I can do this alone."

I brush my hands off on my pants, ridding them of grit and rat hair. "There is no chance in heaven or on earth that I'm going to leave your side, certainly not to hide in a rat-infested tunnel."

He opens his mouth to say something and I place a finger over his lips. "No chance."

"Are you okay to go on? Or do you need to rest?" he asks.

I nod. "Good to go."

He leads the way into the dark, then fumbles with a switch on the wall. Glass panels ignite above us, one after another, filling the tunnel with cool light.

The illumination allows us to see the rats have left dung and hair in every corner. "Eww."

"Yeah." He points to a small cart up the tunnel. "Let's hope that works. I'd hate to walk through this mess."

The cart is narrow and I climb in behind Korwin. He taps the dash and a driving console comes to life. "Good news. This thing is electric, and it looks like this tunnel has its own grid."

"Probably powered with scamped electricity," I say.

"If you'd rather pick your way through a few years of rat dung…"

"No, I'm good," I say, smiling.

"Excellent. Hold on tight."

I lean forward and wrap my arms around his waist. He hits a button and the cart glides into motion. It coasts along a track at a quick but even pace.

"That wasn't so bad. Why did you tell me to hold on tight?" I ask.

"Because I like the feel of my wife's arms around me." He flashes me a half grin over his shoulder. I squeeze him tighter.

A few minutes later, the cart slows and then stops. This part of the corridor is dark, aside from the light of the dashboard. Ahead of us is a white door, the high-tech type I've come to relate with the Stuart compound.

"It's unlocked," Korwin whispers as the door gives slightly under his touch. He ignites one hand. The other finds the pistol tucked into his waistband. He uses his toe to push the door the rest of the way open. The antechamber is dark and quiet. The interior door is also shut but unlocked. No illusions. No force fields. No blood or codes to get inside. This is wrong.

Carefully, we venture into the hall. Korwin turns left and I follow close behind, unsure where we are in the Stuart compound. Unlike the last time we were here, it's dark, and Korwin must use his spark to see. The air is close with a slight musty odor.

As we round the corner, we pass the windows overlooking the gardens. Korwin pulls up short. I stop and follow his line of sight. Once thriving and green, the indoor paradise is dead and gone. In the light of Korwin's glow, I can barely make out the white marble of the statue of Pandora through the branches of dead trees and shrubs. On what was once the walking path, the body of a goldfinch lies limp and rotting in the dark.

"They've cut the emergency power," Korwin says. "No water. No sun. No security. That's why the doors were unlocked."

"I'm sorry. This is devastating." He once told me the gardens at Stuart Manor had perfect conditions and contained a host of rare and unusual plant species.

"Only because it's the site of our first kiss." He pecks me on the cheek and gives me a weak smile. "Let's go."

It bothers him more than he's letting on, I'm sure. Korwin grew up playing in these gardens. Just like everything else, it's a concession we must make, another sacrifice to the god of war. Nothing angers me more than the sight of that dead bird. A free thing trapped inside an artificial Eden, never understanding its prison until it was too late.

With a sigh, I follow Korwin through the labyrinth of hallways to the stairs that lead from the compound to the main part of the house. The vault door hangs open. We climb the steps to the wood-floored great room where we shared our first dance. All the furniture is gone. The metal shields are down, blocking the windows. Without a sound, we search the remaining rooms until we find ourselves in Maxwell's first-floor study, one of the only areas that is still sparsely furnished with a desk, a chair, and a garbage can.

"I don't understand," I say, eyeing a hodgepodge of books and paperwork on the desk. "It looks like there was someone here until recently."

Korwin bends over and snatches a crumpled piece of paper from the garbage can. He flattens it on the desk and turns it toward me. "Not anymore."

I take the paper from his hands. "*Notice of reassignment,*" I read. "*Due to threat of war, all nonessential personnel are ordered to report immediately for reassignment within capital boundaries.* This is dated the day after Pierce was killed."

"They've been planning an attack. Conserving their resources. Organizing their troops. They must've known where we were all this time," Korwin says.

"Konrad knew. He always knew. Only after Pierce died, he found a benefactor who believed him. Elias Fitzgerald has been planning this for weeks." I shake my head. "And I lured the drone to the reactor."

Korwin frowns. "Don't blame yourself. The attack was inevitable. Come on. Let's hope we don't have to walk to the capital."

Easier said than done. I do blame myself for our discovery, both by my confession on Konrad's table and the incident with the flashers. It drives me forward. I have to succeed in destroying the hub and ending the Green's control over the Deadzoner army. Only by completing this mission can I make it up to those who trusted me.

In the garage, Maxwell Stuart's coupe is still parked in the third bay. Korwin gives the garage door a little juice and it rumbles open. When we get in, I tap the dash.

"Fuel cells are empty," I say.

Korwin shrugs. "We're on the grid. A little juice to get us out the driveway and we should be good. He places his hand on the dash and the engine purrs to life. We roll out of the garage, then down the hill to the open gate. But when we're on the main road, Korwin frowns. "The grid should be here."

I scan the surrounding area. "It's like a ghost town." There are cars abandoned in the street. Houses dark with lack of power. Overgrown yards. The entire neighborhood is evacuated. "What do you think happened?"

Korwin keeps driving using his own power to fuel the vehicle. I can tell it's getting difficult for him. Probably like being hooked to a drainer. I put my hand on his skin to help, but he shakes his head. "We can't wear you out. I might need you later." I remove my hand.

A few slow miles later, Korwin smiles. "Hot damn. The grid." He removes his hand from the dash and the car snaps on. Even so, our pace is pitifully slow as we head toward the capital.

"They've run out of power," I say. "They've abused the system too long. With everyone scamping and the waste, I think it finally caught up to them."

Korwin nods. "The Deadzone's been growing for years, but I had no idea it was this bad."

"They short-circuited themselves," I murmur.

"Huh?"

"At the ball, I saw picketers across the street from the Ambassador's Club. Their signs said *Stop Wasting Energy* and *Equal Allocation for All*. What if the people did this? If they don't trust the Green Republic anymore and the capital starved the provinces for energy, maybe the provinces struck back? Massive scamping could be responsible for the blackout."

"Makes sense. There is definitely something going on here."

My stomach tightens and my cheek aches. I try to ignore the nagging suspicion that I'm a balloon with a slow leak. I have to stay strong. I have to do this. Too many people are counting on me. Korwin types the address for CGEF into the dash and we exit the grid for downtown Crater City.

Chapter 25

"Hold it right there." A Green officer, a boy who looks younger than me, trains his rifle on us. "CGEF is closed today. You need to go home. There's a curfew."

"Why? What's going on?" I ask innocently. He doesn't seem to recognize Korwin or me.

"Are you kidding? Are you from the Deadzone or something? There's a war. Rebels found in the Outlands."

We nod and continue to walk toward the building.

"Hey. Did you hear me? You can't go in there!"

Hand in hand we approach the glass doors.

"Stop!" The boy has his gun raised. We've finally garnered the attention of additional officers stationed to the right and left. They raise their weapons too.

Korwin and I glance at each other and draw our power to the surface. There's no way into CGEF but through the front door. We don't have the equipment or support to try for the roof and the access from below was destroyed when Konrad blew up the garage. While touching, we can block a bullet in a split second if we have to, but sparking out too soon would be a mistake. The longer we can go without being recognized, the better.

The guards don't shoot. It's too risky with the building so close. If the bullet misses us, it will plow into the mirrored glass and potentially strike someone in the lobby. Instead, the officer closest to us reaches for his scrambler—not because he knows who we are, but because it's the safest course of action. His naiveté is apparent when the probes fall short. We're out of range. As we pass through the double doors, he drops the scrambler and reaches for his radio.

Inside, the guards behind the security counter are not as patient or as inexperienced. *Pop! Pop!* We spark and the bullets dissolve in our shield. The guards draw their scramblers, mouths gaping. Now they recognize us. In the blink of an eye, Korwin takes out Guard One. I face off with Guard Two. Mine pulls the trigger. Ducking, I knock his arm up over his head with both hands. His scrambler fires straight up. I curse; what goes up must come down. I grab the man by his neck and waistband and drop to the floor, using him as a human shield against the scrambler probes that coil toward the ceiling before descending. I roll out from under Guard Two's body before the probes hit him in the chest and thigh.

As Korwin finishes off Guard One, I make it to the stairs. But when I open the door, Green uniforms and stomping feet greet me. I slam the door and solder it shut.

"No good!" I yell to Korwin, now behind me.

He drags me by the arm to the elevator and punches the call button. The officers from outside have arrived, scramblers in hand. I throw my power, cutting them down at the knees. Among the screams and moans, we board the elevator and Korwin selects the fourth floor.

"After what happened downstairs, they'll know we're coming," I say.

"It doesn't matter. We can handle anything they throw our way." Dark with determination, his eyes flick to the black glass bubble in the corner of the elevator that houses the security camera. "Get behind me." He sparks out as the elevator slows.

We stop. The doors open. Without hesitation, Korwin strikes, a lightning bolt barreling through the widening space at anything that dare stand on the other side. It should be enough. It's not.

An officer with a long, metal rod in the shape of a T braces himself as the tool absorbs Korwin's strike. The force dissipates harmlessly, and the Green officer slams the bar of the T through the open door and into our chests. Whatever the device is, it makes the hair on my arms stand on end. I can feel the weapon drawing on my power like a leech on a fresh wound. I've never seen or heard of this technology.

It drains me with every breath. I take a step back.

Elias Fitzgerald's portly frame moves into the space behind the officers. He chuckles wickedly. "Lydia Lane and Korwin Stuart, I thought Emile would have taken care of you by now. Dr. Konrad must be losing his touch."

"You're his benefactor," I accuse.

"Of course. We've been working together, since Pierce went soft. A useful man to keep on the payroll." Elias runs his hand over the T holding us against the wall. "He provided us with this particular device, as well as a lovely version of Slip perfect for mind control."

"How are you controlling the Deadzoners?" Korwin asks.

I don't expect Elias to answer. When he does, I know it's a bad omen.

He sniffs and raises his chin. "Brilliant piece of technology. The men and women are controlled using ultrasound. Another Dr. Konrad invention. Radio or electromagnetic signals would be useless. Easily blocked. But ultrasound? The perfect tool to circumvent your defenses. We can control an entire army of Slip addicts from the comfort of CGEF. And the best part? The Deadzoners fighting our war for us won't stop until their bodies give out. Brilliant bit of chemistry."

"Konrad is dead," I say, although I have no idea if it's true.

Elias blinks slowly, seeming to digest this piece of information. His heavyset physique threatens to burst through his tailored shirt, rolls of flesh bulging at the cuffs and collar. His long face has a decidedly horselike appearance. He licks his thick lips and dabs under his nose with a handkerchief. "No matter. Our need for his services has diminished. You know, when he told me you two were living in the Outlands, I didn't believe him. But then the drone analysts brought me your picture, Lydia. I thought it was strange how careless you'd become." He sniffs and lowers his voice. "Perhaps you wanted us to find you? Was it bait? An attempt to lure us to war? It worked, only to your detriment. I am told our troops are quelling the rebellion and bringing the Liberty Party to its knees as we speak."

"You won't win," Korwin says. "Even if you defeat us in the Outlands, our supporters are everywhere. The people want justice."

Elias draws his two furry black eyebrows together. "Justice?" He gives an exaggerated laugh. "People want what I tell them they want. Do you think the Green Republic has survived this long by being honest and fair? Do you believe the bit about saving the earth and energy efficiency?" He snorts. "We maintain control of the masses by perpetuating the virtue of the few who really matter. We preserve our way of life by keeping the story alive. The Great Rebellion was never about saving the world; it was about shifting the power. All war is about power and making the masses believe in their heart of hearts that those who have it are acting in their best interests. It's a game of words. An illusion. And today, you become part of that illusion."

"What do you mean?" I ask.

"Chancellor Pierce's murderer is still on the loose. You and I know that Dr. Konrad is responsible…" He lowers his voice. "But the people don't." He gestures toward the wall, indicating the city. "It could very well have been you two."

"You have no proof," I say.

"Hmm. Normally there would be a trial requiring evidence, but we are a nation at war. We are a nation who needs a leader who protects its citizens. Finding Pierce's murderers and bringing them to justice will be an act of leadership that will bind our communities and bolster us as a nation."

I bristle. What is he saying? Korwin takes my hand.

"As the leader of this Republic, I must make difficult decisions," Elias continues. "For example, I've made the decision that you two are guilty of murder. Tonight, the Green Republic will know that I am a swift and decisive leader, delivering justice when justice is due. You will be executed publicly at 2200 hours for the murder of Chancellor Pierce."

I take a step back, but there's nowhere to go. We're boxed into the elevator. All I can do is shake my head.

"Your execution itself causes a bit of a quandary. Based on past experience, we can't shoot you, and electrocution is out of the question." He pulls the white handkerchief from his pocket and wipes his nose with it again. "Draining would take much too long in public. No. Something poetic. Something to show the people what happens to rebels. For you, we look to the past for guidance into the future. Beheading."

"You can't do this," Korwin yells.

Elias turns on his heel, placing one hand on the shoulder of the guard holding the draining device. He whispers in his ear.

A blast of power hits us, filling the elevator with light as bright as the flasher drones. Only, once the light fades, there is only darkness.

* * * * *

My eyes open. Korwin's face hovers above mine and he's smiling.

"Why are you happy? I'm pretty sure we were just sentenced to death." I let him help me sit up and assess the situation. We're in a holding cell. I'm on a concrete bench without so much as a padded mat. We're alone. The cell is inside a larger locked room. My eyes flit up to the black bubble in the corner. Security camera.

Korwin sits down next to me and leans his forehead against the side of my head. "He underestimated us," Korwin whispers.

"No handcuffs," I say under my breath.

"Without Konrad around he has no idea what we can do. He has draining technology on the cell though. Don't touch the bars."

"What's your plan of escape?"

"I haven't figured that out yet."

I stand and turn a circle, taking in our surroundings. "We can take out the power to the bars if we find the source." I search the wall making up the rear of the cell.

Korwin shakes his head. "It's not back there. I checked. It's on the other side of the bars."

"Did you try throwing it?"

"Yeah." He winds up and casts a bolt of electricity toward the wall. When it reaches the space between the bars, it fizzles and scatters, absorbing into the cell.

"We could blast through the back wall." I place my hands on the only place in our cell not covered with bars. The ribbon at the back of my brain asks the molecules under my fingertips to move. By the reaction of the atoms to my call, I can tell what they are made of. Air answers quickly, the molecules virtually ricochet against my touch. Stone barely hums in response to my energy. I've blasted through a concrete wall before. It is possible, but there was space beyond, a place to blast into. This is different. "I don't feel any space at all on the other side."

He tests the wall too and frowns. "We're underground. Maybe I should have given Elias more credit."

"Maybe we can hurl something against the bars?" I try to lift the concrete bench.

"There's nothing in here. That bench is poured into the floor."

I kneel down and place my hands on the concrete under our feet. "This is definitely the basement. Nothing below us either," I say.

Korwin paces beside the bars. I cross my arms over my chest and concentrate on every detail of the cell. As the minutes tick by until our execution, I hope the Liberty Party is faring better than we are. I try to keep my mind from picturing Laura dead in the dirt or Caleb struck by a bullet.

I tip my head back in frustration and find myself staring at the ceiling. "Up?"

"Excuse me?"

"What about the ceiling?"

He looks at the smooth white paint above us and jumps on top of the bench. I wait while he flattens both hands against the ceiling. After a few seconds, he frowns and shifts his palms to a new section. "Hmm."

"What is it?"

"The good news is, there's space on the other side."

"And the bad?"

"Whatever material this is, it's dense and strong. It won't give easily."

"Stronger than concrete?" I ask in a "could be worse" sort of way.

He licks his bottom lip and frowns. "Worse."

I can't accept it. I leap on top of the bench and stretch for the ceiling. My fingertips just barely reach, but it doesn't take me long to confirm his statement. "This will take a consistent and concentrated blast. I'm not sure…"

"I'm not either," he says. "We'd have to work together. Open it up."

I know what he's suggesting when he says *open it up*. When we first met, we almost melted a flameproof room in Maxwell Stuart's compound with a deep kiss. Maxwell warned us that our connection had the potential to produce as much energy as a nuclear bomb. That was his theory anyway. The night Maxwell died, Korwin and I called on our connection. We took out an entire battalion of Green Republic soldiers, but we almost lost our humanity in the process. Unchecked, we became killers.

Since then, Korwin and I have practiced controlling the spark within. We can touch without fear of hurting those around us. What Korwin is suggesting is that we drop that control, that we get close and stay close in hopes that his father's theory is true. It could work, but it's not what I want. Our intimacy is something sacred to me, not a weapon, and I fear losing myself to that dark place we once were. And there's another, more pressing reason.

"I still haven't completely healed," I say. My throat is sore and there's a bruise starting on the inside of my wrist. "If we do this, I could lose my power, if not my mind. It could kill me."

"We won't do it then. There has to be another way." He looks away.

I jump down from the bench and pace the room. It won't help anything, but I weep. Allowing myself a good cry seems like a reasonable indulgence given the circumstances.

Korwin's arm slips around my shoulders. "Don't cry. We'll find a way." He cups my cheek in his hand. "There has to be a way."

That's when I see her, my wolf. She stalks toward me, promising to make me brave. Promising to take away the horror that saving myself means flattening a building and everyone in it. If I welcome her in, she'll take away my guilt, my shame. I close my eyes and shake my head. "No. I don't need you anymore," I murmur to her.

"What?" Korwin asks.

When I open my eyes the wolf is gone. I did it; I've sent her away. I raise my eyes to his. "There's only one way, and you know it."

"It's too risky."

"It's our only hope."

"No." He shakes his head. "It's too dangerous and too... awful."

"It's not ideal. True. But I've flipped this problem over in my head in every direction. I can't think of any other way out."

Korwin strokes my hair back from my face. "Are you sure?"

"Yes. I won't be myself when we're done. If I don't come out of this whole, I want you to escape without me."

He shakes his head. "I'll get you out, and I'll find a way to make you whole again."

I swallow hard and reach for his hand. On contact, heat climbs my arm, over my neck, to my ear. It's crushed velvet on raw skin, liquid fire. I give myself to it, leaning in to meet his lips. The kiss opens and our mouths meld. Electric current runs down my throat into my stomach and lower, where it becomes a deep tangle of attraction. My hands move to his hair. I close my eyes against the gathering blue, the spinning stars that revolve around us.

There's no space between us. I open myself to the engine that is us. Power flows in; power flows out. My skin is alive with energy. Korwin pushes my jacket off my shoulders. His eyes are solid blue. The walls beyond the bars begin to scorch, their nonmetallic material melting at the edges. I wrap my arms around Korwin's neck and pull him closer.

All the time we've been together, we've always held back, guarded against things going too far for the sake of those around us. We've practiced control and self-denial at every turn. Now there is no holding back. I give him everything.

The bars drip to the floor. Skin touches skin and every atom dances, charging and purging, moving faster, creating more energy. I moan at the weightless feel of our connection. Like our first kiss in the garden, heat builds between us, caged lightning. Time stops. Has it been a minute? An hour? A decade?

Hotter and closer, the fuse burns. There's a noise at the room door. I ignore it. Closer. Hotter. Faster. The pressure builds until it detonates.

WIRED

We don't blow apart, not like we did in the garden so long ago. Instead, I cling to him in a tunnel of light as waves of energy ripple into the beyond. I am sure we've passed into heaven, chest to chest and breath to breath. I don't let go. I only hold him tighter.

Chapter 26

It's the way of things that what goes up, must come down. What begins must end. Korwin and I retract. Well, I do. My glow fizzles and fades. The hair on my arms burns away. Korwin senses my withdrawal, opens his eyes and pulls his power back inside. It isn't easy. He grunts with the effort. I'm in awe of his restraint.

The air around us cools. He holds me in his arms as I tremble violently, not from the cold but from the sudden loss of energy. I search for the ribbon at the back of my brain, the power that has become my crutch and my friend, and can't find it. Leaning back from his embrace, I hold my hands between us. "It's gone." My voice cracks.

He gathers my face in his hands, our noses touching. "Are you still here?"

My gaze darts from his face to the utter destruction around us. We are no longer in the cell but in a pit of scorched earth, peppered with metal and glass. The building that once surrounded us is gutted, the night sky above, barely visible through the still standing walls. It is as if God himself has drilled a hole in the building from the top down. A green-uniformed arm sticks out from the rubble, dangling from a floor above us.

"I'm still here," I murmur. "I haven't gone mad. There's no wolf. There's... nothing." I start shaking again.

Korwin's hands turn my face toward his. "Look at me."

I do.

"I love you." His words are as sincere and intimate as if we were in our marital bed rather than a crater of our creation.

"I love you too."

"Let's get out of here."

He helps me up. Each of his movements seems extraordinarily fast and graceful. Mine, on the other hand, are painfully human. We are both naked, standing in a disaster of our making, and I feel as helpless and scared as a newborn.

Screams filter through the walls. "I need something to wear," I say. My bare foot comes down on something sharp and I retract it.

Korwin scans the rubble and then digs. "Don't look."

I turn my face away. A few strangled minutes later, he places a Green uniform and boots in my arms. One pant leg is torn and there's blood. I don't ask. I dress, thankful to have anything at all. When I turn back to Korwin, he's dressed too, but not in a uniform. He's wearing Elias's oversized suit. The material adjusts to his size.

"He must have been coming to get us," Korwin says. "Mission accomplished."

I roll my lips together and squeeze my eyes shut. So much death. So much destruction. And by my hand! But in my heart, I know I've done the right thing. I've defended myself.

Korwin's fingers wrap around mine, and he helps me climb out of the crater onto what remains of a hallway, although I have no idea what floor it was originally attached to. We navigate the wreckage until we can squeeze out a window. When we do, we drop into utter chaos.

"There's one!" a man yells. Another runs at me with a pipe. Korwin hits him with his spark and he crumbles.

"Take the jacket off," Korwin says, tugging at the Green uniform jacket.

I do as he suggests, ending up in green pants and a bloody, sleeveless T-shirt. It's a cold night, but once I leave the jacket behind, I understand why he asked me to lose it. Crater City residents are rioting, beating the Green officers and waving blue flags.

"Blue, Korwin. The flags are blue!"

"These aren't Liberty Party soldiers," he says to me.

"Revolution!" screams a man standing on top of one of the many cars stalled in the street. He waves his flag and shakes his fist at CGEF. There is no power, but the crowd makes do with candles and lanterns. We navigate the sea of people hand in hand, smiles breaking out across our faces as we put distance between CGEF and ourselves.

"We've done it," I say. "When CGEF fell, the people revolted."

Korwin pulls me into a hug and kisses the side of my face.

"Do you think the others…?" I want to say *survived the war,* but I can't bring myself to consider the alternative.

"Only one way to find out."

Korwin weaves between the cars parked in the street. When he finds one that's not boxed in, he pulses it open and climbs behind the wheel. No one says a word to us. The crowd is celebrating in the streets. With a spark, Korwin gets the tiny car running and navigates the parked cars until we are able to reach the highway.

We are the only ones on the grid. The only ones with power. "How are you feeling?" I ask, noticing him wince as the power drain continues.

He smiles. "Are you kidding? After being with you, I could do this all day."

"It was wonderful." I lean my head against the window and shut my eyes.

"Earth shaking."

"Literally," I slur.

His smile fades as we take the exit toward Willow's Province. I feel his hand on mine. "Stay with me. We're almost there."

I force my eyes open, anxious to know the fate of our friends. We reach the site of the battle in the dead of night. A tank is parked sideways to block both lanes of the road. Neither of us recognizes the man in the Liberty Party uniform who approaches Korwin's window.

"Oh!" he says when he identifies Korwin and me. "Jonas is going be relieved to see the two of you. He's ordered a search party but we're having trouble finding the manpower. He's about to come out of his skin."

"Can we pass?" Korwin asks, gesturing toward the tank.

The man shakes his head. "Sorry. You've got to go on foot from here."

"But the reactor is miles away. I can't walk that in the dark." I look down at my hands, my powerless hands, and then at Korwin.

"Don't have to make it to the reactor. Reactor's gone. There's a camp just inside the line." He gestures with his head toward the tank.

We thank the man and Korwin pulls off the road to park. He helps me from the car. I can hardly move. Everything hurts and my legs cramp with each step. As we pass through the ring of military vehicles guarded by Liberty Party soldiers, I lean on Korwin. "I can't go any farther," I murmur. "Something's wrong."

He sweeps me into his arms and carries me. Inside the border, military tents dot the road and landscape. Each flies the Liberty Party flag, navy blue with five silver stars. One tent is significantly larger than the others and in a central location. There's a light on inside. Korwin heads toward that one.

Blue uniforms pass us by with hurried greetings. Some recognize us. Others seem to be too busy to notice. I lean into Korwin's chest and rest my eyes. I'm so tired I can hardly think.

"Hello?" Korwin calls inside the tent.

"Korwin! Lydia!" Jonas's voice precedes a firm hug that encircles both of us. I try to respond but my eyelids won't lift and I can't get my lips to move.

Shuffling feet. "What's wrong with her?" Laura asks.

"I don't know," Korwin says. His voice is laden with panic. "Where's Charlie?"

"He's dead," David says.

Korwin gasps and I slip slightly in his arms.

"You have the bedside manner of a viper," Laura hisses.

"Why sugarcoat it? It is what it is," David says defensively. "He died saving an entire platoon of our people. Distracted the Deadzoners. He was a hero."

"Stop," Jonas commands.

There's a moment of silence. I can't open my eyes or speak, but I can cry. Tears trickle out of the corners of my eyes.

A hand strokes my hair. "She's crying. She can hear us," Laura says. "Korwin, set her down on the cot."

He lowers me to the firm sling of a military bed.

"What happened to her?" Jonas asks.

"We had to use our power. All of our power. We blew up CGEF."

"It *was* you," Jonas says. "We got word that CGEF was bombed. That was the turning point. We were losing until then. The Deadzoners stopped their attack as planned, but that was just the beginning. Once people saw the building go down, they rose up. The Green Republic has been abusing the masses for so long, the people were waiting for an excuse. When you two took out the hub, they rose up and joined forces with us. Some of the Green soldiers even switched sides."

"At what price?" Laura asks near my head.

"The Nanomem shorted her system," Korwin says. "All of her energy went out and she can't take any back in. Charlie warned us it could happen, but I'm not sure why she can't move."

David groans. "The medical tent doesn't have the kind of technology to find out, Korwin. Without Charlie and the facilities we lost with the reactor, I'm not sure what's going on or how to help her."

Fingers run through my hair again. "She's human," Laura says. "Maybe she's just exhausted." A hand presses against my forehead. Two fingers grip the inside of my wrist. "Her pulse and respirations are strong. I don't think she has a fever."

"So, we let her sleep and see if her body can heal itself?" David asks.

"We'll take shifts watching her," Laura says. "Make sure she keeps breathing. If she stops, we provide life support."

"I'll have the medical crew hook up an IV. She could be dehydrated," Jonas says. Footsteps recede into the distance.

"It's going to be okay, Lydia. Just rest." Korwin squeezes my hand. His lips press into mine. The kiss feels warm and soft. It is a comfort to me, but there's no spark and the only tingle I feel is the tingle of affection, not the pull of electricity.

I drift toward oblivion, my breath evening out, my tears stopping. I'm almost asleep when Jonas returns and the inside of my arm is assaulted with the sharp prick of a needle. I cannot jerk or call out from the pain. The procedure is over in a matter of minutes.

After a stretch of silence, Laura says, "I think she's asleep."

"How many did we lose?" Korwin asks.

"We don't have a final count," Jonas answers. "Two thousand would be a close estimate."

Korwin inhales deeply. "Warren and Mirabella?"

"Fine. They joined other business owners in Crater City. They'll be establishing a new governing body under Liberty Party rule."

"Hannah and Caleb?" he whispers more softly. He's asking for my sake. They come from where I come from.

"Caleb suffered a blow to the head. He's in the medical tent but they expect he'll make a full recovery. Hannah doesn't have a scratch on her. Caleb was protecting her when he was hit."

"Thank God."

"There's something else you should know," David says.

"David," Laura interrupts. "This isn't the time."

"She's unconscious, Laura, and even if she wasn't, she's going to find out sooner or later."

I want to scream, to demand he tell me right away, but my body doesn't respond. I go on silently, my breathing even.

"Tell me," Korwin says.

"The first wave of Deadzoners made it to the wall. They blew it up. There is no longer a barrier between here and Hemlock Hollow."

"Was anyone hurt?" Korwin's hand squeezes mine, although I sense it's an involuntary reaction to the news and not intentional.

"We don't think so. Our troops took them out soon after. The Greens used the Slip addicts first, because they were afraid of the radiation."

"You were right about the Deadzoners. Lydia and I discovered it was Dr. Konrad who designed the Slip to have mind control properties. Elias and the Greens were controlling them using ultrasound."

"Ultrasound?"

"He knew we wouldn't think to block it."

"Block it? We didn't know it was possible."

"Elias said the Deadzoners wouldn't stop until their bodies gave out."

"I don't think he appreciated how quickly that end would come. Some of those people hadn't eaten in days," Jonas says. "They dropped as soon as CGEF fell, but some were useless before that."

"But not before they made it to the wall around Hemlock Hollow," Korwin mumbles. "Trinity and Jeremiah went there with SC-13. Do you think any of the Greens or Deadzoners made it inside?"

"We don't think so," Laura said. "We took them out soon after the wall came down. I'm sure they're okay. Trinity is an exceptionally smart and cunning young woman. She'd fight if she had to. I could see it in her, even in the short time I knew her."

Korwin sighs. "I'll go in the morning, just to be sure."

"Bring back SC-13. I don't like the idea of a gamma out there unprotected," David says.

Laura clears her throat. "More importantly, Charlie told me the baby helped stabilize Lydia's condition."

"Stabilize," David says. "Not reverse."

"If there's any spark left in her, he might help."

"I'll bring him," Korwin says. "It can't hurt."

There's a rustle of papers, more footsteps, the hiss of someone adjusting a gas lamp. "You need to get your rest," David says. "I can take the first shift."

"I don't want to leave her," Korwin says.

"You won't have to. There's a cot right over there."

Korwin's hand slips slowly from mine and his footsteps cross the room. There's a creak and groan as he lies down on the cot.

"You too, Laura," David says.

Her hands leave my head. "I'll be right next door." Her footsteps exit the tent.

David's rough hand slips into mine and there's a creak from a stool or folding chair. "I'm sorry," he whispers in my ear. "I never meant for the Nanomem to do this to you. I thought I was helping you." There's a sob in his voice. "From the first time I saw you, looking so much like your mother, I knew they'd underestimate you. You're not just a pretty girl with a spark. You're a warrior. You're a survivor. And you should be a leader. Who else has a heart like yours? No one." Rough fingers stroke my face. "Michael would have been so proud of you. I'm so proud of you. Please get better. Please forgive me. I'm not sure I can live with myself if you don't."

There was a time I hated David. I blamed him for every bad thing that happened to Korwin and me. But now, lying here, having killed an unknown number of people in CGEF, right and wrong take on new meaning. I think back to David's actions with as much pity as judgment. Blessed are those with the option of absolute morality; pity to those like us who have to choose the lesser of evils.

I do forgive you, I think in the dark and silence.

He shifts in his chair.

I am alone inside myself in the quiet of the room. I can't move or speak, but suddenly I am overcome with gratitude. We've won the war. I'm alive and married to Korwin. I am surrounded by the people who love me. If I die tonight, I will take with me the knowledge that I played an instrumental part in bringing peace to this world. I loved and was truly loved in return. Most importantly, I have God. My faith has come back to me in inches, not miles, breathed to life by Korwin, Charlie, SC-13, and the cross that gave me comfort. I know in my heart my death will not be the end. Perhaps Bishop Kauffman waits for me on the other side. Maybe I'll meet my biological father for the first time in heaven. Will my dear, heroic friend Charlie welcome me into my next life?

I give myself over to the newfound peace in my heart and pray. I'm ready. If it's my time to die, God can take me.

Chapter 27

*D*weet, weeet, dwit, dwit, dwit, dwit.

A bird singing outside the tent wakes me. I am familiar with its song, the call of a cardinal, and I open my eyes to the light-filled tent. Blinking, I silently thank God that my eyes opened. Silently, because Laura is asleep on my chest.

I slide out from under her, gently lowering her head to the cot. My limbs are sore but working and I scoot off the cot to test them out. My feet hit the floor and my legs obey my commands. A few experimental steps and I stretch my arms above my head. The IV line attached to my arm slaps against the pole. I roll the wheel to pinch off the line and carefully remove the catheter. This time, I find a tissue and put pressure on the resulting puncture.

Aside from the pain of overworked muscles, my body seems to be responding normally. Perhaps Laura was right and I suffered from human exhaustion.

My mother is the only one in the tent. I consider waking her but then decide against it. She still has blood on her uniform. After being on the front lines of a world at war, the telltale bruises of early electroscurvy cover her arms. She needs her rest. With Charlie gone, I wonder if she has enough serum.

My stomach growls, and I place both hands over my abdomen to muffle the sound. I set out to find Korwin and breakfast. I am still wearing a Green Republic uniform, and I'm covered in blood. The camp is quiet but I manage to find a wash tent and get cleaned up. There's a pile of freshly laundered uniforms on a table outside the showers. I find one that fits and pull my hair through the navy blue cap.

A few more minutes of searching and I give in to the hunger. I follow a small group of soldiers into the mess hall.

"Have you seen Korwin?" I ask the cook, an old woman by the name of Judy who I've met only in passing. She shakes her head.

"He hasn't been in this morning. Glad to see you two are still with us. I'd heard you were injured."

"I'm okay," I say. "But thank you."

As she loads my tray, the hunger is almost unbearable. I start eating even before I sit down. By the time I'm done, I've consumed two bowls of oatmeal, three meat patties, a cup of fruit substitute, and a slice of bread. I stop, not because I'm full, but because I'm embarrassed about the sheer quantity of food I've consumed.

Once I've scraped my tray and left it for the cleaning crew, I wander the camp again looking for Korwin. Most of the soldiers are sleeping off the events of yesterday. I ask the few on duty but no one has seen him. A young woman sends me to a tent she thinks is his, but when I poke my head inside, it's occupied by a gray-haired soldier.

Only when I see three motorcycles parked on the edge of camp do I remember what Korwin said the night before. He planned to go to Hemlock Hollow to make sure everyone was okay and to retrieve SC-13.

Hemlock Hollow... my father, Jeremiah, Trinity... my heart aches to know if they're okay. Surely, Korwin is already there. I climb on the bike and smile when my fingerprint unlocks the dash. These must be general use. The fuel cell is half full, plenty to make it to the wall from here. I start the engine in silent mode and advance toward Hemlock Hollow.

I'm not prepared for the feelings I experience when I reach what used to be the wall. It's been reduced to a pile of rubble and Hemlock Hollow's cemetery is visible on the other side. There's no way I can get over the remains on wheels; driving through it or over it is not an option. I could round the wall to where the gate used to be, but the rubble goes on as far as I can see. It's possible the gate has been destroyed too. If it is, I will have wasted the drive and still have to scale the pieces and walk a greater distance. I park the motorcycle and walk toward what used to be the wall.

With more effort than it should take, I climb on a chunk of concrete and jump from section to section. I'm tired and my legs ache by the time I reach the other side. I can't rest. If I stop moving, I might not be able to start again, and I have a long way to go.

I have a choice to make. I can either go right— the shortest way to my father's house, where Korwin will likely be—or go straight to my tree. I asked Jeremiah to hide SC-13 there in its hollow heart. It's the place I've always kept my secrets. Did he do as I asked? Or did he press on for home with the war at his back, planning to make good on the promise later? Did he look in the bag? Did he know he was carrying my child if he did?

SC-13 has been unplugged for more than twenty-four hours. His pod has a battery, but I have no idea how long it will last. It is very possible he'll be dead by the time I reach him. Not to mention, without my spark, I won't be able to charge his pod if the battery is low.

Time is my enemy. I must find SC-13. I decide to head for the tree.

It's late in the year and the wheat has already been threshed. I traverse the stubble of the former field, remembering the way the feathery crop once tickled my fingers and tugged at my skirt so long ago. Once the growth stops, there's nothing left to do but cull the plants and start over. Everything changes. It has to change to make room for something new.

By the time I'm a stone's throw from my tree, I'm exhausted. Each step is a monumental effort. I grip and lift my leg at the knee, trying to help my weakening stride. Eventually, I give up and crawl the rest of the way.

She's beautiful, my tree. Her dead side reaches its twisted branches against the bright blue beyond, while her living half remains green and strong, even though other trees around her have changed color for the season. She's even taller than I remember.

I dig my fingers into her bark and pull myself up to the large hollow where I've hidden a secret stash of Englisher contraband since I was small. When I reach inside, my fingers immediately bump leather.

"Thank you, Jeremiah," I breathe. I pull the satchel from the hole and collapse to the ground with SC-13 in my lap. Propping my back against the tree's trunk, I hold my breath as I unbuckle the straps and remove the artificial womb. *Please, Lord, let him be alive.*

The glass is still foggy and the side button glows green. I press it. *Blink. Blink. Blink*

SC-13's heart beats, slowly but evenly. One hundred sixty-five beats per minute. I smile, and then a great laugh of joy bubbles up through my throat. I laugh until I'm distracted with SC-13. He's moving, tumbling inside his protective fluid. Can he hear me laughing? Is he reacting to me?

"I love you, little one," I whisper, and press the button to fog the glass again. I hug the pod to my chest. A flood of warmth fills me. How can I love someone I've never even met? Is it the potential of SC-13 I love? The idea that someday he could be ours, Korwin's and mine? No. I love him now. I want to protect him now, for what he is, not what he will be. And it doesn't even matter if he lives only one more day. I will always love him, no matter what. I can't explain why. It just is.

Exhausted, I lie on my side at the root of the tree and curl around the pod. A nap and I will find Korwin, check on my father, and make sure the Green mercenaries from the Deadzone didn't reach Hemlock Hollow. I'm useless like this anyway. A nap will make things better.

I rest my head on one arm, the other curled around SC-13, and I sleep.

* * * * *

I wake ravenously hungry and blink at the blue sky above me. The sun is west. It's past noon. I've been asleep for hours, but I'm stronger. I rise easily and tuck the baby back into the satchel. Loading him onto my back, I set out for my father's house.

It takes me a good forty-five minutes to reach the white farmhouse, longer than it used to even before I became a Spark. I'm still weak. I'm relieved when I arrive at the edge of our farm.

Something is wrong. The black door hangs open on its hinges. I run, taking the porch steps in one leap.

There's blood on the doorjamb.

"Lydia, run!" Jeremiah yells from within. There's a smack of flesh against flesh.

I step inside to a scene out of my worst nightmare. My father is unconscious and tied to the kitchen table. Jeremiah is bound to a chair in the family room, pronounced dark circles under his eyes and a cheek stinging red. Trinity is on the couch, head bleeding and eyes closed. Korwin is unconscious, handcuffed to the stove with draining cuffs. And the man standing in front of the fire, staring at me, looks hardly human. Dr. Konrad.

He is a series of yellow parts stitched together like Frankenstein's monster. The hair on half his head is missing, and thick black stitches run the course from temple to ear. Another row of black marks his nose and down his cheek. One of his arms hangs shorter than the other within his tattered shirt. It's the eyes I recognize. Those cold, gray eyes. And the smell. Blood and sulfur.

"Why, Lydia. I thought you'd never join us," he says through thin, tight lips.

"Dr. Konrad," I say.

"You remember me."

"How? You should be dead."

"When you pulled that little trick in the Deadzone, I was trapped in the rubble for hours. Brilliant, using my own bomb against me. I underestimated your will to become a martyr." He rolls his eyes. "I might have given up. I was badly injured." He paces to the fire and leans his forearm against the mantle. "Of course, I couldn't move at all, buried alive as I was, but then I heard voices. Your friend Sting and a small army of his closest friends dug me out. It seems my condition produces a slight glow. He thought I might be a scamper like you. He was hoping my life would be worth something. Slip addicts have deplorable incomes, you realize. In exchange for a few units, he connected me to the help I needed to survive. Seems he shares a hatred for you that rivals mine."

Sting. I see his face sneering at me from the shadows. "Was he among the Deadzoners you and Elias used to draw out the rebels?"

He shrugs. "Probably. His death was inevitable. But I digress. When he pulled me out of that pile of concrete, I still had this." He reaches into his back pocket and retrieves a square of paper, unfolding it and turning it to face me. It's Korwin's sketch of me in the buggy, wearing my dress and *kapp* and drinking hot cocoa, the same one he showed me in the Kennel. "Your father was a genius to hide you here for all those years. The only place long forgotten by the Greens and underestimated by civilized culture." He steps toward me. "When the Greens attacked, it provided the perfect opportunity. I was the one who brought the wall down. From there, it was all too easy to find your father's house. I knew, if I waited long enough, you would come."

"I'm here now. Take me and let my friends go."

He snorts. "Give me SC-13. I need the gamma to fully heal."

"You've come for nothing," I say. "The baby died. You were right. I couldn't keep him alive."

Konrad laughs. "You've become such an accomplished liar since the first time I met you. Should you have survived, you might have made quite a politician. Too bad you have no idea what you are dealing with. Even if I couldn't read your mind, I can feel him in this room. Every cell in my body is focused on the hum coming from the pack on your shoulders." He beckons me with his yellow fingers and I notice dried blood caked under his fingernails. I have a morbid curiosity about whose it is. "Hand over SC-13."

315

"No."

"I will kill you. I will tear the skin from your flesh," he seethes. A clatter from the kitchen sends me diving behind the sofa. A knife grazes my ear as I fall.

"You can't hurt me without hurting the baby," I warn, huddled behind the furniture.

"Then I'll hurt your friends."

Slowly, I rise, peeking over the back of the sofa. Konrad has the knife pressed against Jeremiah's throat. My friend's eyes are closed, but his lips twitch with the prayer I know he's reciting in his head.

"Leave him alone."

"Give me SC-13!"

I'm so angry, I can feel the emotion like a twenty-pound weight resting between my eyes. Slipping the satchel from my back, I think of the wheat and how it is Dr. Konrad's day to be culled. He should have died long ago. Along with the Greens, it's time for him to go, to make room for something new. I can't allow him to kill Jeremiah, nor can I give him my son. I am paralyzed with fear and loathing as I stand and slip the satchel off my shoulders with shaking hands.

He narrows his eyes and lowers the knife. Konrad can't resist the draw SC-13 has over him. Holding the knife between us, he rounds the sofa and approaches me, reaching his hand out for SC-13. I have no plan accept to engage, hand to hand.

A blast of lightning comes from behind me and plows into Konrad, who seizes as the blue works its way through his body. How? Who? I turn, pulling SC-13 back into my chest.

"David!" I gasp. Pale and sweating, David stands in the doorway, an open electroscurvy sore on his left cheek.

"Run, Lydia! Run!" he yells.

I do, barreling down the porch steps and throwing SC-13 over my shoulders. My human legs are slow and the satchel feels heavy on my back. I need to hide him. If I can hide SC-13, I might be able find a way to help my friends.

David's muffled scream comes from the house and I choose the closest place of concealment, our barn. Slipping inside the doors, I close and latch them behind me. Our horse, whinnies when he sees me. He stomps his front hooves, obviously hungry. If Konrad has been here since last night, he hasn't been fed.

"Shhhhh," I plead, quickly tossing a clump of hay and a scoop of feed haphazardly into his stall. Thankfully, he quiets and lowers his head to feed.

I climb the ladder to the haymow and flatten myself behind the stack of hay.

"Lydia!" Konrad's call filters through the walls from a distance. He's searching for me. "Don't make me kill the rest of your friends."

I wince at his words. Is David dead?

"SC-13 is as good as mine. Give him up and we can go our separate ways."

Desperately, I try to dig in the back of my brain for the hot ribbon of power that has protected me since becoming a Spark. It's not there. Even in SC-13's presence, I can't muster it from the depths of my brain. Charlie's voice comes back to me, *stabilize, not cure. Temporary reversal.* I can't rely on my own power. I'll have to rely on another.

I slip the satchel from my shoulders and cover it with hay. The cross Korwin gave me melted at CGEF, as did our rings, but my roots run deep, especially here where my faith began. I pray from the heart. Crawling, I put space between SC-13 and myself. I cower behind a hay bale, heart pounding.

The latch on the door lifts of its own accord, and the doors fly open. Dr. Konrad walks into our barn, smiling banefully.

"Lydia. Tsk, tsk, tsk. You don't get it, do you? You can't hide from me. I can *feel* him, and I can hear you. The stuff he is made of runs through my veins.

It keeps me alive. SC-13 is mine, just as you are. I own you. You are my creation!"

The rush of my breath matches the pounding of my heart. With raw courage, I stand, revealing myself, and face him from above. "I'm not yours, Konrad, and neither is SC-13. I have one creator, God. I am His and always will be."

Konrad narrows his eyes and my body flies off the haymow, yanked by the invisible force of his telekinesis. He drops me. My newly human legs aren't strong enough to withstand the impact. I collapse onto the straw-covered floor, unable to catch my breath.

With a snort, Konrad moves for the ladder. "The difference between me and your God is I exist." He steps onto the bottom rung and uses his normal arm to pull himself up. The other must not work because it remains limp at his side, slowing his progress up the ladder. He reaches for the next rung. Pull, step, step. His slow ascension gives me time to think.

I blink against the pain in my ankle and leg and manage a shallow breath. I have to get up. I have to do something. I drag myself through the straw to the base of the ladder just as Konrad clears the top rung. As best I can, I pull myself to standing, intending to follow him. But my eyes catch on the hay behind the ladder and I reconsider. I am too weak to fight him with my body. I must use my mind.

Konrad descends, the straps of the satchel visible on his shoulders as he lowers himself from rung to rung. Using one arm requires him to pause on the ladder at regular intervals. Foot, foot, arm. Foot, foot, arm. I position myself in the shadows and clear my mind. Closer... closer.

Foot, foot... With a howl, I dive from the hay and the shadows, driving the pitchfork between the rungs and into his chest. Blood sprays across my face. I thrust forward with all my strength and weight, feeling the iron hit ribs and then slide between them with the angled force of my thrust.

His body falls backward, taking the pitchfork with him. The handle catches on the ladder and it tears from his flesh. I gasp as he lands on SC-13, blood gushing from the wound. I wrestle the pitchfork from the rungs and use it as a cane to limp toward Konrad, who gurgles and coughs. He turns his head and narrows his eyes on me. Thinking fast, I scoop the hay near my feet and toss it between us. It intercepts his telekinesis, meant for me, and is thrown against the wall of the barn. The distraction is enough.

I hop forward on my good leg and stab the pitchfork through his neck, bending his body over SC-13's pod. I drive the fork to the floor, careful to position myself so he cannot make eye contact with me. Hay whips around the barn, stinging my cheeks and hands. The doors open and close as Konrad's power frantically claws at anything it can reach. The gate on the stall flies open and slams shut, sending our horse stomping to the rear of it. I lean my weight into the pitchfork, wailing at the feel of iron against bone, the pain in my leg, my fear for SC-13.

The cacophony of destruction ebbs. The hay snows to the ground. The doors creak to a stop. Blood pools below Konrad. I wait, clutching the handle of the pitchfork and crying until full minutes have passed without a hint of struggle from Konrad. I yank the prongs from his throat. He doesn't move. Frantically, I pull off my military jacket and throw it over his face. There is no struggle.

Through vision blurred with tears, I work the strap to the satchel off Konrad's short arm, then roll his body off SC-13 with a kick.

"The pods are strong," I say to myself. "Charlie said the pods are strong." I weep as I fall to the floor and pull the bloody satchel into my lap, on top of the lame leg whose pain is almost too much to bear. I slide the artificial womb from the leather and tap the side.

Blink. Blink. Blink. SC-13's heart beats the tune of our victory. His pod is whole. He's alive and well.

I lay back in the straw, hugging the artificial womb to my chest. Overwhelmed with pain, I close my eyes and repeat a prayer of thanks for the miracle in my arms.

Chapter 28

I t's Laura who finds me. She rushes to my side and tries to lift SC-13 from my chest.

"No," I whimper. "He's mine."

"You're in a pool of blood."

"It's Konrad's."

"He's dead. Really dead." She places a hand on my head. "Are you injured?"

"My leg."

"Do you think you can use me as a crutch? I have a medical team at the house, but they are caring for the others. David is injured. I'm afraid to call anyone away."

"I can do it." I sit up and am surprised that my leg doesn't hurt as much as it did. I look down at SC-13, wondering if my healing, while not complete, is his doing. Laura helps me slide him into the satchel and sling him over my back. She seems resigned to it, even though it would be easier for her to carry the womb herself.

"One… two… three." She lifts me onto my good leg and we limp toward the door to the barn. I take a second to glance back at Dr. Konrad, his face still covered with my jacket, the pitchfork thrown into the bloody hay beside him. "You're sure he's dead?" I ask, shivering.

Laura's hand cups my cheek. "He's stiff and cold. No heartbeat. He's dead."

I meet her eyes. "I want to burn his body."

She nods. "We will."

I expect to feel guilty about killing a man, especially in the brutal way I took out Konrad. After all, I was born and raised a pacifist. I don't have my wolf to blame either. For a long time, she's protected me from the full weight of guilt about what I had to do. But not anymore. She is gone for good. The only one who wielded the pitchfork was me. I don't feel guilty as we make our way to my father's house. All I feel is relief. I thank God for giving me the strength to protect my child and myself.

Inside the farmhouse, David is unconscious on a cot in the center of the room. A bag of blue fluid drips into his arm. A man and a woman in Liberty Party scrubs are stitching a wound in his shoulder.

"The blue solution contains serum, as much as we could spare. He risked his life coming here. We've been living on half doses until the new doctor can replicate the formula," Laura says.

I bite my lip. A wave of loss over Charlie's death almost brings me to my knees.

"Where's Korwin? My father? Jeremiah and Trinity?"

Laura answers. "They're fine. The medics are stitching them up. Korwin is still unconscious but healing." She gestures toward the bedrooms.

I move in that direction, needing to see for myself that they're okay, but I stop when David shifts on the gurney. "Lydia?" he rasps. His eyes flutter.

Laura races to his side and grabs his hand. "You're okay, David, just rest."

His sunken eyes find my mother's face. "Liar."

A tear cuts a trail down Laura's face.

"Lydia?" he says again. He blinks and doesn't open his eyes fully. His head tilts in my direction, but I don't think he can see me. His eyes seem unfocused. "Please."

I limp to his side, lowering myself to the chair near his head. "Thank you, David, for coming for me."

"Owed you," he rasps, each word a pronounced effort.

"No, you didn't. You didn't owe me this."

He blinks slowly. "Sorry for … I did to you. Forgive?" The words are slurred. His body is so still, his flesh raw with electroscurvy. He stares aimlessly at the ceiling. I haven't seen a person in this condition since Natasha.

"I forgive you." I squeeze his hand, my eyes pooling with tears. "I forgive you, David. For everything. I understand now. I understand why you did it."

He swallows and stops breathing.

"David? DAVID!" I shake his shoulder.

The medics rush in. I scramble out of the way, and Laura catches me in her arms when I trip over my injured leg. One of the medics places a rubber mask over David's mouth and nose while another begins compressions on his chest.

"Don't you dare die, David!" I yell. "I won't forgive you if you die!" I sob as Laura cradles me in her arms, stroking the back of my head.

I'm not sure how much time passes until the medics stop working. I raise my face from Laura's shoulder to see them packing up their equipment.

"Is he dead?" I ask.

The medic shakes her head. "Not today."

I limp to his side. He's even paler than before, but he raises his eyelids, and this time, he's focused on me. "Konrad?"

I nod. "I killed him, David. He's dead."

"How?" His voice peters out, but I can tell what he wants to ask by the shape of his lips.

"With a pitchfork," I say solemnly. "No spark. No Nanomem. Just the tool I used to use to shovel manure."

David's eyes close but the corner of his mouth lifts into a slight smile.

"An appropriate end for him, I think," I say. He squeezes my hand and then slips into a needed slumber.

"You saved us, Lydia," Laura says, coming to my side and placing a hand on my shoulder. "All of us, including that little guy on your back. Don't ever forget that." The look she gives me is knowing and empathetic.

I kiss David on the cheek and watch his chest rise and fall evenly.

"Wait!" a Liberty Party medic yells from my father's bedroom. "I need to examine you!"

Korwin staggers into the doorframe, a bag of ice pressed to his head, and locks eyes with me. "Thank the Lord!" He limps across the room to wrap me in his arms. "Konrad knocked me out. When I woke, I was afraid… I…"

"I'm okay," I say. "Konrad is dead."

He squeezes me tighter.

There's more yelling from the bedroom and my father appears. War-torn but alive, he hobbles to me, and I embrace him. "I wasn't sure I'd ever see you again," he says.

I squeeze him tight. "It's going to be okay. You're safe now. Konrad's dead."

Trinity, head bandaged, emerges from my room, pushing Jeremiah in his wheelchair.

"Did I hear Konrad's dead?" she asks.

"Yes," I say, breaking into a grin.

Jeremiah shakes his head. "I, for one, don't reckon I'll miss him."

With one arm around Korwin and the other around my father, I break into a slow, painful smile and shake my head. "I don't think you're alone in that, Jeremiah Yoder."

Chapter 29

Later, after the medics have had their say and everyone is bandaged and hydrated, it becomes clear that Korwin is in the best shape of any of us. His spark has healed him in a way that isn't possible for me anymore. He rests his hand on my shoulder. "I'll take Jeremiah home."

My father points out the window toward our driveway. "Take the buggy."

"Thanks." Korwin moves for the door, and I realize he'll have to go to the barn to get our horse.

"Wait. Konrad's body is still in there. Don't go alone."

Laura places her hands on my shoulders. "He's dead, Lydia."

I shake my head. "Not until I see him burn."

She nods. "I'll go with him. I'll make sure." She follows him through the door and I watch them head toward the barn.

"I can take him home," Trinity says, one arm on Jeremiah's shoulder. "He can tell me where to go."

Jeremiah seems fine with the idea. If the ridiculous smile on his face is any indication, he'd go anywhere with Trinity. It warms my heart to see it, but there are practicalities that need to be addressed.

"Your head has barely stopped bleeding," I say, spreading my hands in a gentle plea for understanding.

She shrugs. "It's nothing. I'm fine."

"Can you drive a buggy?" my father asks.

"No. She can't," I say.

Through the window, I see Korwin return, horse in tow. He starts readying the buggy with Laura's help. I breathe a sigh of relief.

"You can come back when you're well," Jeremiah says to Trinity. "Ma'am Yoder would love to cook for ya. You've never eaten until you've had a good Amish meal."

Trinity smiles coyly, her cheeks reddening to a soft rose. "I'd like that. I'll ride with you, then, to your place."

Jeremiah beams his consent and she rolls his wheelchair out to the porch where Korwin helps her get him down the steps and loaded into the buggy.

"Hmm," my father says from our porch as the buggy pulls out of the driveway. "She a nice girl?"

"The nicest."

* * * * *

It's late in the day when Laura and the medics load David into the medical truck they arrived in. When the truck pulls away, Laura remains.

"You're not going with them?" I ask.

She shakes her head and looks toward the barn. "I want to see this finished as much as you do."

Without saying a word, my father joins her in the front yard. I watch them disappear into the barn from my seat on the porch step. I'd like to help, but without my spark, I remain injured and helpless. I sit and wait. They emerge a few minutes later with Konrad's body on a board. They take him to the bit of scorched earth in our front yard where I'd once seen a doll dressed as me burn at the stake. Laura helps my father construct a platform of crisscrossed logs and sticks to support Konrad's corpse.

Our barn is a bloody mess. I'm anxious to clean it and eradicate all evidence of Konrad's existence from my life, but I'm too weak. *Soon enough*, I tell myself. It will take a long time and hard work to put the devil behind me.

When they've finished and Konrad is in place, Laura sprinkles the body with kerosene my father gives her, the kind he uses as fuel for his space heater. She approaches and hands me a box of matches, the acrid smell of the combustive agent thick in the air. "I think you should be the one to do this," she says.

I nod my agreement. With her and my father's help, I hobble to the logs. The match strikes against the flint and I toss it on Konrad's chest. The pile explodes into flames, a plume of fire rising toward the heavens. I take a step back, away from the heat and then take a seat on the porch to watch him burn.

After some time, my father breaks the silence. "You can come back to Hemlock Hollow. You and Korwin both. I'm the bishop. You can be married and raise your family here." He motions toward his house.

Laura glances at me from her place on the step. She doesn't say anything, but her face gives her feelings away. Each of them wants me to remain in their world. Understandable. I have no comfort to offer. At this point, I'm not sure where I belong.

She stands up and brushes her hands on her pants. "Please excuse me," she says. "I'm needed back at the base."

"Korwin will return with the buggy soon," my father says. "We could give you a ride to the wall."

"I have a ride on its way. I think I'll meet them halfway and leave you to catch up with Lydia." She leans down to give me a hug, and then shakes my father firmly by the hand. With quick steps, she moves around the fire and sets off at a jog toward the wall.

"Is it true, about you and Katie Kauffman?" I ask my father.

He nods and raises an eyebrow. "You didn't notice the beard?" He runs his hand over the stubble on his chin.

"Not too long yet." I smile.

"It's a good match, the kind you would approve of."

What he means is, he loves her. Really loves her. I can see it in his eyes.

"So, I live at her place now, and you can have this place."

"Why were you here?" I ask, suddenly aware that he shouldn't have been. He should have been with Katie.

"The explosion." He frowns slightly. "Most of the *Ordnung* went into hiding. I'd been an Englisher. I thought if someone needed to defend Hemlock Hollow, it had to be me. I'm their leader. Plus, this place is nearest to the wall."

"You sacrificed yourself to make sure the *Ordnung* was safe?"

"I'm one of the few who would fight back. I know I'm not supposed to, but things look different when you've lived as an Englisher. I figure God put me here to help in a way the others can't."

"I married Korwin, Dad." I stare intently at my toes, unable to look him in the eye. I'm ashamed. Not only did I not invite him to the wedding, I didn't even send a messenger to tell him. I had reasons, good reasons, but somehow, in person and in hindsight, they don't seem good enough. "We couldn't wait. We are married, in every sense."

"An Englisher ceremony?"

"Yes."

"You happy with your choice?"

"The happiest."

He puts one arm around my shoulders, squeezing me into his side. "Then I'm happy for you."

I give him a firm hug. "Looks like we both have what we want."

The flames lick toward the sky, Konrad's body fully consumed now and unrecognizable. I breathe a long sigh of relief.

"What is SC-13?" my father asks abruptly. "I heard talk of it. Is that what's in your pack?"

I slip the satchel from my shoulders and unbuckle the straps. When I pull the artificial womb out, my dad's eyebrows knit together.

"This is SC-13," I say gently. "This is an artificial womb and the baby inside is the product of Korwin and my genetic material."

"Genetic..." My father looks at me, confused.

"He's my son. He wasn't made in the traditional way, but he's Korwin's and mine. You're going to be a grandfather."

My father's face pales and he stares at the womb, running his hands along the glass.

"This is a happy day," he says, voice cracking. "The blessing of a married daughter and a grandchild all at once." I can tell the sentiment is a bit forced, but only a little. He's overwhelmed. I don't blame him. So am I.

"I don't think it's as simple as all that," I say solemnly, wondering if SC-13 will continue to grow. If it's possible that he'll be born healthy.

My father raps his knuckle on the wood of the step under us. Turning his face toward the pyre, he says, "It never is, Lydia. Never."

Epilogue

It has been six months since we burned Dr. Konrad's body. Six months since the war and the new government took power. What used to be the Green Republic is now called the United Provinces, and the war we helped win will go down in history as the Fight for Liberty.

The wall was destroyed and hauled away. Already Englishers seeking a simpler existence have built homes just inside where the wall used to be. They buy fresh milk and vegetables from the *Ordnung*. Amish and Englisher live in community with each other, separated by nothing but culture and belief.

The principles of individual freedom balanced with responsibility to the greater community have replaced the Green's hierarchal structure. Thanks to better allocation methods as well as lifting the ban on new energy technologies, everyone has enough energy. My mother, Laura, recently ran for senator and won.

I have my own role in this new government.

"Case 4821 will come to order." The provincial elect stares at me over her glasses. "The United Provinces have raised concerns over the health status of Amish and the natural food stuffs they have newly introduced to the nation. Council proposes immediate vaccination of the entire population of Hemlock Hollow. What say you, Ambassador?"

I stand and take the podium, smoothing the asymmetric jacket of my teal suit. "As the report you've been provided suggests, the residents of Hemlock Hollow choose to be in the world, but not of the world. Most voluntarily keep themselves separate from regular contact with Englishers. The rising demand for natural foods has changed that. Englishers are settling inside the former confines of the wall. While the United Provinces have a right to protect the health of their population, up until recently the population of Hemlock Hollow was governed independently. The leadership of Hemlock Hollow proposes that only those who have regular contact with a predominantly English population outside the border of Hemlock Hollow require vaccination. Englishers who voluntarily move into the community do so at their own risk to susceptible children and elderly."

"And those who refuse vaccination will self-confine to the area?"

"Yes, ma'am. As ambassador, I have already been vaccinated as have the sellers of milk and pork."

At the mention of animal products, one of the council dignitaries gags. She covers her mouth with her hand.

"I mean no offense to Ms. Gladwell. I am aware that many in modern society feel farming is barbaric, but the increasing demand for these products suggests that others disagree. And under the Historic Preservation Act, the United Provinces have chosen to protect and maintain the Amish as one of the only religious communities to have survived our turbulent past. These people are a human record of a different time, a lighthouse as we sail into the future, to measure just how far we've moved."

"I'm aware of the terms and purpose of the HPA, Ambassador." She purses her lips. "I agree with your assessment. Council's proposal will be edited to your proposed terms."

Ms. Gladwell scowls at me from the council box. I bow, as is procedure, and return to my seat.

For the first time in a long time, I feel good about this world. Which is why I haven't rejoined the *Ordnung*. I have a job, one no one else can do, an ambassador for the Amish, a bridge between two worlds.

When the Englishers found out about the community living behind the wall, the *Ordnung* was met with fear. Many people felt that Hemlock Hollow should be assimilated into secular culture. Only by lobbying the new senators and speaking the truth about where I came from was I able to convince the new government to leave the *Ordnung* alone. Without a wall, I am the only barrier that preserves Hemlock Hollow from the greater world.

But it is at my own sacrifice. To keep the *Ordnung* from being "of the world," I must be. I am wired into the very society they admonish for the sole reason of preserving their right to stay separate. I live on the edge of who I was and who I have come to be, and thankfully, I've been accepted as I am, by both sides.

* * * * *

"How did it go today?" Korwin asks. He sits at his easel in what used to be my father's house, a smudge of orange paint marring his cheek. The canvas in front of him depicts a sunrise over a wheat field. It's good. His paintings are popular with Englishers everywhere.

"As expected," I say. "Dad will be pleased. It could have been worse. I thought Gladwell was going to need medical attention."

"I'm happy everything came out okay." Korwin smiles at me, eyes twinkling.

"What? You look like the cat who ate the canary."

"Something happened today. Something we've been waiting for."

I leap from my chair and run into the bedroom. SC-13's artificial womb no longer has a green light on the side. The display has changed to a twenty-four-hour clock. It blinks 22:34... 22:33... "Korwin, does this mean what I think it does?"

"I called Doc Nelson. Judging by the manuals..." He shrugs. "He'll be here soon with the others."

A wave of joy floods through me and I squeal with delight, throwing my arms around Korwin. A flash of blue passes behind his irises as he lowers his lips to mine. There's a mild shock as our lips connect. Nothing like it used to be, but purely ours, stronger in some ways.

My spark has never returned. I hardly miss it anymore.

"I'm glad the doctor is coming," I say, pulling back.

"Me too. I have no idea what to do."

"That and…" I run my hand over the tiny bump in my lower abdomen.

Korwin's face freezes, locked in a look of surprise.

"If one is good, two is better, right?"

He laughs and spins me in his arms. "Two is definitely better."

* * * * *

We stand over the artificial womb, watching and waiting. We're in our bedroom, the womb between us, resting on the corner of the bed. SC-13 has slept near us for six months, our presence fostering his growth as before. Although my spark has never returned, SC-13 thrived. The miracle happened moment by moment, day by day. He grew. He moved. His heartbeat was the drum we lived our lives around.

The clock on the side of the artificial womb reads 00:10. SC-13 is bigger now, almost too big for the glass enclosure. Doc Nelson stands beside Korwin. He's as excited as we are. No one knows what to expect. SC-13 is the first gamma baby in existence and only the tenth baby of any genetic makeup to be born via artificial womb.

Korwin squeezes my hand. "Five... Four... Three..."

I join him, counting down. "Two... One..."

The light turns red and a loud click comes from inside the womb. The sound of a vacuum and whirring gears ends with the foggy glass clearing and the lid popping open a quarter of an inch. A rush of fluid splashes out of that gap and onto my pants. Trembling, I place my hands, thoroughly washed and gloved per Doc Nelson's instructions, on the lid and lift. It opens easily. Inside, I see the back of a head with fine light brown hair and a spine, like a string of pearls, arching from neck to tailbone.

For the first time, I see my baby. I've looked inside the womb a thousand or more times, but the opaque sac of fluid SC-13 developed inside means I've never seen him clearly. The sight of his normal, healthy spine fills me with joy.

The baby is facedown on its knees. I slide my hand under the chest and turn the head to the side. Doc Nelson uses a device from his bag to suction the mouth and nose. And then the most beautiful sound I've ever heard.

Waa. Waa. Waaaaa.

A good strong cry fills the room. Korwin holds a towel open, and I gently roll the baby into it. Doc Nelson cuts the cord attaching our son to the diminished pink sac inside the womb and uses another tool to seal the cut. He places a device on the baby's chest that runs a series of checks. "Normal. Healthy. And a boy, just as you suspected," he says. "How did you know?"

Korwin and I share a smile. I'm not sure how we knew, but we did.

I help the doctor clean the remaining fluid off the baby's body and we wrap him in a feather soft blanket Katie made for the occasion in unisex mint green. I wrap him up and lift him into my arms, Korwin coming to my side. We take the first good look at our child. Brown hair, green eyes, ten fingers, and ten toes.

"Do you have a name?" Doc Nelson asks.

"Samuel Christopher," I say.

He plugs the information into his tablet and has us sign the birth certificate. "He'll need feeding. NGA has a formula. Although with your current pregnancy, you might be able to try it the old-fashioned way." He hands us a can of powder from his bag. "Call me if something doesn't seem right."

I nod, barely able to remove my eyes from my son.

We watch Samuel's chest rise and fall for a moment, touching foreheads over his blinking eyes and button nose. Doc Nelson collects his bag. "Congratulations. You can dispose of the womb. They can't be reused." He walks out the door as if he delivers babies out of pods every day.

"Let's go introduce Samuel to the family," Korwin says. He guides me into the main room.

My father and Katie stand shoulder to shoulder in the kitchen, hands folded as if they've been praying. David and Laura turn in their chairs near the fireplace. Jeremiah, sporting the beginnings of a beard, rubs Trinity's shoulders as she sits at the kitchen table. She adjusts her *kapp,* no doubt still getting used to the feel of it on her head, and smiles in our direction.

With Korwin's hand on my shoulder, I tilt our son up for all to see. "I'd like to introduce you to our son, Samuel Christopher."

My family applauds and hollers, hugging each other in relief. I look at Korwin and I am filled with joy. When I think back to the winding road that brought us here, I can't help but wonder at the journey. We've come full circle. And while my life is not what I once thought it would be, my life is my own, and more than I ever dreamed.

Rooted in faith and family, I kiss my son's forehead. I thank the Lord for my past, for my trials, for the pain and the change. I know without a doubt that although it wasn't easy, I am wiser. In suffering, I've found purpose. I walk the wire between my faith and the future.

This is where I belong.

About the Author

G.P. Ching is the bestselling author of The Soulkeepers Series and The Grounded trilogy as well as a variety of short fiction. She specializes in cross-genre novels with paranormal elements and surprising twists. G.P.'s idea of the perfect day involves a cup of coffee, the beach, and her laptop. She splits her time between central Illinois and Hilton Head Island with her husband, two children, and a Brittany spaniel named Riptide Jack.

G.P. Ching is the owner of Carpe Luna Publishing, an independent publishing company.

Sign up for her exclusive newsletter to be the first to know about new releases and news about her novels.

Learn more about GP and her books at www.gpching.com.

Acknowledgements

Writing a trilogy about an Amish girl in a futuristic dystopian society is not an easy endeavor. It's not a matter of learning how the Amish live today, but projecting how they might live tomorrow and how it might matter to a futuristic society. When it came to learning about the variety of Amish living in America, I'd like to thank Erik Wesner at Amishamerica.com for his enlightened blogging on the topic.

From a futuristic perspective, much of my inspiration came from exhibits inside the Museum of Science and Industry in Chicago. I highly recommend a visit if you are in the area. The concepts of the grid, adjustable clothing, and the attraction between Korwin and Lydia were born in the Science Storms exhibit.

Huge thank yous to Gayle Evers (Real Time Edits) and Hollie Westring. (Hollie the Editor) for editing all three books in this series. This was a complex story that truly blossomed under your care.

Finally, thank you to the fans, book bloggers, and everyday readers. No one expects Young Adult, Amish, Sci fi, Dystopian fiction to sell. NO ONE. I wrote these books based on an internal drive and fascination with how traditional and religious cultures, while strange to some, contribute to society in a unique and grounding fashion, how those who want to do good are often corrupted by power, and the difficult balance between diversity, freedom, and community. I've been awestruck at the reception of the trilogy and am thankful for every single reader.

Made in the USA
San Bernardino, CA
24 November 2015